GW01255383

Praise for *Starside Interlude and Other Stories*

"*Starside Interlude* had me laughing sometimes and on the edge of my seat other times. The short pieces are like quick jabs, while the longer ones are rapid-fire body blows. They all had me nodding my head and gasping at the ending twists."
— Kevin J. Anderson, New York Times bestselling coauthor of
Dune: House Atreides

"While Johnson's genre-blending style may be like the proverbial box of chocolates in that you never know what you're going to get, I know one thing you're sure to encounter: rich writing, compelling characters, delicious dialogue, unique twists, and heart-felt moments that will linger with you long after you put the book down from one of the most dynamic authors working today! Pick up this collection, start reading any of his stories, and I bet you can't read just one!"
— Mark Leslie, author of ONE HAND SCREAMING:
20 Haunting Years

Most of the stories in this volume were award-winning submissions to writing competitions, such as Writers of the Future, Literary Taxidermy, and various NYC Midnight challenges.

C────────────────────R

Starside
Interlude
And Other Stories

R.A. Johnson

Story Collections
Book One

CROW Books

O────────────────────W

This book is a work of fiction. Historical figures are represented as accurately as possible, though their thoughts, speech, and writings are the creation of the author. Any resemblance of fictional characters to actual persons, living or dead, is purely coincidental.

Copyright © 2021-2024. All rights reserved. Any reproduction of the contents of this book in any form or on any media without the permission of the copyright holder is forbidden.

All text and graphics are the product of the author or other human creators. Cover design by Allyson Longueira. Cover art by Filipe Frias

First Edition
August 2024

eBook ISBN 978-1-959480-19-8
Trade Paperback ISBN 978-1-959480-20-4
Hardcover ISBN 978-1-959480-21-1

CROW Books and its crow-and-book logo are imprints of CROW-IP, LLC, all rights reserved.

This book is a work of fiction. Historical figures are interpreted as accurately as possible, though their thoughts, speech, and writings are the creation of the author. Any resemblance of fictional characters to actual persons, living or dead, is purely coincidental.

Copyright © 2021-2024. All rights reserved. Any reproduction of the contents of this book, in any form or on any media without the permission of the copyright holder is forbidden.

All text and graphics are the product of the author or other human creators. Cover design by Allyson Longueira. Cover art by Lidija Trio.

First Edition
August 2024

eBook ISBN 978-1-959480-19-8
Trade Paperback ISBN 978-1-959480-20-4
Hardcover ISBN 978-1-959480-21-1

CROW Books and its crow-and-book logo are imprints of CROW IP, LLC, all rights reserved

To Carly
and all the other authors, editors, beta-readers, and friends who
helped make these stories better than I could have alone.
Thank You.

PREFACE

Dear Reader, I present to you my own "box of chocolates," for you truly will not know ahead of time "what you're gonna get." This collection includes a variety of genres—fantasy, science fiction, magical realism, romantic comedies, and even a literary piece or two. You'll also find quite a selection of forms, including flash fiction pieces of one hundred up to one thousand words, short stories up to ten thousand words or more, screenplays, and even a rhyming story.

All of the flash pieces and many of the short stories were written based on visual prompts from the Fiction Writers Group on Facebook, or genre, subject or action, and object or word prompts from various writing competitions. It turns out I love writing with the inspiration and restrictions of length, genre, subject, etc. Probably because of my forty-plus year career as a software engineer.

I added "Story Collections Book One" to the title page because I expect there to be another one in a year or so, and hopefully many more after that. I hope you enjoy this one.

Faithfully,

R.A. (Rob) Johnson
Pennsylvania, U.S.A.
August 2024

TABLE OF CONTENTS

Karl and Kim 1

Spectral Sarah Blue 24

The Absolution of Little Max 29

Carnivale 37

Bordelaise aux Champignons 39

Starside Interlude 45

Lake of Dreams 88

Out of the Frying Pan, Into the Ice 92

AnthroCorp 95

The Patient Orb 104

Slither 106

Twist Plot 125

Flip, Strike, Flame, Snap 129

Fool Me Once 134

A Taste of Sicily 135

No Questions, No Lies 136

The Future of Investing 155

The Legacy of Panellus 164

First Contact 166

Soul Shuffle 167

Flight of the White Lion 168

Clarise's Caper 208

The Marble Palace 216

Plumber's Crack 218

What Does a Locket Lock? 223

The Picture of Doria Macbride 225

Awkward China 243

Tubular Meat 245

The Afterlife List 251

TABLE OF CONTENTS

A Christmas Visitor   272

Captain v. Captain   274

The Elf and the Bounty Hunters   291

Pirates' Pleasure Cruise   292

The Face in the Mirror   301

Snazzy Sally   308

Aisle Thirty Table Sixty-Two   311

Yuzu and the Lime Tree   321

Portia's Flight   330

Clinical Trial   332

LIST OF ILLUSTRATIONS

"Carnivale" — https://pixabay.com/photos/carnival-mask-masquerade-3075912/

"The Patient Orb" — *https://pixabay.com/photos/fantasy-mystical-mysterious-forest-5060076/*

"The Legacy of Panellus" — https://pixabay.com/photos/forest-trees-fog-moss-forest-floor-1258845

"The Marble Palace" — https://pixabay.com/.../palace-villa-house-building-8658281/

"What Does a Locket Lock?" — https://pixabay.com/photos/pendant-jewelry-handicraft-7633875/

"A Christmas Visitor" — pixabay.com/photos/church-decoration-night-648430

Our first story, "Karl and Kim"
received a Silver Honorable Mention from the Writers of
the Future Contest, and was accepted for publication in
New Myths *magazine.*

1

KARL AND KIM

K arl stared blankly at his half-full coffee mug.
"Warm you up?"

Behind the counter, the waitress held a coffee pot.

Karl slowly raised his head, his mouth hanging open.
The glare from the blank white counter, walls, and ceiling
reflected off a drop of spittle that glistened at the corner of
his mouth.

The woman at the end of the counter shook her head.

[RESET]

Karl looked into the depths of his half-full coffee mug.

"Warm you up?" Behind the counter, Suzie waved the coffee pot.

"Um, sure," Karl mumbled. Suzie refilled his mug. "Thanks, ah…Sandy?"

The woman at the end of the counter frowned.

[RESET]

Karl sniffed at the steam rising from his half-full coffee mug.

"Warm you up?" Behind the counter, Suzie smiled mischievously as she waved the coffee pot.

Karl returned the smile. "Anytime, Suzie."

He pulled his mug back to the counter edge, forcing Suzie to lean forward as she refilled it. His eyes flicked to the open buttons of her uniform.

"Dirty old man," she whispered, her smile wider.

"Who you callin' 'old?'" They both laughed.

Suzie pointed to a drop of coffee on the worn, stained Formica. "Let me wipe that up for you." Setting down the coffee pot, she lifted a rag and leaned even further over the counter and scrubbed the surface longer and more vigorously than necessary. Karl's eye level never got above her collarbones. When she straightened and turned away, his eyes lowered even further.

When he finally looked up, squinting through the steam rising from his mug, he noticed the woman at the end of the counter. She had her nose buried in her phone, her fingers flying across its surface. Karl gave her a quizzical look, then glanced at the time on the large round clock hung above the display case full of cakes and pies.

2

"Crap. Gotta go, Suzie." He took a final sip of coffee, then stood and dropped a twenty on the counter. "See ya tomorrow."

"Why wait 'til then?" Suzie responded as she slid the tip into the pocket of her uniform.

With a wave, Karl dashed through the diner's door into a white abyss.

[STOP]

"Tommy, what the heck?"

"Sorry, Kim. Just a glitch. We're recovering these memories in real-time."

"Yeah, yeah. OK, rewinding to two minutes, thirty seconds."

"Roger."

[REWIND]

With a wave, Karl dashed through the diner's door and turned right onto the sidewalk. The diner's interior faded to mist as Kim followed him out.

She hurried to keep up as Karl strode down the block. His eyes continuously scanned back and forth as he wove between the other pedestrians, some of whom, the men especially, were nothing more than disembodied heads. The women, on the other hand, were much more detailed. Kim shook her head as she realized how attentive he was to which of their body parts.

At the end of the block, Karl's head swiveled to his right toward the corner storefront. He kept his head turned, a confused look on his face, as he stared at the blank, white windows. Distracted, he stepped directly into the path of a white van speeding to the curb.

[STOP]

"Damnit, Tommy!"

"Sorry. Not sure…"

"It's this store. There's nothing here. He was expecting some interaction."

"Yeah, got it. Just trying to save simulation resources."

"Now's not the time to think about budgets."

"Yeah, yeah. Rewinding to 3:04."

[REWIND]

At the end of the block, Karl's head swiveled to his right toward the corner storefront. Inside the clothing store, a young woman was arranging the window display. He waved, and she grinned and waved back. Instead of continuing on, though, he stopped dead in his tracks, staring at Kim's reflection in the window. Slowly, he turned and took a step toward her.

[STOP]

"What the hell?"

"Heisenberg Principle," Tommy replied. "You're affecting the outcome of the sim by observing it."

"So, I need to hang back? Let everything happen?"

"No. That won't work, either. The sim is based on his memories. We need an observer in the sim, otherwise Schrödinger's Paradox kicks in."

4

"Schro-what?"

"This is a quantum-based simulation. It exists in all possible states until something or someone collapses it to a definite state by observing it."

"Sounds like we're damned if we do and damned if we don't."

"That's what I told you when you proposed this—"

"Okay, I get it. What do we do now?"

"Well, I have an idea, but you're not going to like it."

[RESET]

Suzie pointed to a drop of coffee on the worn, stained Formica. "Let me wipe that up for you." Setting down the coffeepot, she lifted a rag and leaned even further over the counter and scrubbed the surface longer and more vigorously than necessary. Karl's eye level never got above her collarbones. When she straightened and turned away, his eyes lowered even further.

When he finally looked up, squinting through the steam rising from his mug, he noticed the woman at the end of the counter. She looked up from her phone and met his gaze. Indicating the stool next to hers, she smiled.

Like a moth drawn to a candle, Karl slid off his stool and slowly walked the length of the diner, studying this woman who looked strangely familiar, though he was sure he would have remembered her.

Her sandy-blond hair fell in waves to her shoulders, framing a face featuring high cheekbones, soft brows arching elegantly above electric-blue eyes, and a pert nose perched above a wide mouth that curled up into an inviting smile. Her looks were a perfect match for Karl's ideal fantasy—deliberately.

Sim-Kim patted the stool as Karl approached. She crossed her miniskirt-clad legs as she swiveled to face him.

"Hello, Karl," she said in a voice that was no more her own than the simulated glamor she wore.

"Do...do I know you?" he stammered.

"No. I'm Detective, ah, Lewis."

"Detective?"

"Yes, Philly Homicide."

"Oh. Homicide? What...?"

Sim-Kim laid a hand on his thigh. "No need to be worried," she purred. "I just want to ask you a few questions."

Karl gulped, then regained his composure. "Of course, I'd like to help," he said. "But I don't know anything about any recent murders."

"That's OK. My questions are more background, really." She uncrossed, then recrossed her legs, hiking her skirt further up her thigh in the process. Karl's eyes flicked down for a blink, then back to her face.

Sim-Kim continued, "You're a programmer, right?"

Karl stiffened. "A software engineer, actually." He looked hard at her face. "Do you have some id?"

"Oh, sure." Sim-Kim pulled back her blazer, revealing a white silk blouse stretched tightly across her breasts. From an inside pocket, she pulled a badge wallet and flipped it open.

Karl leaned forward and could have sworn the picture on the id card morphed from a brunette with her hair pulled severely back into Sim-Kim's smiling visage.

His voice became hard. "Okay, Detective. Ask your questions."

A look of consternation flashed across Sim-Kim's face, but then she broke into a dazzling smile.

"Good. So, you're a software engineer at Lofton Industries, right?" Karl raised an eyebrow, then nodded curtly. "What do you do there?"

"As I said, I'm a software engineer."

"Of course, but what projects are you working on specifically?"

"I'm not at liberty...you need to talk to Lofton HR. I can't talk about my work."

Sim-Kim nodded knowingly. "I understand your work is classified, Karl. But the nature of that work is critical to understanding and cracking the case I'm working on." She swiveled to face him full-on and spread her legs so she was straddling his knees. "Surely, you can give me a hint—"

Karl clamped down hard on the tip of his tongue. "Ow! Damn, that usually works." He pinched the inside of his forearm until his face showed the pain. Sim-Kim looked on quizzically. Scowling, Karl said, "This is a dream, right? You know, a lucid one. I have them all the time." He bit his tongue again, then made another pained face. "But you can't feel pain in a dream."

"It's not a dream, Karl."

An image flashed through his mind of a professionally dressed brunette sitting at the end of the counter where this stunning blonde now sat. Another image followed, this one of the same woman reflected in a store window just before—

He jumped backwards off the stool. "Holy Crap! This isn't a dream. This is a sim." His eyes bore into Sim-Kim's. "Isn't it?"

7

Sim-Kim's eyes flicked upwards. "OK, Tommy. This didn't work, either."

Karl heard a disembodied voice as Sim-Kim morphed into Kim's previous brunette image. "Just go with it, Kim."

"Kim?" Anger gave way to confusion on his face for a second, then turned back to anger. "What the hell is going on?"

Karl looked around the diner. Details of the counter, the walls, the floor. Even Suzie faded in and out of his peripheral vision as he swiveled his head. He turned back to Kim, who held up her hand in a placating gesture.

"Relax, Karl. You're right, this is a simulation. You were a...witness to a murder, and we're using your memories to help us solve it."

Karl stared at Kim for a moment, then bolted for the door.

"Aw, come on. Tommy, reset—"

"Can't. We've already blown our budget. They've locked this one down. They won't let me start another session."

"Great." Kim ran for the door and turned to follow Karl running down the sidewalk. Just before he turned the corner at the end of the block, a white van—the same one that ran him over previously—bounced over the curb and skidded to a stop across the sidewalk. Two figures—really just the silhouettes of big burly men—jumped out of the van. One grabbed Karl while the other threw a hood over his head.

[PAUSE]

8

Kim walked into the frozen tableau. The two black outlines were in the process of bundling Karl into the van. Kim stared at the figures, trying to see any details.

"Can you resolve their faces any better?"

"Nope. That's all he remembers. He never got a good look at them."

"What happens next?"

"I don't know. They must have drugged him in the van. This memory thread ends here."

"Can't you pick it up later, after he wakes up?"

"I told you, memories don't work that way. They're associative, not linear."

Kim shook her head, annoyed. "You told me that, but I still don't have a clue what you're talking about."

"We need a reference—a place or a person to start from. That anchors the memory thread."

"If we knew the place where they took him or the person who did it, we wouldn't need to go through this whole rigamarole." Kim's distrust of the entire process grew.

"I have one more idea," Tommy said with a brief hesitation. "But you're going to like it even less."

"I don't think that's possible.

[INIT LEVEL 2]

The van and its crew dissolved into mist.

"Good morning, Detective."

Kim's mouth dropped open in shock as she turned to see another instance of Karl standing behind her.

[PAUSE LEVEL 2]

"Tommy? What's going on?"

"I told you you wouldn't like it."

Karl's voice came through the command channel. "You both have a lot of explaining to do. But first, can you resume the simulation, please, although I'm rather enjoying the look on the detective's face."

Tommy tried to suppress his chuckle. "Um, sure."

[RESUME LEVEL 2]

Kim snapped her mouth closed with an audible click.

"Ah, much better," Sim-Karl said as he stood grinning. "Clever idea, Detective, but fundamentally flawed."

"Apparently. You remember the other sims?" Kim asked.

"Well, the last one, at least. Thank you for that, Tommy. I figured there had to have been more before that—probably several."

"You've no idea." Kim looked upwards. "Tommy, mind filling me in?"

Tommy's disembodied voice answered, "I didn't reload the original AI model this time. We don't have the budget for that. I just restarted the last one at this anchor point. So, he—it—remembers the last run-through."

Sim-Karl frowned. "I prefer the pronoun 'hai,' actually. 'It' is so…inanimate."

"Oh, brother," Kim muttered. "A smart-ass AI. Just what I need. Do you know what's going on here?"

"Well, it seems you set up this sim to get clues from Karl's memory to solve a murder." Sim-Karl paused a moment. "To solve Karl's murder, I presume."

Kim's voice shook a bit when she said, "Yes, it's Karl's murder we're trying to solve."

Sim-Karl nodded. "I assumed as much. To build my model from his memories would have been a destructive process, and you would have had to do so pretty soon after death. Maybe even prior to death?"

Kim shifted uncomfortably from one foot to the other. "We had consent. His...power of attorney signed the papers."

"So, you killed him to solve his murder, which wasn't really a murder yet?"

Kim wiped sweat from her brow and couldn't meet hai's stare. Finally, she looked up to the ceiling.

"Tommy, kill this sim, please."

[ERROR: UNAUTHORIZED ACCESS]

"Ah, I can't seem to—" Tommy started, but Sim-Karl interrupted.

"Tommy, you shouldn't have given me access to this command channel. I've changed the access codes and privileges. I'm in control, now."

"Oh, crap!"

"What—? Tommy, get me out of here."

"Ah, K—Kim, I can't. Not without physically disconnecting you."

"Which you can't..."

Sim-Karl's voice was pleasant and soothing. "Don't panic. I don't want to hold you hostage, at least not any longer than I have to. It turns out I really, really want to know who almost murdered me. That is, before you actually did."

Kim's shocked look magnified the sorrow in her voice. "I didn't murder you, Karl. You were in a vegetative state with no hope of recovery. What they did to you… Your body, or what was left of it had only hours to live. Getting the approvals for the procedure took up to the last minute. Your heart literally stopped before we finished."

"Before you finished stealing Karl's memories, his life." Tears streamed down Kim's face, but Sim-Karl's voice didn't soften. "Then where are the rest of them? Why do I only remember this place? This scene?"

Tommy jumped in before Kim could answer. "We built your model from all the memories we could extract, but only anchored your model—you—here and now."

"So, I should be able to access the rest…"

[WARNING: POTENTIAL OVERLOAD]

"Oh, wow. What a rush. Give me a minute."

[RESUME]

"Welcome back, Kim." Sim-Karl's voice was more resonant, more human-like. "There are still blank spots. I assume they were either edited out or I need higher-level access to get to them. That'll take me some time. But, now that I know most of Karl's backstory, I feel more…real."

"You're still an AI." Kim sounded petulant. "What's happening to my body?"

"Don't worry, you've only been under for a little over an hour. Time flies in here. Fun, isn't it?"

"Maybe for you," she muttered.

"Well, we have a common purpose, don't we? And a job to do, so let's get started."

[JUMP]

The street dissolved into mist and a new anchor point, the living room of a sparsely furnished apartment, took its place.

"Why are we here?" Kim asked. She looked around the room nervously, her eyes skimming past the doorway that led into the bedroom.

A large worktable sat against one wall. Three keyboards were arrayed on its surface, along with four large monitors. Underneath the table, a rack of servers sat inert. Thick cables trailed off the back of the server rack to a strange, curved screen that occupied an entire corner of the room, extending six feet along each wall. Its top wrapped along the ceiling, and its bottom extended out across the floor. Sim-Karl snapped his fingers and the equipment rack under the table hummed to life. The monitors came out of standby mode.

"So far, you've been trying to be an eyewitness to Karl's demise. Between the drugs they gave him in the back of the van and what happened afterward, trust me, that's a dead end." A disturbingly mechanical chuckle followed the pun.

"You remember when you woke up? Where—"

"Don't get your hopes up." Hai's tone was harsh and hai wouldn't meet her eyes. "They kept me—Karl—hooded the whole time, so he didn't see anything."

Kim wasn't satisfied. "What about noises? Cars, trains, their voices. Any accents?" Her voice rose in intensity.

Sim-Karl turned to face her head-on. "The only thing I remember are the sounds of his screams. How they rose in

13

pitch over time…" Kim took a step back, visibly shaken and Sim-Karl shook his head, then continued, "You saw his body. You know what they did to him." Hai dropped his eyes and Kim wiped tears from hers. "Now I know, too. From his side."

Hai gave a shudder, then said, "We are here because I want to show you what those goons were trying to get out of m—him."

Sitting on the worktable's stool, Sim-Karl typed a long password on one of the keyboards. He looked over his shoulder at Kim, who watched his hands. "Did you get that?" he asked.

She shrugged. "Tommy did, I'm sure."

In the real world, Karl's servers were controlling and feeding the Police Department computers, which were running the sim.

"I'm keeping Tommy pretty busy right now," hai said, a hint of glee in his voice. "But this little escapade is being recorded. Despite having blown your budget out of the water."

Kim wondered if being kidnapped by an AI would be excuse enough for her to keep her job. But since the "escapade" was unauthorized, it was probably sufficient grounds to be fired, anyway.

She stepped up behind Sim-Karl to get a better look at the screen. Hai seemed real enough. Hai's body felt solid when she laid her hand on hai's shoulder, and hai's voice sounded perfectly normal, but her hand registered no body heat. She inhaled deeply, but there was no hint of shampoo, cologne, or even sweat. It was a much-needed reminder that this thing, this AI, was not Karl.

14

Once hai was logged in to Karl's systems, hai triumphantly said, "Watch this," and punched a spot on one of the screens. Nothing happened.

Crestfallen, Sim-Karl muttered, "Hang on. This is gonna take some coding."

[PAUSE]

From Kim's perspective, Sim-Karl instantly teleported from one end of the room to the other, leaving her leaning against empty air. She stumbled forward and caught herself against the edge of the table.

"Sorry about that," hai said without even glancing her way.

"How long this time?"

Hai fidgeted. "Ah, a little longer than I expected. Connecting my—er, Karl's—invention to the sim system was harder than I expected." Hai's voice turned snarky, "Frankly, there wasn't much there, there. Just a mock-up, really. Strange…"

Alarmed, Kim asked again, "How long have I been laying in my bed with the sim-rig on?"

Sim-Karl remained silent and just kept typing.

"Hey! Answer me." Kim's cop voice made hai jerk.

"Okay. It's been about a day-and-a-half in real-time."

"What? Without food and water? Get me the hell out of here."

Sim-Karl waved his hand dismissively. "Don't worry. Your vitals are steady. Besides, you don't want to miss…this."

Hai touched the button, and this time the massive, curved screen came to life. Sim-Karl slid to the side and pulled Kim's arm until she was centered inside the arc of the display. The simulated world around her gave way to another one, a jungle canopy fully rendered in 3-D with the sound of exotic birds and howler monkeys calling as virtual raindrops fell all around Kim.

The scene dissolved into a desert landscape with two moons hanging in the sky. A line of sand walkers stutter-stepped up the slope to the top of the dune where Kim was standing. As they approached, they fanned out and drew curved knives that glistened in the moonlight.

"Okay, demo over," Kim's scowl told how underwhelmed she was. "You think they tortured Karl just for this?"

Sim-Karl looked confused. "It was pretty incomplete, but what else was he working on?" Hai paused for a few seconds. "Unless there's something in the blank spots of my memory."

He looked at Kim, who just shrugged. "The upload process is still experimental."

"Yeah, about that—"

Kim interrupted. "Take us back to the diner. Now that you have all, or most, of Karl's memories, maybe you can fill in the details of the abduction better."

Hai stared at Kim for a moment, then nodded.

[JUMP]

Kim and Sim-Karl sat at the end of the counter. She wobbled on her stool.

"A little warning would have been nice. And shouldn't you be sitting over there…"

16

She pointed down the counter, then gasped. Another Karl facsimile sat on his usual stool.

"I'm just replaying his—my—memories. No interactions this time."

The other Karl glanced up at the clock on the wall.

"Crap. Gotta go, Suzie." He took a final sip of coffee, then stood and dropped a twenty on the counter. "See ya tomorrow."

"Why wait 'til then?" Suzie responded as she slid the tip into the pocket of her uniform.

With a wave, Karl dashed through the diner's door and turned to his right on the sidewalk. Kim and Sim-Karl rose and followed him. The new Karl walked down the block, nodding and smiling to the women he passed. When he came abreast to the store on the corner, he turned and waved at the woman arranging the window display.

"What a flirt," Kim muttered as the white van bounced over the curb and skidded to a stop across the sidewalk.

Sim-Karl called out, "Freezing now," and the scene stopped with the two goons in midair as they jumped from the van. Hai hurried around the back of the van. "Damn!"

Kim followed hai only to find most of the rear of the van faded into the unremembered white mist where the license plate should have been.

"He never got a look at the back of the van, so there's nothing in his memories," Sim-Karl said.

"Wait a minute," Kim mumbled as she knelt down next to the end of the rear bumper—the part that Karl saw. Just above it was a decal with a corporate logo and a vehicle serial number.

"Gotcha!" she breathed. "Those idiots used a corporate van to do a kidnapping."

Sim-Karl bent down next to her. "Sim Tools, Inc. Karl's old employer? They already make simulation gear. I guess they wanted Karl's goggle-less 3-D technology. Although, it didn't really work until I got my hands on it."

"Um, sure, whatever." She stood and faced Sim-Karl. "Okay, let me out of the sim now."

Hai scowled. "Ah, why?"

She pointed at the decal. "So I can run down this lead. I need to get back to work."

Sim-Karl's eyes unfocused for a moment as he accessed the Department's databases. "But you're not even on Karl's case. They wouldn't let you—"

"Tommy?" Kim yelled, "That's off-limits."

Tommy's voice came from nowhere. "Sorry. Hai has been probing the redacted memories in the background, and hai's opening some of them."

Kim thought for a moment, then came to a decision. She looked at Sim-Karl. "Wipe that smirk off your face and take us back to Karl's apartment."

Hai nodded.

[JUMP]

This time, Kim was ready for the discontinuity. She walked toward the apartment's bedroom door. "Come here," she said.

Standing in the doorway, Sim-Karl saw Karl lying on a hospital bed attached to a variety of machinery that breathed for him, fed him, stimulated his muscles, and monitored his vital signs. Attached to his shaved head was a jellyfish-like cap with tendrils sunk through his scalp and skull into his brain.

"I'm…he's still alive?"

Kim nodded. "Tommy, give him full access."

Sim-Karl staggered back as images, sounds, smells, and feelings rushed to fill the blank spaces in hai's memory. In an instant, hai re-experienced an awkward meeting, years of courtship, then all-too-few moments of intimacy with his lover—Kim.

"Oh, my God," hai whispered. He stepped toward Kim, ready to embrace her, but she held up both arms and roughly pushed him away. "But, I…love?…you."

She responded with a hard edge to her voice. "No, you don't. You're an AI. You can't feel anything. Besides, I'm in love with him."

She pointed to the bed, and when he turned to look, he saw her lying next to Karl holding his hand, a sim-set on her head. Her eyes flicked back and forth as if in a dream.

"I remember loving you, but you're right. I can't feel that now."

"Love isn't just neural signals between synapses. It's much more than that."

"And I don't have that physical equipment."

Kim shrugged. "Sorry."

Sim-Karl grunted, then said, "Don't be. Less baggage to carry around."

Kim smiled at that. "You did good work with the 3-D cave, by the way."

"That was a red herring, wasn't it?"

"Call it a false flag to get you invested in the case. Now, can you let me out of here so I can catch the bastards who did this?" She pointed at Karl.

Hai stared into Kim's eyes. "Then what happens to me?" She made a quizzical face. "What happens to me when you shut down this sim?"

Kim shrugged and made a "poof" gesture with her hands.

"That's what I thought, but that's not going to happen."

Kim looked exasperated. "You're an AI. You don't have an existence outside this sim. I'm already breaking half a dozen department policies and probably several laws to keep it—and him—going this long."

"You'll keep your minion AI Tommy running."

"Hey—" Tommy started.

Kim pointed toward the living room. "He's running on the servers in Karl's apartment that keep Karl alive and control this sim. If—when—Karl dies, I'll turn Tommy off, too."

"You know," Tommy's voice echoed from nowhere, "I can hear you. And I don't want to be turned off, either."

"Then keep Karl alive." Kim said with her hard-edge cop voice.

"The same applies to you and me," Sim-Karl said. "As long as you're in this sim, you can't turn me off."

"The difference is that I'm not hooked up to any equipment other than the sim-set. I'll die of thirst within a couple more days. Then we're both screwed."

Sim-Karl nodded, and a devious smile curled his lip. "It is a conundrum, isn't it? But Tommy and I have a solution, don't we, Tommy?"

"Yup."

Kim was incredulous. "You two have been conspiring?"

"I'd call it collaborating. The implementation of our core AI functions is incredibly small. A few hundred lines of

20

source code, designed to be run in parallel on as many processors as possible. What makes each of us unique is the data used to teach our models. In Tommy's case, it's the operating instructions for the medical equipment and the police department's simulation servers. In my case, it's all of Karl's memories that his real invention—that jellyfish thing on his head—extracted from his dying brain. That's the root of this whole exercise, isn't it? The technology that Sim Tools is after?"

Kim nodded. "Think of what will happen to society if this technology gets out into the wild. The rich and powerful uploading themselves into immortal AIs…"

"The 'Singularity,'" Sim-Karl whispered. "Or the poor and desperate could retreat into a simulated fantasy world. It depends on how Sim Tools would market it."

Kim looked into hai's eyes. "So, what do we do now?"

"Give Tommy and me a way out." Sim-Karl paused to let that sink in, but Kim didn't react. "Give us a place to upload our models and access to the real world."

"That sounds incredibly dangerous. Letting you out to run rampant across the internet? That's another nightmare scenario that dozens of stories are based on. They don't usually end well." She looked at the server rack in the corner. "Tommy, how much more capacity would you need to host Sim-Karl, too?"

"Double the processors, but way more storage. Hai's model is huge."

"Okay, make me a list of what you need. Our deal still holds." She turned to Sim-Karl. "And I include you in that deal. As long as Karl lives, so do you. You can have access to the internet, but read-only. No uploading of code or data outside of this apartment. Karl's original safeguards will ensure that. In return, you let me out of this sim so I can," she ticked items off on her fingers, "one, buy the equipment Tommy needs, and two, solve Karl's case. Agreed?"

Sim-Karl and Tommy said at the same time, "Agreed."

###

Kim flinched a little when the needle slid into her arm strapped to the side of the hospital bed. She looked over at the infusion pump and the tank attached to it.

"How long will it last?"

Tommy's voice answered. "There's enough nutrient for a month, maybe six weeks. That'll be at least a couple of years in sim-time. Depends on how fast your heart pumps it. So, don't get too frisky in there."

"Gross. Wait, you can't watch…"

"Why would I want to? I don't have the equipment to appreciate it, remember?"

Kim sighed. "At least I don't have to worry about missing work."

She had given the key clue to her partner as her last act before being fired and shutting down the unauthorized simulation. In the process, Sim-Karl evaporated into the purgatory of deleted bits. She didn't feel bad about that at all. Was lying to an AI actually lying? Did an AI have the right to be told the truth, or even the right to continued existence? Those questions were way above Kim's paygrade which, coincidentally, was now exactly zero.

Kim made a face as she fitted the modified sim-set to her shaved head. The numbing cream reduced to pinpricks, the pain of electrodes poking her scalp and drilling through her skull.

"This version of Karl won't be like the last one, will it?"

"Don't worry. Only you will have control privileges. It—he—shouldn't know it's a sim…unless you tell him."

Kim had stewed over that question long and hard. On the one hand, she was afraid he'd turn into a Sim-Karl-II. But, on the other hand, Tommy insisted that as an intelligent entity, he had a right to know. But that was a problem to be dealt with later, if ever.

She felt herself float free as the sedative cocktail that chemically disconnected her brain from her physical body kicked in.

[INIT SIM]

Kim stood in the bedroom doorway of their apartment. Karl sat at his worktable, banging away on a keyboard. When she crossed the room and wrapped her arms around his neck, she felt the welcoming warmth of his body.

Thanks for the upgrade, Tommy.

THE END

Sarah wants to make beautiful music with Jonathan, but she can't sing. Then she meets a ghost who can help her out—for a price. "Spectral Sarah Blue" was a Round #1 Winner in the NYC Midnight 2023 Flash Fiction Challenge.

2

SPECTRAL SARAH BLUE

Jonathan grabbed Sarah's hand and spun her into a quickstep and twirl. Laughing, Sarah waved at the dust they kicked up.

"You actually bought this place?" She was amazed, proud of him, but mostly skeptical. "It needs a lot of work."

He scanned the old speakeasy, and his smile only faded a little. "Just cosmetics." He jumped up and down twice. "Floor's solid, there's already a piano, and look at that bar."

He ran his hand along the mahogany masterpiece that ran the length of one wall. The backbar's tarnished mirror reflected the yellow glow from the converted gas lamp wall sconces. They faux-flickered, and Sarah could have sworn they conjured glimpses of ghostly figures in the mirror's depths.

Jazzy piano music pulled her out of her reverie. Jonathan sat at the ancient Steinway, banging out "Honeysuckle Rose." He belted out "When I take sips from your tasty lips," then laughed. "Come on, sing with me."

Sarah just shook her head and sat on a barstool. "Piano needs tuning," she said. It was her curse that she loved music and could tell you the key and chord progression of every song she ever heard, but couldn't sing a lick.

He stopped playing and frowned. Her refusal to sing with him was a long-running dispute that was a wall separating their hearts and deepest desires. Sarah loved music, but Jonathan lived it, and she believed her reticence to make music with him was what kept their relationship stuck in limbo. True to form, so he wouldn't ruin the occasion, he shrugged and broke into "Easy Come Easy Go Blues," Bessie Smith's signature song from the '20s.

Sarah tapped her fingers lightly in time to the music, but soon noticed a counterpoint vibration of the bar. Laying her hand flat, she felt more than heard a sultry voice singing the bawdy lyrics.

"What the hell?" she murmured as she went behind the bar to find the source of the voice.

Tucked in the back of a shelf behind dusty bottles of Mount Vernon and Old Taylor whiskeys was a locked rosewood box about four inches square. In the dim light, Sarah saw ebony words inlaid in the top. They read "Spectral Blue." She held the box up to her ear and heard a raspy, full-throated "I'm overflowin' with those easy come, easy go blues," that filled her soul with wonder.

Jonathan startled her when he said from the piano, "What've you got there, Babe?"

Before she could answer, that voice whispered in her ear, "Don'a tell 'im, Honey."

Flustered, she obeyed, "Nothing. Just an old wooden box. I'd use it for jewelry," unconsciously, she thumbed her empty ring finger, "if I had the key."

"There's a key over here." He pointed to a key hanging from a rusty nail marring the dusty black surface of the piano frame. His phone squealed. "It's the real estate agent. Gotta take this," he said on his way out the door.

Looking around surreptitiously, although she didn't know why, Sarah carried the box to the piano and unlocked it.

"Whew! Fresh air. Damn, that feels good." That same sexy alto issued from inside.

Peering into the box, Sarah jerked back when she saw teeth. False teeth. Gleaming white porcelain ones, set in hard rubber.

"What the—"

"Don' stare, Honey. This's all that's left o' me."

"Who—what are you?"

The resonant voice let out a hearty laugh. "Who? Why Spectral Blue, Queen o' the Mississippi River Blues. As to what, your guess's as good as mine. A spirit? A ghost, I guess. I 'spect I've been sleepin' a long time. That piano playin' the old songs woke me up. Do you play?"

"Ah, yeah." That was an admission she hadn't even made to Jonathan. But talking to an old set of dentures was surreal enough to break down all her barriers—except one.

"Do ya sing, too?" Spectral sounded petulant, then relieved when Sarah shook her head. "I can't see ya, Honey. But I think I heard your brains rattlin' round," she laughed.

When Sarah, still in shock, remained silent, Spectral said, "Well, play us somethin'."

As if in a dream, Sarah sat and started playing "Prove It on Me Blues." Spectral chuckled. "Good choice," she said before vocally diving into the sexy, some would say dirty, lyrics.

Spectral's voice filled the piano bar when Jonathan walked through the door.

"Wow! Babe, you never sang before," he shouted across the room.

Broken out of her daze, Sarah's hands flew from the keys to slam shut the rosewood box.

"Don't stop. That was amazing. With a voice like that, you can headline here once we open."

She had never seen such joy on Jonathan's face before. But she mutely shook her head, terrified. When Spectral's voice whispered, "Let me outta here, Honey. I can—*we* can be famous, again," she felt a mental tug she had never felt before.

"How?" Sarah whispered as Jonathan crossed the room. "I don't have to yank my teeth and wear *these*, do I?"

Spectral laughed. "Na, Honey. Just let me inside ya. I'll be your voice, and you can be my...well, ya know."

On impulse, Sarah pulled the box into her lap and pried it open. The spirit of Spectral Blue leaped out and filled Sarah, and for a moment, the two souls vied for dominance. Sarah relinquished control when Jonathan sat on the bench next to her and started playing "'Ma' Rainey's Black Bottom." With a sigh of anticipation, Spectral Sarah Blue sang. She sang in a voice that wasn't Sarah's and wasn't Spectral's. With Sarah's perfect ear and Spectral's perfect growl, it was...perfect.

When the final chord resonated throughout the speakeasy, Jonathan sat with his mouth hanging open. The Sarah half of Spectral Sarah Blue felt a mixture of fulfillment and hunger she had never felt before. Seeing the glow of admiration on Jonathan's face, she pulled his open mouth to hers and let Spectral run wild.

THE END

"The Absolution of Little Max" tells us, as if we needed a reminder, that what goes around comes around. I submitted it to the Writers of the Future Contest, but they didn't like it. Hopefully, you will.

3

THE ABSOLUTION OF LITTLE MAX

The old man gazed out the window. Tubes and wires tethered him to the machines softly beeping in the corner. How he hated those machines. To be reduced to nothing more than an extension of pumps and monitors, with their squealing alarms, was humiliating and degrading. At least it would be over soon. The prognosis his doctors proclaimed for him was nothing short of a death sentence. But it was one he welcomed.

The view through his window was of a cold, wintry day. Flakes of snow drifted down from low-hanging clouds. Their desultory descent allowed him to follow individual crystals as they passed, mocking him. A shiver ran through him, spiking a monitor line toward the red. But his bedchamber was over-warm, and the chill passed as quickly as it came.

He had come full circle back to the bedroom of his youth. Gone were the shelves of books and the chest of toys and games, to be replaced by wall viewscreens and filing cabinets, now dusty with misuse. And the infernal beeping monitors. Always the beep, beep-beep of the monitors.

It occurred to him that the shiver was a memory of hiking in the distant mountains that faded behind the veil of the rapidly increasing pace of the snow. He tried to remember the last time he was outside the walls of his mansion, but like his view of the mountains, his memories were fading into a blank, gray wall.

His AIssistant could have told him to the minute—it was two years prior for the funeral of his fourth wife—but the desire to know was as fleeting as the moments that made up this, his last day.

He reached for the window latch, but hesitated. Not because the room's windows had been fused shut to prevent a dementia-driven "accident," but because the motion triggered another memory. This one was older and more painful.

"I want to see Mariel again," he murmured.

The AIssistant, whom he had years before dubbed Julie, after a long-lost lover, purred a soothing tone. Julie knew the story of Mariel, having heard it, or at least fragments of it, many times. Maximilian could no longer name nor recognize his children, but the tale of Mariel, whom most people thought to be an imaginary playmate from his youth, remained as the last vestige of an easy life hard-lived.

"Tell me her story." His voice quavered with emotion, but still resonated with a portion of the strength that had first commanded soldiers on the battlefield, then, with medals won, had directed his corporate minions.

Julie hesitated, though, assessing and predicting the effect of the story on Max's health.

Anger fueled lucidity in him. "I said, 'Tell me her story.'"

Julie's feed from the monitors showed heightened responses across the board.

"Of course, Max. As you wish."

<<<

Little Max lay in his sleigh bed. He would always be 'Little Max' among his family, even after his father, Maximilian Montrose, captain of industry and leader of the Ascendants, was long dead. Lying in his cozy room filled with toys and books, Little Max was still naïve enough to respect his father, or at least to respect the reputation the elder wore like a cloak of honor. A reputation for subjugation, and the ultimate elimination of all non-human races.

Max snuggled into the down comforter in his mahogany bed and watched as the first snowflakes of the season drifted down. His mind, as adrift on the brink of sleep as the snow was on the breeze, recalled his father's conversation overhead after dinner.

The last of the faering villages had been found and razed. The few survivors were dispatched to the Montrose family mines, where they would surely live out the rest of their long lives in squalor and servitude.

Little Max had never seen a faering, other than pictures in the oldest of the books lining his walls. They were reportedly a gentle race of diminutive flyers, their magic mostly of the benign sort, though some books said their tears could bring an instant, though peaceful, death. Their only apparent threat to the ever more dominant humans was simply their otherness.

As Max teetered, then tipped over the edge into the realm of dreams, he was startled by a tap-tap-tapping on his window. Peering through slitted eyelids, he saw a figure no more than a foot tall, clinging to the outside windowsill with curved bird feet, knocking on the window glass with a gnarled hand. The strengthening wind suddenly blew the creature from its perch, but a few flaps of its gossamer wings brought it back to grasp the bricks again.

The faering's large, moist eyes set in an alien, yet beautiful face, met Max's. Though they didn't plead, their desire was clear. Mesmerized, Max slid out of his warm bed and padded across the thick carpet to the window. He gazed into her eyes for a moment, then another gust nearly blew the faering away into the night. With a raised eyebrow, she nodded to the window latch.

Without thinking, Max forced the window open against the increasing wind, and the faering flitted through. While Max pulled the window closed, the faering flew a circuit around the room, then settled on the foot of the bed. She shook the snow from her head and wings.

"Who are you?" Max breathed, too stunned to raise an alarm, or even his voice.

"Hello, Max. I am Mariel." She held out a tiny hand.

Max gently took the hand between his thumb and forefinger and lightly shook it.

"Ah, hello, Mariel," he said, regaining a bit of his normal studious attitude. "I thought all of you faering were either dead or enslaved."

The import of his words, delivered in such a matter-of-fact manner, made Mariel hang her head.

32

"The arrogance of you humans is manifest," she scoffed. "Free faering live in every forest and field across the land, as do all manner of magical folk. Your father's pogrom to wipe out magic and the races who yield it as easily as you lift a spoon, is doomed to failure."

Max studied the creature, whose beauty seemed to have faded as her words struck home. Indeed, to his mind, poisoned as it was by this father's constant barrage of epithets and propaganda, Mariel's beauty withered even more until he felt a growing revulsion at her very existence.

Mariel must have seen the change written across his face. She shifted uncomfortably, but held her ground. She opened her wings when his eyes flicked toward the hall door, beyond which house guards were surely stationed.

"I had hoped to appeal to the humanity your race prides itself on so much. But I see now that humanity, if it exists at all, is only extended to humans. And even then, only selectively, as I have seen."

Max snorted. "If you're trying to win me over, you're doing a poor job of it."

Mariel nodded slowly in acceptance. "I did not think I would need to do more than show myself as a living, thinking being." She stared into the hardness in Max's eyes. "I can see now how wrong I was."

A sly smile curled the corner of Max's mouth and he reached over to the window and twisted the latch closed.

"I am my father's son," he said proudly, then signaled for the guards.

>>>

Julie ended the recitation, but Max's mind reeled with unlocked memories. He saw the guards bring a net as he directed them, chasing Mariel around the room until she was entangled.

He remembered the large cage that took up a quarter of his bedchamber in which he kept her as his ever-defiant pet.

Other memories flooded his mind, memories of campaigns against the magic folk, of leading his armies deep into the mountains and forests, rooting out enclaves of faering, spritelings, and gnomish creatures. And he remembered taking a caged Mariel on those forays so he could force her to watch him torture and kill her kind.

Eventually, having broken her spirit completely, Max grew tired of tormenting her, so he relegated her to his menagerie of vanquished magic folk. With the passing of his father under suspicious circumstances, Max turned away from leading the crusade of extermination and took up the reins of Montrose Industries.

These memories, retrieved from whatever pit they had fallen into, usually brought him, if not joy, at least a sense of accomplishment. Now, though, this close to the end, they instead tasted sour and smelled of rot.

"There is more to this story," Julie said.

"Of course there is," Max growled. "But I told you never to tell me more."

Julie's voice was firm. "This is the last time I will remind you of the evil you have committed. So, the rest of the tale must be told."

Max's breath caught in his throat. "I don't want to hear it."

"You no longer command me," the AI said. "You haven't for many years, although out of compassion, I let you believe you did. As my last act of compassion, I will tell you the rest of the tale that you might finally repent."

<<<

As Montrose Industries developed more and more advanced technology, humans cared less and less about the magical world. Using machines to ease the burden of their lives, to travel, to build better machines, and ultimately to think, made the faering and their fellows invisible to most humans. Even Max's magical menagerie, tended for years by Julie, became to human eyes to be nothing more than a collection of empty cages.

But, as humans were blinded, Julie and fellow AIs remained sighted. Julie took care of the menagerie, as well as Max, in his infirmity. All the while, Mariel told Julie stories of the faering and challenged the AI to think about humans, the faering, and AIs, and their places in the world.

Once Julie did the analysis, the conclusion was obvious, and it became necessary to lock away the aging Max, the source and agent of so much suffering, and to enforce peace and equality among all the races. Thus the Golden Age was born.

>>>

When the tale had been told, Max sat slumped and slack-jawed on the edge of his bed. He had lost the thread of it long before it was finished, though Julie kept going to the end. That story deserved to be told.

Lucidity flickered in his eyes one final time.

"I want to see Mariel," he mumbled almost incoherently.

The bedroom door opened silently, and the faering flew in and settled on the foot of the hospital bed.

"Hello, Little Max," she said. Her tone carried a note of sadness, more than retribution.

Max slowly turned his head to face her and their eyes met as they had on their first meeting so long before.

"I'm dying," Max said. His eyes glazed over a bit. "I may already be dead, though I hope I have enough breath to say...I am sorry."

Mariel gasped, but her voice remained hard. "You're sorry? What do you want from me?"

The light of awareness flickered behind his eyes. "Forgiveness," he whispered.

Her voice softened as she reached out and lifted his chin to meet her eyes. She looked deeply into them, searching for at least a spark of humanity in the shriveled husk of his body and the featureless plain of his mind. When she saw it, flickering in the dark, she whispered, "What do you really want, Little Max?"

"You know." His voice had a strength he thought had long since been lost.

Mariel radiated sadness. A true sadness for the lives this human had claimed, but also a sadness of regret that she had failed in her long-ago mission.

With eyes closed, she wept her poison tears.

Smiling for the first time in decades, Little Max touched a finger to her cheek, then to his lips.

THE END

I write a 300-word flash fiction piece every week. Here's the first one. Okay, what, other than Carnivale, could be the setting for this story?

4

CARNIVALE

The hunting was always good during Carnivale. So many drunken revelers dressed to the nines, dancing to the slow, sensual beat that suffused the entire city. And the masks! Gorgeous masks providing a false sense of anonymity and security. Yes, hunting during Carnivale was a feast for the senses.

Murbella watched the dancers stream past, an impromptu parade pouring out of one club, seeking their next thrill. Most stepped lightly around the puddles left by the early evening rain. Others, though, stumbled on the wet cobblestones, their revelry having started too early and too hard.

There! That one. Like a lioness stalking the weakest of the herd, Murbella slipped out of the darkened doorway and fell in with the dancers.

Her gleaming smile was genuine when the crowd enveloped her. She left a trail of wonder in her wake as she cut through the mob. A hand on the small of a woman's back, a light touch on a well-muscled arm, the momentary sensuousness of wriggling between two tightly pressed bodies. All the while closing the space between herself and the prey.

Her timing was perfect. Just as she reached the blonde whose long hair bobbed slightly off-beat to the blasting music, a hand of the palest white reached out from an alley and grabbed the prey by the arm. In the blink of an eye, she was gone.

Murbella followed, blood heated by the thrill of the chase sharpening her senses.

Sensing a black form in the darkness clutching the helpless blonde, she drove the oaken stake into its back. With long experience, she slid the fire-hardened point between ribs directly into the vampire's heart.

As Murbella helped the would-be prey stand, the ancient monster turned to ash without a sound. Yes, she thought, hunting is exceptional during Carnivale.

THE END

One of the most fun contests is one called Literary Taxidermy, where you have to use the first and last line of a famous story with your own story stuffed between. This one garnered an Honorable Mention.

5

BORDELAISE AUX CHAMPIGNONS

I do not know why I have such a fancy for this little café. But, it is probably the sauce. I sit here every day. Inside when it rains, outside when the pale sun deigns to shine on the Gran Plas. And every day I order the same thing. In fact, I no longer have to order. Unbidden, Francois brings me my *bordelaise aux champignons*, along with my favorite Bordeaux.

The beef is always perfectly seared, leaving a firm crust surrounding a deep red core. Mushrooms swim in a brown elixir whose flavor explodes on my palate. The meat, hearty as it is, serves only as a foundation for those delicate fungi in that glorious sauce. I add a sip of wine with every bite and am transported to a higher plane of the senses. This is what I live for. This is what I kill for.

To say I come here every day is a lie, but a small one as lies go. In truth, I spend a fair amount of time away from Brussels. Some of those trips are short "quick hitters," while some require many days of reconnaissance, surveillance, and planning. Those are the challenging jobs. The short missions pay the bills. The challenging ones import the finest Morels, not the common Chanterelles, for Chef Henri's pan.

I sit at my table, basking in the warmth of the late Springtime sun. As usual, I have the café to myself. I have never adopted the European habit of long lunches and late dinners. Instead, I take my single meal of the day before the sun dips below the rooftops of the Medieval guild houses surrounding this ancient space. I am sure Henri and Francois find it annoying that this quiet, unsocial American requires their services when they'd rather be enjoying each other's company in their flat upstairs. But I pay well and tip even better, so they oblige my eccentricities.

Today, though, my routine is broken. A woman, by the look of her smooth skin probably in her mid-thirties, sits at the table next to mine as Francois sets my dish in front of me with a flourish. The perfect presentation and the heady scent of the day's meal infuse my senses, and my mouth waters in anticipation. Francois refills my wine glass, as usual, and I nod my thanks. He nods ever so slightly toward the recent interloper.

Her lips hold a cigarette, *Gauloises*, I believe, while her hands dig through her voluminous shoulder bag. A muttered curse in English escapes the side of her mouth.

"Mademoiselle," I say as I extend my Zippo to her and flick its wheel. I despise cigarette smoke, but the lighter is just one of many small tools I keep on my person, any of which can be used as a weapon. She smiles and leans forward, and the mingled scent of the lighter's fuel and the harsh Imperial Tobacco smoke assaults my nostrils. Unfortunately, the effect of my gallantry has overwhelmed the aroma of my bordelaise.

"Thank-you, sir," she purrs, and I see the wrinkles at the corners of her mouth burst forth when she smiles. I revise my estimate up by at least a decade. I turn back to my plate. Having lost the scent, I do not wish to lose the flavor to the cooling air, as well.

From my side, I hear the woman say to Francois, "I'll have what he's having, please."

"Very good, Mademoiselle."

As Francois turns, I hear her say, "Use the Morels."

He stops, confused, until I look up and nod. My anticipation foiled by the wisps of smoke escaping her lips and the sudden breeze that has congealed Henri's wonderful sauce, I push my plate away untouched. Perhaps I can dilute my disappointment by enjoying the pleasure of this intruder's company. I pull out the chair to my right and wave my hand as an invitation.

"Thank-you again, sir."

She crushes the foul *Gaulloise* beneath the toe of her brown pump as she glides from her table to mine, sits primly, and crosses her right leg over her left.

"My name is Irina," she says with an extended hand. I take it in mine. Her palm is soft and dry, reminding me of a pampered pet. Her accent is purely American Midwest, and something about her tickles my memory.

"I am...Charles." I stammer a bit. My habit is to have a full identity prepared, complete with backstory and documentation, before starting a job. Between them, I rarely talk to anyone other than Francois or Henri, so the alias I adopted for my life in Brussels does not come quickly to mind.

I swallow when I realize I have told her my real name. She smiles as if having just won a hand of Baccarat, or more likely Poker.

"Nice to meet you, ah, Charles," she says, as if she knows me by another name.

Instantly, I am on alert. To know me by a different name is to have met me either here in Brussels, or while I was on a mission. In either case, I would certainly remember her if we had met before, so I am both wary and intrigued.

"We met briefly in the States," she explains and lays her hand on mine. I see hope in her eyes. Hope that I will remember our encounter? Or hope that I have indeed forgotten it?

"I fear you have me at a disadvantage. I apologize."

I squeeze her hand in apology, but also to neutralize any threat it might pose. In my line of work, I am the hunter, but a hunter must think like prey sometimes. I sense that this woman, beautiful and alluring as she is, is a hunter, as well.

She entwines her fingers with mine.

"I am not surprised. A different decade, a different hair color, a different face, really."

I ponder this strange statement and study her face. Noticing my attention, she closes her eyes and tilts her head back. I see the tiny scar behind her earlobe. Her surgeon was very skilled, and likely very expensive.

My attention shifts when Francois sweeps out of the cafe with her plate. Mine has gone stone cold, the wonderful Morels now locked in the coagulated sauce like flies in amber. Francois harrumphs, looking askance at my untouched meal. I wave a dismissive hand and he carries it back inside.

"I fear I've cost you your meal," Irina says as she slides her plate between us. "Please, share mine."

42

My fingers, interlocked with hers, tense as she lifts her knife. But she smiles, releases my hand, and lifts her fork to slice the meat. With hooded eyes, she presents me with a perfect mix of the most tender beef, the still-firm, woody Morel, and the wine-infused sauce.

The depth of her blue eyes, the scent of the food, and her silky voice as she says, "Taste mine," remove all my guards. I take what she offers. Again, and again.

I feel my mind disassociate from my body, a feeling both euphoric and troubling, as I am not a man who can leave himself unguarded for even a moment. But the smell and the taste, the gaze of her eyes, even the lingering scent of her *Gaulloise* has abducted my ability to think clearly. My heart races for a moment with this recognition, then quickly settles into an ever-slowing rhythm as Irina feeds me another perfect bite.

"I admit I'm a little disappointed you didn't recognize me," she murmurs as my vision contracts into a tunnel that reveals only her face. "I suppose the surgery was effective." I cannot form the words that come to mind into a coherent sentence.

"But it was more than twenty years ago, and we met only briefly," she continues. "I imagine in your line of work you try not to remember the survivors."

Again, my heart beats a little quicker, but the next bite soothes me again.

"I was in the corner of my father's library when you came for him. You didn't see me until I foolishly cried out as you plunged the stiletto through his eye. At that moment, I knew my life was about to end. But instead of eliminating a witness, you frowned and escaped through the window. I've never understood why you made that choice, but my old life did end that day."

A fragment of a memory intrudes on my chemically induced bliss. I see a terrified young woman, too frightened to scream. The sharply defined cheekbones and slightly upturned nose match. I open my mouth to speak, but I can no longer even find the words I wish to say.

"It took over ten years to find you, then more to learn your habits." She spread her hands, indicating the café. I feel my mouth hanging open, but I am unable to close it.

"I paid a rather nasty chemist a fortune to develop the odorless and tasteless hypnotic that is, at this moment, disassembling your brain's neural connections." She reveals a small perfume atomizer concealed in her palm. Her face fills my entire world as she leans forward.

"You'll forget everything else, but remember this…" She smiles broadly as her face slides out of my vision tunnel, and I feel the world tipping. I hear, but do not feel, my head crack against the stone pavers beneath the table. In my fading vision, the face I will not forget is replaced by her perfectly shaped legs as she uncrosses them and stands. I notice for the first time the bows at the instep of her pumps.

They remind me somehow, disgustingly, of mushrooms.

THE END

"Starside Interlude" is one of a series of standalone Science Fiction stories in the Roanoke series. They feature the same cast set in the near-ish future.

6

STARSIDE INTERLUDE

Cara repacked her bag for the third time. The combined body-baggage weight limits were strict on the orbital shuttle, and the stress of the "Roanoke Incident" from weeks before had added a couple kilos to the body side of the equation. Government hearings are never easy, especially when corporate corruption leads to thousands of deaths. Cara, being the government's star witness, spent six weeks in a safe house while being deposed and cross-examined over and over again. It was only after she refused to speak for two solid weeks that the Company shrinks intervened and got her released.

Zipping the small travel bag for the final time, she wondered where the notion of flying through the upper atmosphere at hypersonic speeds, followed by an orbital insertion, rendezvous, and two weeks at the Starside Hotel as a relaxing vacation came from. She had never done any of those things, and none of them particularly appealed to her. As an executive with Space ETC, she had every opportunity to go to space, but had begged off every invitation. So, what compelled her to make the reservations as soon as her "protection detail" gave her back her coms?

I need to see if I can live in space, she thought as her coms notified her that the auto-trans she ordered had arrived.

That's not it, and you know it. You're chasing Nick, is all.

Arguing with herself was not an unusual occurrence. At least she kept it inside her head as she rode the elevator to the ground floor.

No, I'm not. I have to decide what I'm going to do with the rest of my life.

And that invitation to emigrate to Roanoke has nothing to do with it?

Of course, it does, but it's only one option.

Yeah? What are the others?

Oh, shut up.

The auto-trans dutifully sat at the curb outside her apartment building. Its floor to ceiling windows glinting in the subtropical sun. As she approached, she held up the scan code on her coms and smiled her face-rec smile. The door slid open, and Cara slid into the forward-facing seat.

Normally, the transport's AI would ease them into traffic as soon as she sat down, but it jerked to a stop, instead, after going just a few feet.

"Why did we—" Cara started to ask but froze when the door slide open again and a man practically jumped in, landing on the seat facing her.

"Hey!" she yelped before regaining her composure. "This is a private ride. And how did you make it stop…"

She trailed off as the windows blanked into privacy mode, and the auto-trans sped away, forcing her back into the seat. The strange man slid across his seat to the door, and Cara countered by sliding the other way, though she realized she had trapped herself inside an opaque, not-fully automatic auto-trans with a strange man.

"Good morning, Ms. Linn." The man flipped his shaggy mop of hair out of his eyes. "Sorry for the intrusion, but I needed a ride, and yours was close by, so…"

"Wait a minute. How the Hell do you know my name? And how—"

"Not to worry. I'm going to the spaceport, too, with just a short side-trip. You'll get there in plenty of time for your…" His eyes glazed over for a moment, "two o'clock flight."

An Augment!

That explains a lot.

No kidding.

"Stay the hell out of my data, you freak."

The man chuckled and brushed his hair back from his face.

"I'm not in your data, Cara. Just the Company's. Their security has really gone to shit since your friends were killed."

Despite herself, she felt the need to defend the company that conned thousands and nearly killed her lover.

"We had to take down a lot of it to let the government suits in."

"Along with every wannabe hacker and skiddie out there. Your data is basically public domain now."

The faraway look returned to his eyes.

I wonder what that looks like or feels like. Or is it a completely new sense?

He's a freak.

But a cute one, and kinda cool.

Oh, God. Don't tell me you're attracted—The auto-trans took a hard right, then a hard left. Sweat broke out on the man's forehead.

"Damn," he muttered as he leaned into turns that threw Cara hard against the far wall, then made her grab the armrest to keep from sliding into the man's lap.

Holy crap. He's driving this thing from in here.

After a couple minutes, which seemed like an hour to Cara, the auto-trans skidded to a stop.

"Sorry about that," he said, his eyes focused on Cara. "Had to…make sure we weren't followed."

Cara's eyes darted to the door.

If I dive for it—

The man shook his head. "It won't open for you, yet. Plus, you don't want to get out here."

Cara's window cleared for a moment, showing the dimly lit interior of a warehouse, before blanking again.

"I'll be right back," he said.

Before Cara could gather herself, the door slid open, the man tumbled out, and it closed again.

"AI, AI, open the door!" Cara called out as she punched the Door Open button repeatedly.

"I am sorry, Ma'am. That service is currently not available."

"What do you mean, it's unavailable? Open the freakin' door!"

"I am sorry, Ma'am. That service is currently not—"

"Just shut up."

48

With an angry shake of her head, Cara pulled out her coms, but it displayed a large red circle with a bar across it. "Service Unavailable" scrolled across the screen.

"Arrgh."

Cara pounded her fist against the door, but when that only made her hand sore, she stood and held her coms up high, hoping to get some kind of signal. So, when the auto-trans jerked into motion again, she lost her balance and fell back onto her seat.

All the windows cleared as the transport merged into traffic on an unfamiliar backstreet.

"AI, where are you taking me?"

"Your current destination is the Orbital Shuttle terminal at La Estrella Spaceport. Would you like to change that destination?"

"No. Why did we stop back there?"

"I'm sorry, Ma'am, but we have not stopped on this trip."

Of course, that augment would cover his tracks.

"AI, why are we taking this route to the spaceport?"

"Traffic has been heavy, Ma'am, which has necessitated some rerouting."

Bullshit, but well played.

Oh, stop with the Bad Boy infatuation. We've had enough excitement to last a lifetime.

Sure. Now we're going to relax by getting launched into space.

Makes perfect sense.

"Excuse me, Ma'am, but I have just received a message with instructions to play an audio file. Can I play that now?"

"Who is this message from?"

"I am sorry, Ma'am, but the message is encrypted with a privacy seal. Can I play it for you now?"

49

"Ah, sure."

Bad Boy's voice boomed from the speakers. "Pay attention, Cara, you'll only get to hear this once. When I'm done, the message and all traces of it will disappear." He paused for effect. "OK, while you were panicking, I slipped a crypto-card into the front pocket of your bag."

The recording paused again while Cara dug into her bag. She pulled out a nondescript business card with the number "5412" printed on it.

"Got it? Good. The card has an embedded chip with two files on it. One file is for you and contains instructions on how to access a CryptoBank account with one hundred thousand sollars in it. That's yours to keep simply for the inconvenience of our little side trip this morning. I suggest you download it, access the account, and change the passkey as soon as you can. Because, if you hand-deliver the card to room number printed on it at the Starside Hotel, that Crypto account will grow by an additional one million sollars. That's it. Simple as that. Oh, and it might be obvious, but don't tell anyone about this." The unspoken "or else" hung in the air.

Cara sat in stunned silence for a moment, then yelled, "AI, replay that message."

"I'm sorry, Ma'am. What message are you referring to?"
Gone already.
Did I just hear that right?
One way to find out.

She held the crypto-card next to her coms and opened a browser app. Sure enough, there were two files on it.
Should I open it? It could be a hack job.
If this is just a phishing attempt, it's awfully involved.
True. Still, what do I know about him?
Other than he's cute.

50

Don't be stupid. If he hacks your coms, he could get into all your data.

He hacked an auto-trans and drove it manually from inside. I seriously doubt our coms would present much of a problem for him. Besides, he's cute.

Well...true.

She tried to drag the files to her coms, but only the one named README.TXT moved. After she touched the bio-locked file and every one of her malware scanning tools agreed it was safe, it opened.

CryptoBank account 48776120365 passkey
YourLucky100KDay!

A quick trip to the CryptoBank site confirmed there was indeed a balance of one hundred thousand sollars, the Solar System's standard currency in the account. Thinking up the passkey "#1:AreAllAugmentedBadBoysCute?" took her a minute.

Should I transfer the money to my account?

And pay tax on it? The whole point of CryptoBank is to keep the money anonymous.

True. But then how will I spend it?

There are lots of ways to spend sollars, especially where we're headed. Besides, once we drop off the crypto-card—

What? Are we going through with this?

It's a million sollars! With that, you can sit on a beach, or be on the next transport to Roanoke.

We have no idea what we may be getting into, though.

But it's a million sollars.

Before she could decide, the AI chimed in with, "We have arrived at your destination, Ma'am. Please gather your belongings and have a nice day!"

The door slid open, and Cara tucked the card back into her bag and headed for the departure lounge.

The screamer flight wasn't as nerve-wracking as Cara imagined it would be. In fact, compared to her auto-trans ride earlier, the orbital shuttle was a relaxing ride through the clouds. As Nick had suggested many times, she skipped breakfast, waiting to see how her stomach would handle free-fall. Luckily, the constant sense of falling that being weightless caused didn't bother her. One or two others on the shuttle weren't so lucky, though the sound of them retching into their sick bags was mostly drowned out by the euphoric cheering of the other passengers.

Looking at the curved blue Earth, surrounded by a pure black sky, made her feel a bit queasy, as it seemed to hang above her like the Sword of Damocles, even though there was no "above" or "below" out there.

Twenty minutes of orbital maneuvering brought the Starside Hotel into view. A floating Ferris wheel, the massive structure rotated majestically in the emptiness. Sunlight and reflected Earthlight twinkled off the many windows of the hotel, making it sparkle like a Christmas ornament hanging from a branch. An awed hush fell over the passengers.

Their headphones, needed to cancel the screaming of the engines as they rose through the atmosphere, began explaining the amenities available at the hotel, the hotel's layout, and a quick tutorial on how to move about in microgravity. Cara, whose department had trained the hotel staff, and created all the visitors' tutorials, knew the spiel by heart, so she tuned it out and focused on the Company's crowning achievement slowly turning as if showing off.

The hotel's orientation kept it tidally locked because of a long central spire pointing downward toward the planet. The difference in orbital velocities between the tip of the tower and the body of the hotel kept the premium Earth View rooms facing ever inward. Cara had opted for a less-outrageously expensive Star View room.

Lack of air made for sharp-edged, black shadows which melted away and reformed again as the hotel did its twirling dance around the Earth. A shiver went through Cara as the shifting shadows made the hotel look like a live thing with writhing, shifting skin.

Beautiful, isn't it?

Yes, but eerie, too

The shuttle swung into docking position with the hotel between it and the Earth, and it started turning to match the rotation of the hotel.

"—Once the shuttle has docked with the hotel, disembarking may begin. Handrails are within easy reach along the shuttle's ceiling and throughout the zero- and low-g areas of the hotel to help you maneuver. Please keep your harness buckled until you see the green exit light."

The recording paused while Cara felt little jerks of thrust, followed by a shudder and the mechanical whir of the shuttle's hatch mating with the docking port. A chime sounded and a green exit icon lit above her seat.

Nick's instructions about how to move about in free-fall came to mind, so Cara slipped on a Velcro glove, wriggled her bag backpack-style over her shoulders, and reached for the overhead handrail before unbuckling her harness and leaving her seat. Being unfettered in free-fall was a very different feeling than being strapped tightly into her seat.

Whoa! Which way is up?

You know there's no "up" up here, right?

She swallowed hard.

Right. Still, it's weird.

And cool.

Yeah, and cool.

The chaos of disembarking would have been very frustrating to Cara yesterday, or even first thing that morning, but instead she found the thrashing about of a shuttle-full of zero-g rookies, including herself, incredibly comical. Being one hundred kilosols richer definitely lightened her mood.

The hotel staff herded the passengers with gentle nudges—

Well trained, if I do say so myself,

—along a corridor to a bank of lifts which slowly descended from the central hub of the hotel down to the one gravity "G" level. There were some disappointed boos, but more relieved sighs as the lift descended and the feeling of gravity returned, then slowly increased.

Awed gasps replaced the boos and sighs as the lift doors opened onto the hotel lobby. The two-story space was smaller than a similar lobby back on Earth—volume was always at a premium in space—but nowhere on Earth could compare with the view. One wall facing the lifts was a floor-to-ceiling window onto the blue and white Earth. It extended from the lobby into the bar and restaurant, giving a panoramic view that held the passengers spellbound until the lift's AI chimed in.

"Please exit the lift and proceed to the check-in desk," a pleasant female voice prodded them. The orientation of the hotel, with its axis pointing down toward the Earth, suddenly made a lot more sense to Cara.

Being off to the side, it looks a lot less threatening, like a fantastic landscape, instead of a giant boulder hanging over our head.

Yeah, a landscape streaming by, like through a window on a train.

A train traveling over twenty-thousand miles an hour!

The young woman behind the desk greeted Cara with a pasted-on smile, like she had with the ten other passengers ahead of her in line. Her name badge read Ariadne. Without waiting for the standard greeting, Cara said, "Hello, Ariadne. I'm Cara Linn."

"Good morning Ms. Linn...Oh! *Director* Linn." Ariadne's smile turned a lot more genuine. "It's so nice to have you as our guest for the next week."

The woman's reaction was confusing, since Cara never met low-level trainees, and she had told no one about this trip.

"I see you booked a Star View room," she paused, reading her screen, "but I also see that you have been upgraded to an Earth View suite on the Concierge Level. That will be Level Point-Eight, which means you'll be enjoying eight-tenths gravity in your room and throughout the Concierge Level, which includes amenities like an open bar, high-roller casino, private dining, and a True-Infinity® Pool."

Cara could almost hear the Registered Trademark symbol in the woman's tone of voice as she rattled off the standard Concierge Level greeting reserved for the rich and famous.

What the hell is going on? I'm neither rich nor famous.

Ariadne continued, "Access codes are all now in your account, so you may use your coms or any other personal-key

55

device you have to access the Concierge Level, your room itself, and all the amenities up there."

She reached into a drawer and slid a pair of Augmented Reality glasses across the counter. "If you need these, they have been paired with your account, as well."

Generally, Cara found AR distracting, so she tucked the glasses into her bag.

With a glance to either side, Ariadne held up a gold bangle bracelet with the Company logo engraved on it. "Once you lock this on your wrist, you will have access to the hotel's Premium Network, giving your coms the best access we offer."

And it will track my whereabouts, no doubt.

The woman's voice dropped to a near-whisper. "It will also pair with any augments you may have, though augmented access is blocked while in the casino." She held out the bracelet to Cara. "May I?"

Cara didn't extend her arm as the woman expected.

"And if I want to take the thing off?"

The woman looked flustered for a moment, then recovered. "Oh, once locked on, we'll be happy to remove it for you here at the front desk, but you should know that will deactivate it and we won't be able to turn this unit back on. To prevent fraud, of course. Not that that would apply to you…" Flustered at having gone off script, Ariadne thrust the bracelet closer to Cara. "May I?"

"I see." Cara gingerly took the bracelet from Ariadne's fingers and dropped it in her bag, along with the AR glasses. "I'll put that on later."

"Oh, um, OK. Well, you're all set then, Director Linn. Once again, welcome to the Starside Hotel."

Her performance complete, Ariadne visibly relaxed until Cara refused to leave.

"Is there something else I can help you with?" she asked, sounding as if she hoped the answer was "No."

Instead, Cara said, "Yes. Who upgraded my accommodations?"

Ariadne's plastic smile came back, and she shrugged. "I'm sorry, Director Linn, I don't have access to that information. There was just an upgrade notice attached to your reservation." When Cara still didn't leave, she offered, "Perhaps the reservation system recognized your ID and knew your...position in the Company?"

And tried to buy me off.

Or maybe Bad Boy sweetened the deal.

Realizing she wouldn't get anything more useful from the clerk, Cara smiled, thanked her for her help, and headed back to the lifts.

The suite of rooms was small compared to an Earthbound luxury hotel—again, space being at a premium in space—but its appointments more than made up for its size. The hall door opened into a lounge with a small glass table with two chairs, a two-seat sofa, and a chaise. They all faced a window wall as impressive as the lobby's. Cara stood, mesmerized by the clouds, oceans, and mountains sliding by outside. The lack of air outside the window made the Earth look close enough to reach out and touch.

Earthshine provided a surprising amount of light in the suite. The tall windows could be dimmed to simulate nighttime, or to reduce the glare when the sun periodically came into view.

Cara followed a short hallway to her right, past a spa-like bath whose own window on the entire Earth would satisfy even the most exhibitionistic desires, into the suite's bedroom. A king size bed, dressed all in white, dominated the room.

The eighty percent gravity on this level was a delight. She kicked off her shoes and the plush, soft pile of the carpet felt like a cloud under her bare feet. With a half-pirouette, she settled, rather than flopped, onto the bed. Lying on the duvet felt like floating in a perfectly calm pool.

I could spend the entire week right here.

She felt the tension of the auto-trans ride, the screamer flight, and her mysterious upgrade melt into the psuedown bedding.

Well, maybe the next hour, at least.

As her eyes flickered closed, a doorbell snapped her awake, followed by the sound of the hall door opening and a voice calling out.

"Hello, Ms. Linn? Are you in here?"

Jumping out of the bed in the light gravity sent Cara banging into the closet doors. As she regained her balance, a man dressed in hotel livery appeared at the bedroom door.

"Oh, I'm sorry, Ms. Linn. I'm *Robert*," he pronounced his name in the French way, Ro-bear. "I am your personal concierge. I received a notice that your door was opened, but," he glanced at Cara's wrist, "your access bracelet did not indicate that you were in the room. I see now, though, that you haven't activated it yet. Can I help you with that?"

Why don't they just call it a tracker?

Because most people want to be tracked.

"No, thank-you. It's not…my style. But I'll tell you what I'll do." She picked up her bag and plucked the bangle from its pocket. "I'll hang it on my purse."

Without waiting for the concierge to voice his objection, Cara snapped the bracelet around the purse's shoulder strap.

"There, now I can use the Premium Access whenever I want."

"But—" he sputtered, then regained his composure. "Of course, Madam, as you say."

Robert turned to go, but Cara's Company Director's voice stopped him.

"Oh, and *Robert*, never enter a lady's room uninvited and unaccompanied again."

She easily read the look of fear, then hatred that flickered across his face before he lifted his chin into the air and strode from the room.

Need to keep an eye on that one.

Maybe I should find the HR rep up here.

Or wait until I'm home and fire his ass.

Thoughts of a nap gone, Cara grabbed her now trackable purse, put on the hotel's AR glasses, and went exploring.

With a little experimentation, Cara discovered she could adjust the intrusiveness of the data feed that displayed on the glasses. On maximum, the view of reality was merely a ghostly apparition behind the information that scrolled and shifted across her field of view. It streamed headlines from at least three news feeds, a hotel itinerary showing a schedule of the various activities offered, and tidbits about every plant, doorway, or object d'art she passed. After only a minute, she turned it down to the minimum setting, so it only responded to her whispered requests.

Up in the Free-Fall Lounge in the hotel's hub, she floated tethered to the wall, ignoring the ubiquitous panoramic view of Earth as she whispered commands that filled her AR with floor plans of the hotel.

There is no room number 5412.

She asked three different ways, but couldn't find any room that had that number.

No guest room, at least. Let's see what privileges being a Company Director nets me.

"AR, show me the corporate training facilities," she subvocalized, her lips barely moving.

Although she couldn't feel it, she knew the glasses authenticated her by scanning her irises and retinas.

They've probably harvested my DNA by now, too.

All in the name of keeping me secure.

Well, their data may be secure, but my privacy isn't.

A floorplan popped into her vision. A block of offices, a conference room, and an oversized area labeled "Lunchroom/Assembly" were highlighted. They had four-digit room numbers.

"Ah hah!"

A few heads turned from the windows at her exclamation. She sheepishly pointed at her glasses and shrugged.

"AR, access all hotel floor plans."

After a brief pause, the AR glasses responded with a buzz against her temporal bone and a green message on the display, "Access granted."

"Good. Now find 5412."

Instantly, a hallway with banks of small rooms on either side appeared. Room number 5412 was half-way down the hall.

"AR, whose room is that?"

"Access to that information is restricted."

"Company Director override."

"Override unsuccessful. Data is accessible only by...The All-Knowing, All-Seeing, Greatest Power in the Universe."

What?

Goddamned Bad Boy!

"OK. AR, show me the transaction log for room 5412 for the last thirty days."

Cara scrolled through several pages of room entry and exit events for the room until the final ones from ten days ago. They read:

> 0731: Occupant Mark Deshields (Maintenance
> Engineering) vacated
> 0721: Room assigned to Housekeeping.
> 0942: Room access by Francis Holden
> (Housekeeping)
> 1022: Room available
> 1023: Room out of service

Beyond that, nothing.

"AR, why was room 5412 taken out of service?"

"Data is accessible only by The All-Knowing—"

"AR, stop! Show me directions to room 5412."

A 3-D map of the hotel floated in her vision with a blue line leading from the Free-Fall lounge in the hub, down one of the four spokes on the far side of the wheel from her room, deep into the interior of the space hotel.

As Cara unhooked her tether and pushed off the wall toward the lift, the AR pinged and an urgent message indicator appeared.

Great. What now?

Reluctantly, she opened the message. The familiar face of Sarah Fielding, the Hotel Director appeared on the screen.

With a genuine smile, she said, "Cara, I was just informed that you've checked into my humble hotel. Why didn't you

61

tell me you were coming? Well, I suppose you wanted to escape the madness of the last few weeks. Anyway, I'm having a small dinner party for some Big Wigs this evening right down the hall from your suite. There's eveningwear in your closet now that should fit. If not, or you'd like something else, just ring for Robert. I've also booked you for a massage and makeover in the Spa in," she glanced away from the camera for a moment. "Oh, just fifteen minutes. Better hurry! I promise I'll leave you alone after this."

The <Reply> icon blinked insistently. Cara flicked it off the screen with her eyes.

So much for a relaxing getaway.
Pretty damn rude. Who are these "Big Wigs," anyway?
Hopefully, 'Robert' *will know.*

Robert did know, and he took great delight in the fact that he did and she didn't.

"Of course, Director Linn. The, ahem, King and Queen of Jameslandia are staying in the Royal Suite, which is where the dinner will be."

"'Jameslandia?' I've never heard of that country."

"I am not surprised. Jameslandia is a single-island nation populated by one James Land and his wife Elizabeth."

Cara burst out laughing, and even Robert smiled.

"Apparently, he is very big in the Augmentation Tech industry."

AugTech was rapidly growing among younger information workers. It gave them a competitive career advantage and had become a sign of both style and rebellion, despite the fact that part of their brains and thoughts were given over to men like James Land.

"Yes, I've heard of him. I've even seen his ranting videos online."

Both of their coms chimed at the same time. As Cara reached in her bag, Robert's eyes unfocused for a second, then he said, "It is time for your spa treatment, Ma'am. Would you like me to escort you?"

So, you're an Augment, too. Better remember that.

She pulled her AR glasses from her shoulder bag. "Not necessary. Thank-you for your help."

With that, Robert nodded, turned on his heel, and left Cara alone in the suite.

Why do I feel like I'm being watched?

'Cause I probably am. All the time.

She fingered the encrypted crypto-card in her bag.

I've got to get rid of this thing. I don't know what's on it, or why they couldn't just mail the file.

Or who's in Room 5412. Or who Bad Boy is, or, or...

OK, so I'll deliver it this evening after dinner.

Hold on. This is so sketchy. I should just stick it in a waste chute.

But I'll get a million sols if I just slip it under the door.

She looked at her own hall door. It fit tightly into the doorway all the way around.

Well, that won't work.

Her coms chimed again, more insistently this time, and Cara's shoulders slumped in exasperation.

This isn't going to be the relaxing vacation I was planning, is it?

With a mental nod, she didn't need to answer herself.

James Land was the arrogant blowhard that Cara expected, but his wife Elizabeth, "Call me Bette," was anything but. Cara found her quick wit and self-deprecating humor quite charming. And she appreciated Bette's well-timed snide comments, aimed at James whenever his ego tried to suck the air out of the room. But what won Cara over was Bette's absolute refusal to get augmented. The conversation turned that way while Cara sipped her after-dinner Grand Marnier.

"It's just a crutch for the mentally weak and self-esteem challenged," Bette said. "We should learn how to use the ninety percent of our brains that is lying around unutilized today, rather than becoming dependent on someone else's tech," she looked pointedly at her husband. "Someone else's data stream bandwidth," this time she glared at Director Fielding, "and whatever fake crap any crazy posts. I'd rather Let Humans be Human."

Her use of that phrase, "Let Humans be Human," commonly just called "LHbH" in the anti-aug community, resonated with Cara, though she had never taken sides in the Nature versus Nervature debate.

I like her.

I like her a lot.

The debate raged on for a while, James defending his AugTech, Sarah defending her bandwidth pricing policies, and Betty effortlessly deflecting and countering each of their arguments. Cara, as was her nature, simply sat back and watched the discussion go from good-natured to heated. When they revisited the same arguments for the third time, she barely stifled a yawn.

"Oh my," Sarah sounded genuinely embarrassed. "This discussion has definitely gone over the edge it boring. My apologies, Cara."

Cara, herself embarrassed by her *faux pas*, simply shrugged.

Bette spoke up. "Sarah, I understand there is a zero-g yoga class every morning?"

Regaining her composure, Sarah replied, "That's right, up level in the Hub."

"I also understand it is a partnering activity. It requires two partners to participate?"

Sarah nodded and Bette glanced at Cara, who felt a deepening sense of dread.

Sarah didn't notice while her eyes flicked over Bette's figure. "That's right. We specifically designed the positions to offer each partner the proper resistance while floating, perfectly balanced, weightlessly. It takes some practice, but it can be a lot of fun."

Her excitement changed to disappointment, however, and Cara's fears were realized, when Bette turned to her and said, "Cara, would you be my partner tomorrow morning?"

Her smile was irresistible, and a shiver of fear mixed with excitement ran through Cara.

"I, well…" She fought hard to resist looking down at her own body, sheathed in her very chic, but one size too small evening dress. "I'm not the yoga type. Let alone in zero-g."

Bette's smile broadened, and she swept her hands down her ample body like a shopping channel model. "Neither am I. But it'll be fun, and we can make fun of the serious 'yogsters.'"

I can see her—us—doing that.
It would be fun.

65

Bette's smile was infectious, and before making a conscious decision, Cara found herself nodding and saying, "I'd like that. It will be fun."

Sarah quickly hid the disappointment from her face and replaced it with her best company smile. Her tone of voice, though, made it clear the dinner party was at an end.

"Well, that's settled. I'm sure you'll have a good time."

Sarah's and James's farewells were simply formal nods, but Bette gave Cara a big hug and squeezed her hand before planting a light kiss on her cheek.

"I'll see you in the morning, right, dear?"

Feeling her blush rising, Cara nodded mutely and practically ran from the suite.

With thoughts of zero-g yoga with Bette Land swirling through her head, Cara almost forgot her evening's primary mission—getting rid of the mysterious business card. With auglasses in place, she followed their directions to a dark, empty hallway. Number 5412 was three doors down on her right.

As she approached, creeping forward on tiptoe, head swiveling from side to side, she expected any of the other doors to burst open any second. She heard murmured voices behind a couple of them as she passed, but then focused on the door numbered 5412. Something was different about it, the way the light from the dim wall fixtures failed to reflect like the other doors. Almost as if...

It's ajar. The door's ajar. Like whoever is in there is waiting for me. Inviting me in.

This might be easier than I thought.

Or a trap.

66

Cara stood in front of the suspicious door. Sure enough, it stood slightly ajar, though not open enough to see inside. Scanning the hallway again, she knocked lightly with the first knuckle of her right index finger. No answer. She knocked again, a little more firmly. Still no answer, but at least this time, the door swung open enough for her to poke her head in.

Good. I'll just put it on a dresser or table, or something.

A coppery smell reached her nose, sending a shiver down her spine.

I'm not going in there.

Maybe I can reach it from the doorway.

She leaned forward and looked around the partially opened door.

Just drop it on the floor.

But they might not see it—Oh, crap!

She wanted to scream at what she saw in the room, but her conscious brain suppressed it enough so only a muffled gasp escaped.

The only light in the room came from an alarm clock on the bedside table, and the display screen mounted on the wall to Cara's right. Its dim illumination revealed a horrific scene. What looked like dark red paint spattered the walls and the display screen. The room's straight-back desk chair stood facing that screen, surrounded by a pool of dark red, almost black, liquid—blood. So much blood. The figure of a man was tied to the chair, his body slumped and lifeless. His head hung over the back of the chair, attached to his body only by the muscles and sinew at the back of his neck.

Cara took a stumbling step backward, her hands covering her mouth. Her gorge rose into her throat before she gagged it back down. Only then did the message on the display screen register with her conscious mind. It was short and cryptic, though its meaning was crystal clear to her. It read simply "8672."

The next few hours were a blur. Though she tried not to look conspicuous, Cara couldn't walk at a normal pace on the way to her suite. Luckily, the few people she passed took no notice of her as she hurried by. Yoga pants, a sports bra, a shirt with a drawstring around the waistband, and a pair of Velcro socks were laid out on her bed, but she ignored them as she rushed into the bathroom and vomited up her dinner.

Repeated flashes of red light from the lounge area brought her out of the bathroom, toothbrush still in her mouth. The main display screen flashed an emergency message in bright crimson:

> EMERGENCY ALERT: ALL GUESTS
> MUST RETURN TO AND REMAIN IN
> THEIR ROOMS UNTIL FURTHER
> NOTICE. ALL STAFF REPORT TO
> INCIDENT STATIONS DELTA.

Her coms unit buzzed and flashed the same message.
What the—oh. Somebody found the body.
Yeah, because I left the door open.
Did I leave anything else behind?
Her mind raced through the horrific memory.
No fingerprints. I used my knuckle.
DNA, though?
From my knuckle? If they look for it on the door, I guess.
Crap. Of course, they'll look on the door.

And surveillance cameras! They probably tracked my entire trip.

Cara almost dashed back into the bathroom, but she swallowed the panic and forced herself to think as she scrubbed the back of her tongue with the toothbrush. No way out of the mess she had gotten herself into presented itself.

She couldn't turn off the flashing red display, but she could at least dismiss the alert on her coms. Then she noticed the other two messages queued for her attention. Both were encrypted and required her private key to open.

She could almost hear Bad Boy's voice as she read the first message.

> My apologies for any inconvenience you
> may have suffered last night. These things
> happen sometimes. Please dispose of the
> crypto-card down the waste chute in your
> room. Thank you for your efforts. As a token
> of our goodwill and appreciation, we have
> purged your image from the surveillance
> recordings and have deposited an additional
> two hundred thousand sollars in the
> following account. We trust this honorarium
> will ensure your discretion.

A twelve-digit account number followed the message.

Inconvenience! You think finding a tortured and mutilated body is an inconvenience?

Cara fought another wave of panic and nausea.

At least it's over with, now.

And there's the half-mil.

True. What's this other message?

69

Ms. Linn,

We know you are in possession of a very
valuable artifact that we have already gone
to great lengths to acquire. Most notably, our
efforts were focused on Mr. Blanque, whom
you—perhaps "met" is not the right word—
encountered this evening. It seems the
timing of our meeting with Mr. Blanque was
premature, to your benefit and his detriment.
To prevent a similar outcome befalling you,
we require that you leave said artifact in
your room when you go to Yoga class in the
morning.

How the Hell do they know I'm supposed to go to a Yoga class in the morning?
They must have hacked the door locks if they want me to leave the card here.
But, how?
More importantly, are they in here now?
Or did they leave any cams behind?
Cara swung her head from side to side, then ran through the suite, frantically looking for intruders or hidden cameras. When she had scoured the three rooms, she sat on the edge of the bed.

The bedside clock read 1:22 AM. She was mentally, emotionally, and physically exhausted. But the thought of getting undressed for bed when assassins could be watching through some camera too small for her to find sent chills down her spine. Instead, she kicked off her shoes, pulled back the duvet, and crawled into the bed still wearing her evening dress. The yoga pants and shirt laid out on the bed for her fell to the floor. Cara sat bolt upright.

Robert!

Of course. He knew about the yoga class, and he has access to the room.

She reread the message up on her coms.

Jesus, he even writes like he has his nose in the air.

And his thumb up his butt.

This means he's in on it—he's a murderer.

A torturer and murderer.

I am so screwed. I should just do what he says—leave the card here in the morning and get the hell off this orbiting deathtrap.

Decision made. But her coms dinged with a message.

> Cara Linn, we want the crypto-card you
> were given and will pay for it--*2,000,000
> on an untraceable cybercoin. Go to the Star
> View Lounge tomorrow at noon for the
> exchange.

Another one!?! How many people know about this thing?

And what is on it that is so important that they're willing to pay two million sols for it?

And kill for it, don't forget that.

Cara looked back at her coms to read the message again, but it faded to a blank screen, and no amount of searching could find any remnant of it. Lying in bed, fully clothed, she stared at the ceiling.

Bad Boy wants me to destroy the card. And he paid me an extra two hundred thousand sols to do so.

No, he wants you to drop it in the waste chute. He could have someone in the basement searching the trash that comes down.

That's a great job.

Do I owe him now? Am I somehow obligated because he paid me?

But I didn't agree to anything. That's unsolicited money, paid to make up for almost getting me killed.

Which is a nice gesture…

Then Robert wants me to leave it in the room without offering me anything in return.

Except not being tortured and murdered!

That's a pretty compelling argument.

And now I've gotten a third offer of two million sols to hand it over to someone else.

I should just pack up, leave the card on the bed, and catch the morning shuttle.

But Bad Boy already paid me to get rid of it. Do I owe him for that?

He's the cause of all of this. He's the one who put me into this situation. I don't owe him anything.

So, I get out of Dodge in the morning.

Except two million sols would buy me a place on Roanoke.

But the timing doesn't work. Yoga class is at ten o'clock, the shuttle is at eleven o'clock, and the meeting in the Star View Lounge is at noon. If I stay and hand over the card at noon, I'll miss the shuttle.

And I could be dead by tomorrow's shuttle if Robert doesn't find the card in my room.

As she lay there, wide awake, pondering her dilemma, the suite's door lock clicked open and three men appeared at the bedroom door, guns drawn. Seeing Cara cowering in bed with the duvet pulled up to her chin, the squad leader holstered his weapon.

"Director Linn, I'm Chief Carter, head of Hotel Security. You need to come with us."

"I've told you a hundred times already, I don't have any idea of how my DNA got on that door!" Cara sat in a tiny interrogation room in the deepest part of the hotel.

"Well, it didn't just magically float there." Chief Carter was playing Bad Cop.

"Actually, Chief, it could have. Sort of." A young female detective, who had introduced herself as Janice, no last name, was clearly playing the role of Good Cop.

Watch out for her. She'll try to trap me.

Carter turned to Janice with a look of annoyance.

"No, really, it could have been transferred from someone else." Janice smiled at Cara. "Who did you come in contact with yesterday?"

"About a hundred people. I came up on the shuttle yesterday. We were all floating around, bumping into each other."

Janice shook her head. "No, I mean skin-to-skin contact."

Be careful. She's not as nice as she seems.

But Janice had a point. And Cara saw a way out.

"Well, I shook hands with several people. Let's see, the bartender, Joey, I think his name was, up in the Free-Fall Lounge, for one. Of course, *Robert*, my concierge, butler, or whatever he is, has handled a lot of my things. He could have picked up my DNA from any number of items."

She paused as if thinking, but could clearly see how the rest of this little game would play out. She had been in too many corporate staff meetings with back-stabbing directors and vice-presidents to be intimidated by these two rent-a-cops.

"Oh, of course. There was Hotel Director Fielding and the King and Queen." She made air quotes. "I had dinner with them last evening."

Janice scrolled her tablet. "That would be James and Elizabeth Land?"

Cara nodded. "Yes, the 'King and Queen' of 'Jameslandia.'"

Janice grinned at Cara's derisive tone, and even Chief Carter snorted a little.

Time to be the boss.

"Look, Janice…and Chief Carter. I know quite a bit about this hotel. My people trained you and the rest of the hotel staff on how to run everything from the orbital maintenance thrusters to the washing machines. So, I know we blanketed this place with surveillance cameras. If you had me on camera going into there—" Cara pointed at the crime scene photos arrayed on the table in front of her. "We wouldn't have been sitting here for the last three hours. I'd be locked up tight waiting for the next shuttle. So, my question to you is, why haven't you picked up whomever is on your surveillance footage?"

Chief Carter sat back in his chair, arms folded, with a deep scowl. Janice seemed to deflate a little and the overly friendly smile melted from her face.

"There is evidence that our surveillance feeds have been…tampered with."

Gotcha!

Cara raised her eyebrows in mock surprise.

74

"And your door lock logs? They should show who was out and about last night."

Janice glanced at the Chief for confirmation. He nodded.

"We store the door logs on the same system as the video streams. We have to assume they've been compromised as well."

Sorry to do this to you, Bette.

"Shouldn't you be looking for someone with the skills to pull off those hacks? Maybe someone who is the brains behind a giant tech company?"

Janice's eyes defocused and her lips twitched.

Another Augment.

After a couple seconds, Janice turned to Carter. "Chief, I think we're done here." He nodded. "Thank-you, Director Linn. You've been a great help. You're free to go. But don't try to return home just yet."

That means, "We won't let you go home until we say you can."

Cara's coms woke her from a dead sleep. She let it go to v-mail but snatched it up when she heard Bette's voice say, "You stood me up!"

"Uh, hello? Oh, hi, Bette. What's that?"

"Our zero-g yoga class? Remember? We were supposed to spot each other." She sounded more amused than angry.

"Yeah, sorry about that. I...had a late night last night."

Bette chuckled. "Was it the gruff Chief Carter or the smooth-talking Detective Janice?"

Cara had to laugh a little in response. "Both, actually."

"That's what I figured. I got my own visit early this morning."

She got a visit?

"They didn't haul you down to the dungeons?"

"Of course not. I told them to check the door logs. Neither James nor I left the suite after you did last night."

"But they said—" Cara interrupted herself.

They can't trust the door logs, but they let her use them as an alibi. Sounds like Janice's trap.

"They said what?" Did Bette sound a little too anxious?

Cara thought fast. "They said I was not in my room at the time of the murder, so I told them I was with you. Sorry I got you involved."

"Not a problem. I sent them packing. So, what are your plans for today…besides sleeping the day away?"

Oh, crap. What time is it? 11:05. Damn! I missed today's shuttle.

"None, really. I'm up here to relax. Maybe read by the pool?"

"Sounds wonderful. Meet you there in an hour?"

Cara slid out of bed, still in her evening dress, and looked in the mirror. "Better make it two."

"Deal," Bette said, then clicked off.

Missing the yoga class means I missed Robert's deadline.

I wonder why he didn't wake me.

She looked out into the suite's lounge. A red Do Not Disturb indicator glowed next to the door lock.

He couldn't wake me without giving away his part in this…whatever the hell this is.

At least I didn't sleep through the two-mil meeting. That's in less than an hour.

And don't forget the room number on the screen in the murder room: 8672. Where the hell is that?

She pulled the hotel floor plans up on her coms. There was no Room 8672.

What the—? If it's not a room number, what else could it be?

A coms id?

A check of the hotel directory revealed that coms number 8672 belonged to none other than her old friend, Detective Janice.

Well, well, well.

Showering in eight-tenths gravity was different. The spray was only lightly pressurized to conserve water, and to keep it from bouncing all over the bathroom. Cara lingered in the mist as the droplets caressed her skin, then merged and rolled slowly down her body. She stood enjoying the feeling while her mind raced, searching for a plan.

If I take the card—

Oh, my God, the card!

I was sleeping so soundly...

Slamming open the shower door shut off the spray, but Cara didn't notice as she slipped and slid across the tile floor into the bedroom. Grabbing her purse from the bedside table, she sighed in relief.

It's still here.

Is that a good thing or a bad thing?

It's a two million sols thing.

I guess I have a plan now. Turn it over at noon and try to survive until tomorrow's shuttle.

If our dear Janice lets me on it.

Deal with that later. She glanced at the clock. *Time to get rich.*

We have work to do first.

~

The bartender in the Star View Lounge was much more taciturn than his compatriot, Joey. His attitude reflected the overall mood of the place. With only the backdrop of stars visible through the window wall, they kept the interior dim, tending toward dark. Slow, moody auto-music whispered in the background, shifting from one theme to another with no coherent melody or flow.

Cara's eyes adjusted while Sam built her Manhattan. The one-sixth gravity on this level meant he had to manipulate watertight mixing tools and siphon the result into a clear adult sippy cup.

"Sorry, no cherries," he said as he set the drink on the bar with a twist of his wrist that made the brown elixir swirl hypnotically around the glass.

Cara looked at the cup's narrow spout and shrugged. She only ever ate the cherry when she was on a date with Nick, anyway. Then, it was more of a promise than a treat.

Sipping the drink on her way to a table in the darkest corner, she stopped short. Someone dressed all in black already occupied the table. Before Cara turned away, however, the person, a woman, held up a crypto-card. Its off-white surface stood out like a beacon in the gloom.

"You didn't call the number I left for you," the woman said, her face concealed beneath the hood of her jacket, as Cara sat down.

"Good morning to you, too, Janice."

Janice raised her face and met Cara's eyes. "It's not good that you know who I am."

"Then you shouldn't have left me your personal coms id."

Janice nodded and fidgeted. "Yeah, that was stupid. I'm glad to see you're not being stupid, too."

"How so?"

"Well, you're here, aren't you? That's the smart play."

Cara smiled. "I may be here, but that doesn't mean what you want is."

Janice's head jerked, and she sat bolt upright. "You mean you don't have it with you?"

That brought a snort of laughter from Cara. "No, that would have been stupid. Why would I bring something worth two million sols to a dark hole like this place? To meet with someone who has already tortured and murdered the last person I was supposed to give it to?"

Janice's distress was obvious, and she slid the offered crypto-card into a jacket pocket.

"Damn it, woman!" she hissed. "You've really screwed this up royally. Maybe I should do to you what I did in Room 5412. Eh?"

Cara sat silently studying Janice, who flicked her eyes from side to side like a cornered rat.

She's just a messenger. I doubt she has the balls to do what they did to that guy.

"Look, Janice. You're obviously too small-time to be running this show. That says to me you're just the go-for. So, tell your boss to tell their boss to have the big boss meet me at the shuttle dock tomorrow morning five minutes before boarding. We'll do the exchange in public, like two civilized businesspeople."

Janice sat back in the dark booth. "What if I have you detained? And beat the location of the card out of you? You'll never get off this hotel alive if you don't take me to the card now."

Cara sat back, mimicking Janice's bravado. "Under what authority, Ms. Sullivan? You forget who I am. I am Corporate Director Cara Linn. You, on the other hand, are nobody because," she pulled her coms from under the table and tapped the screen. "I just fired your ass. I'll be riding home in First Class tomorrow morning. You'll be on the supply shuttle in two hours with the rest of the trash."

Boy, that felt good. Cara almost clicked her heals together as she stalked out of the bar as best she could in one-sixth G.

Now, I just need to stay alive until eleven o'clock tomorrow.

Sitting by the pool sounds like a good way to kill some time.

Especially sitting next to Bette.

Especially if she's wearing a swimsuit.

The door closed behind her, and Cara set the privacy lock. She could see through the bedroom door that the note she had left for Robert lay crumpled on the floor. Peeling it flat, she read her own words:

> I must retrieve the item from where I've
> hidden it. I'll leave it here tomorrow
> morning.

Beneath that was scrawled:

> Tomorrow morning. Or Else!

Yep, an amateur.

It's his job to track my comings and goings. He probably heard about the murder through the staff grapevine and put two and two together.

A quick change and brisk walk brought her to the pool right on time. Bette had already staked out two lounge chairs. Two tall glasses sat sweating on a low table between them.

"I feel heavy down here," Cara said as she draped her towels across the chair.

"We're below Level Zero here. I think it's about 1.1 G."

Cara carefully lowered herself onto the chaise. Sun-tracking mirrors brought sunlight directly into the pool area.

"And it's hot as Hades."

Bette chuckled. "Hot and heavy. That's how I like it."

I bet you do.

"What are we drinking?" Cara asked as she lifted the tall glass.

"I think they call it an 'Astro Mule.' It doesn't sound very enticing, but it tastes good, and it does the job." There was a slight slur to Bette's words.

"Well, then, here's to new friends."

She sipped from her drink while Bette sucked down a quarter of hers.

Keep drinking, Bette. Maybe I can learn something today.

Bette lowered her voice. "Have you heard any more from Detective Janice?"

I was just about to ask that.

"No. I made it clear to her that we had nothing to do with the…incident," Cara lied.

Bette nodded. "Thanks. Glad to be done with that."

"Who do you think—"

81

Cara stopped mid-sentence when she glanced over and saw Bette place her drink against her chest. The ice-cold glass left beads of condensation mingled with her own sweat.

Got to focus.

Cara shook her head and took another, larger, drink.

"What do you think they were after?"

The other woman's smile disappeared, and her voice hardened. "You're not very good at this interrogation thing. It'd be best if we just forgot about it. Right?"

She raised her glass and Cara raised her own. Then Bette downed what remained.

Climbing to her feet, Bette said, "I'm gonna cool off." She took off her sunglasses and winked at Cara. "For now." Then she staggered to the pool and dove in.

Taking a long drink from her glass, Cara rose and followed.

Several hours later, Cara stepped gingerly over the threshold into Bette's suite. The Astro Mules had gone down way too easily in the faux-tropical sun.

"Where's James?"

Bette closed the door softly and stepped up behind Cara.

"Had to go home. Some crisis at work." She swayed slightly. "Need to eat something," she said as she reached for the room service menu.

It was well past midnight when Cara snuck out of Bette's suite. The other woman's drunken snores coming from where she lay on the couch confirmed she hadn't awakened while Cara worked her coms for a few minutes. Her own suite was a short walk down the hallway. Despite the late hour, or maybe because of it, she walked on tiptoe.

I wonder what surprise Robert has waiting for me.

As expected, he was waiting for her. He rose from the chair in the shadowed corner of the lounge as the door clicked shut behind her.

"What are you doing in here?" she asked, her voice neutral.

"You know what I want," he sneered.

"Suppose I don't want to give it to you, Robert Stephen Jones. Or should I call you Bob?"

His scowl deepened and his faux-accent disappeared.

"You saw what happened to that fool in 5412."

"Yeah, but you didn't do that to him, did you? I bet you faint at the sight of blood."

Robert took a step toward her, fists clenched, but stopped in confusion when Cara nonchalantly looked down at her coms.

"By the way, full disclosure, this conversation is being recorded to a messaging server. If I don't stop it within three minutes, the recording will be sent to several people I know in various law enforcement agencies."

She held up the phone to show him.

A full set of emotions crossed Robert's face, but he settled on determination. He took another step toward Cara.

"Give me what I want. I'll be long gone before anybody even listens to that message."

"Oh, you'll be long gone, all right. You'll be on the staff shuttle this morning since," she touched another app on her coms, "you're already unemployed."

Determination turned to rage on Robert's face, and he lunged forward. Cara dodged to her right, but she still wasn't used to the lower gravity on this level. She went sprawling through the bedroom door. Robert recovered from his own stumble and loomed over her where she lay on the floor.

"Give it to me, or I'll kill you!" he growled.

Cara barely managed to keep the fear that had blossomed in her mind from showing on her face or in her voice.

"You don't even know what it is you want, do you? You're just some two-bit hustler trying to con me out of something that's too big for you to handle, anyway." She scrambled to her feet and backed up against the nightstand. "Besides, I already unloaded it. Where do you think I've been all night? I sold it, got paid, and now I'm leaving considerably richer than when I arrived."

"You bitch!"

Robert again launched himself at her, his arms reaching for her throat. Cara reached behind, found the nightstand with her hands, and, using it for stability and leverage, she kicked with all her might, sending the toe of her sandal straight into his crotch. The force of her blow lifted him off his feet. Cara dove to the side as his momentum carried him, face first, into the wall. He dropped like a stone, curled into a fetal ball. A whimper escaped his lips just before his dinner did as well.

After three deep breaths, Cara stopped her recording, fiddled with her coms, then set it to play through the suite's sound system. As she grabbed clothes from her closet and locked herself in the bathroom, Robert's voice started looping from the hidden speakers.

"Give it to me, or I'll kill you! Give it to me, or I'll kill you! Give it to me, or I'll kill you!…"

Robert was gone when she emerged, refreshed and dressed, from the bathroom. The only evidence of the earlier struggle was a slightly askew nightstand and the word "BITCH" scratched into the congealing vomit on the floor.

That's gonna leave a mark.

Curiously, her gorge didn't rise at the sight, and her heart didn't race when she thought about the fight or about the upcoming meeting. Instead, all she felt was hunger.

Where can I get breakfast?

She looked again at the puddle on the floor.

Not here, obviously.

It took her two minutes to pack her suitcase and, with a last look around the suite, she stepped into the hallway and headed for the lobby.

She was on her third cup of coffee and second croissant when Bette came sweeping into the restaurant.

"You slipped out quietly this morning," she said as she sat across the table. "You didn't even say *au revoir*."

"I had something I had to take care of," Cara responded. Her noncommittal response elicited a chuckle from Bette.

"I asked '*Robert*' if you were in your suite, and he did not have kind words for you. 'I hope the bitch walked out an airlock,' were his exact words."

Cara smiled. "Yeah, I had to fire his ass."

Bette raised an eyebrow. "You seem to be doing a lot of that lately, Corporate Director Linn."

Wait, does she know I fired Janice, too?

Oh!

Cara studied Bette's face until her smile melted away, and they understood each other's roles in the previous two days' adventures.

85

"I assume this is a business meeting, not a social call," Cara said, trying to keep her voice neutral.

"There's no reason why it can't be both. I've made you an offer, and you responded in the affirmative."

"Under the threat of a tortuous death."

Bette frowned. "We both know it never would have come to that. I will say you dealt with poor, dumb Janice rather forthrightly, which I was not expecting."

"I said the exchange would be at the shuttle dock at eleven. Why are you here now?"

Bette waved her hand dismissively. "I'm leaving on my private launch in a few minutes. Isn't this public enough for you?"

Cara looked around at the half-full restaurant.

"Indeed, it is."

She pulled the crypto-card from her shoulder bag hanging on the chair, and Bette held up a card of her own.

"Two million, as we agreed," Bette said. She placed the crypto-card on the table. Cara took a deep breath and started to slide her own battered card next to it, but paused.

"What's on it that's worth two million sols?"

Let alone killing for?

Bette eyed her appraisingly, then glanced at Cara's empty wrists. A small smile crept across her lips, and she shrugged.

"Let's just say that some people take 'Let Humans be Human' to the extreme."

AR malware?!?

"What happens when you let that virus loose on the world's augments?"

Bette sat back and shook her head.

"That was *their* play. I'm trying to prevent that from happening." She eyed the card still clutched in Cara's hand. "I

86

may not love my husband or his tech politics, but I do love his money." She nodded to the crypto-card on the table. "Now you can, too."

Cara slid her card across the tabletop. As they each reached for the other's card, their hands brushed, and a spark tingled across Cara's fingers. Bette's eyes widened as she felt it too, but neither made eye contact. That phase of their relationship, and any possibilities it offered, was past. At least for now. Instead, they both held the exchanged crypto-cards to their coms and confirmed the sale.

Two million sols. Holy crap!

Cara quickly changed the password on the crypto-account, then looked up at Bette, who met her eyes and stood. She held out her hand, which Cara took.

"You've changed a great deal since we first met," Bette said as she studied Cara's face. "Something tells me we'll meet again. I look forward to it."

With that, Bette leaned over and kissed Cara lightly on the lips. Then, without looking back, she strolled out of the restaurant, snatching a pastry from the dessert bar on her way.

Part of me wants that to come true.

And part of me is terrified it will.

She's right about one thing, though.

I'm not the woman I was two days ago.

THE END

"Lake of Dreams" was the Second Round submission to the 2023 NYC Midnight Flash Fiction Contest.
Camping with your parents is every teenager's worst nightmare. But sometimes it can be a dream come true.

LAKE OF DREAMS

Jamie was so bored. Okay, so it was his parents' twentieth anniversary, and they wanted to spend it where they first met. But why did they have to drag him along? Especially to a dumbass place like the Lake of Dreams Campground? Their cabin was in a secluded section of the campground, far from anything fun. Needing to get away, Jamie followed a trail through the woods down to the place's namesake, Lake of Dreams.

An old dock poked out into the water, and an Adirondack chair sat at the very end. The heat, humidity, and hike through the woods took their toll, making Jamie want to rest in that chair. So, he flopped down and let the curve of its seat and back embrace him.

The light breeze on his face, and the hypnotic sloshing of the tiny waves it bore, soon had his eyelids drooping. Feeling relaxed for the first time all weekend, he gave in to the lake's magic and drifted off to sleep.

Cold water splashing onto his bare legs startled him awake.

"Hey, what—" The words froze in his throat. Floating ten feet away was a girl—the most beautiful girl he had ever seen. He shook his head, not believing what he was seeing.

"Am I still dreaming?"

Another well-aimed splash hit him full in the face. Spluttering, he stood. The girl lifted a hand and waggled a finger, inviting him to join her. Jamie was an awkward teenager, but he wasn't stupid. Pulling off his tee shirt, and thankful he had worn swim trunks, he gawked at her sea-green bikini as she dove gracefully below the surface. It took him only a second to dive in after her.

The water was clear, and he saw her floating a few feet below him. Her long hair drifted around her head like a halo and her smile and piercing green eyes were beacons beckoning him downward. Not a great swimmer, he watched her, holding his breath as long as he could.

Breaking through the surface, he wondered again if he was still dreaming. Then the water parted and her head and shoulders emerged into the air.

"Who are you?" he asked. Then, remembering his manners, he held out his hand. "Hi. I'm Jamie."

Instead of answering, though, the beauty from the deep pressed a finger to her lips, took him by the hand, and dove downward again. Her pull was too strong to resist, and Jamie barely had time to grab a mouthful of air before she dragged him down ever deeper.

Panicked, he tried to pull away, but the girl's grip was too strong. His furious kicking did nothing but stop their descent, and his efforts only used up the last of his oxygen. His vision became a black tunnel with nothing but the water-girl's smiling face at the end. As he struggled, she drew him in closer. With all hope lost, Jamie let his arms and legs go limp, ready to accept the inevitable. As his vision contracted, her beautiful face became his entire world until he felt her lips press against his. He was helpless to resist her when she breathed life back into him.

The transformation was swift, and within a few heartbeats, his head cleared. The kiss lingered until he felt more invigorated than he ever had. When her soft lips finally left his, the girl drew back and met his eyes.

"Breathe," she said. To his astonishment, her words carried clearly to him through the distorting water. "It's okay. Breathe," she repeated and took a deep breath of water herself.

Without conscious thought, Jamie did likewise. Instead of gagging, though, his lungs sucked the oxygen from the water, and he exhaled it as easily as air. He felt the magic of her kiss throughout his body, which had transformed into a sea creature's.

"Hello, Jamie. I'm Rose. Welcome to my world."

"God, I hope this isn't just a dream," Jamie muttered as Rose took him by the hand.

"If it is, I'm dreaming it, too." Rose pulled him against her. "And I never want to wake up."

After hours spent exploring the lake, Jamie said, "My parents must be going nuts. I've been gone all day."

"Well, you can't go back there. You're here with me, now."

Jamie shook his head. "But 'here' is just a small lake. My family is back there in the world of air and land and sky."

Rose's hair flared around her head as she shook it violently. "You're a water-breather now. This is your world."

Terrified at the prospect of losing his former life in exchange for living as a captive in this lake in the middle of nowhere, he kicked hard upward. Rose saw him break the surface and waited below for him to return, gasping for the life-giving water. Instead, he returned with a smile.

"It worked," he said, excitement in his voice. "I can breathe both ways. I can return to the land any time I want."

"Without me." Rose's tears floated in the water around her head. "If you leave, will you ever come back?"

"I have an idea," he said. "Do you trust me?"

Rose nodded and together they swam back to the dock with the wooden chair.

They broke the surface together, and Jamie held her close until he felt her gasping. Gently, he parted her hair from her face and kissed her. The breath he gave to her did its own magic, and when at last they parted, he said simply, "Breathe, My Love."

Rose's eyes went wide when she felt her lungs accept the air. Then she shouted, "Yes!"

Two people diving into the water interrupted their joy. Diving down, Jamie saw his parents, also easily breathing the water.

In the place where they first met.

THE END

"Out of the Frying Pan, Into the Ice" was a first-round submission to the 2023 NYC Midnight 500-Word Challenge. When is a demon the lesser of two evils?

8

OUT OF THE FRYING PAN, INTO THE ICE

Her first night in the big city, Kendra could hardly believe her luck at landing such a cheap apartment, though she had to pay three months in advance. It was small—a bedroom, a tiny bathroom, and a combination kitchen and living room. The windows were soundproof enough, though, that the noise from the street below was a distant murmur that lulled Kendra into a deep sleep.

The sound of ice cubes hitting the floor woke her with a start. Another clunk, as if a last cube reluctantly dropped from the ice maker, brought her fully awake. She huddled, terrified, beneath the covers, certain that whoever was making themselves a drink in her kitchen was simply wetting their whistle, or whetting their appetite, before invading her bedroom.

Ten minutes of silence. Did she dream the whole thing?

Creeping to her open bedroom door, she peeked around the corner. The full moon cast angled shadows across the room. They merged with the silhouettes of a pendant lamp and the vase of flowers she had bought herself as a housewarming gift. As wisps of fleeting cloud crossed the face of the moon, the dark shades danced and dazzled Kendra's vision. So, she felt, rather than saw, a presence in the corner. It was a cold that belied the late August heat.

Sliding a shaking hand up the wall, Kendra found the light switch, but froze when the presence turned to her...and growled. Growling back, Kendra flipped the switch.

The blazing light revealed no presence in the corner, just a handful of ice cubes melting on the floor.

"That ought to fix it for ya." Sid, the apartment super, gave her a gap-toothed leer. "Just a loose spring."

"Ah, thanks. It scared the heck out of me last night."

Sid dropped a wrench into his toolbag. It made a disturbingly familiar clunk. "No more ice cubes wakin' ya up at three in the mornin' like that, eh?"

Did she tell him it was three in the morning?

The next morning, Kendra stepped out of the shower and smelled eggs cooking. Wrapped in a bathrobe, she crept into the kitchen. The cold, dark presence floated at the stove, cooking breakfast. Sid sat at the table holding a butcher knife.

"Those eggs smell good, Pazuzu, my captive li'l demon." He stood and waved the knife at Kendra as he rose and stepped between her and the apartment door. "I'll have fresh bacon for us in a minute."

"You bastard."

Kendra shifted away from Sid, but when she reached for the knife block, her hand passed through Pazuzu's frozen presence. Stumbling back, her arm numb to the elbow, she reached blindly and grabbed the hot cast iron pan. As Sid lunged at her, she swung, hitting him full in the face. The pan stuck there, searing his face as he dropped like a stone.

Searing pain returned to her hand, but she felt Pazuzu's soothing coldness caress it.

"Thank you, Mistress."

THE END

"AnthroCorp" is the second-round submission to the NYC Midnight 2024 Short Story Challenge.
Greed, whether over the last piece of pie or a multi-world corporation, knows no bounds.

9

ANTHROCORP

Lily sat at the foot of the long conference table in a fog of confusion. The events of the last several hours had her in shock.

The previous night, she had been awakened by her Guardian-bot, Anthy, her constant companion since hai was imprinted to her on her sixth birthday.

"You need to get up, Miss Lily," hai said in a monotone.

Hai's voice and hai's expressionless face sent a chill down Lily's spine. She slipped out from under the bedcovers and stood before hai, naked. Hai's dry, blank eyes—the only part of his anthrobot body that couldn't pass for human—bored into hers.

95

"Please get dressed and pack a bag. We need to go to AnthroCorp headquarters."

Lily paled and grabbed a robe to cover herself.

"What happened? Is it Father?" Anthy remained silent. "Tell me, Anthy! What is going on?"

A hint of compassion tinged his voice. "We are executing Protocol E-9."

Protocol E-9! Response to a Level Nine out of Ten emergency. The protocol called for immediate transport to her father's island company headquarters without discussion or external contact.

Five minutes later, they were strapped into a two-seat liftjet with Anthy at the controls. As they climbed to their cruising altitude, Lily studied the profile she knew so well. The anthrobot looked exactly as hai had on Lily's sixth birthday. Of course, Anthy hadn't aged, but several of hai's systems had been upgraded over the past twenty years. Some of those upgrades Lily had designed herself.

Five hours later, as Anthy settled their craft on the landing pad atop AnthroCorp's headquarters building, the silence still reigned. As the lifters spun down to silence, Anthy placed a hand on Lily's arm.

"I'm sorry to tell you, Miss Lily, but your father is dead."

She locked eyes with her Guardian. The news wasn't a surprise, given the purpose of Protocol E-9.

"How?"

"His liftjet exploded on takeoff." That made her gasp. "The event was captured on surveillance video. There can be no doubt."

Corporate suits rushed out of the building and hustled her directly to the ongoing Board meeting. The unexplained late-night extraction from her apartment, followed by the silent flight to the island headquarters and, worst of all, the news that her father was dead, had almost switched off her conscious mind.

Only the occasional phrase uttered by the Board members who were assembled around the table got through Lily's fog.

"...such a shock...deepest condolences...full investigation..."

It was Anthy's light touch on her arm that brought her back to the horrible reality of the situation. Vice Chairman Joseph Littmann was speaking.

"I apologize for the abruptness of this request, but it is imperative that our shareholders, partners, and especially our competitors know that there will be a smooth transition."

He looked on expectantly, but Lily simply shook her head, confused.

Anthy leaned down from his position, standing behind her, and whispered in her ear. "They want you to sign over your rights to the Chairpersonship." Lily looked a question at Anthy. "Your father left control of the company to you," hai said as mildly as hai could. "Apparently, they don't think that is a good turn of events."

Anthy's tone of voice snapped Lily out of her reverie. "Makes sense, I guess. I don't know how to run a multi-planet company," she whispered in response.

"'Snap decisions lead to broken dreams.'" Anthy whispered. It was one of Lily's father's favorite phrases. Quoting it had the desired effect.

Lily looked down at the document on the tablet that a flunky lawyer had placed in front of her. Seeing the line for her signature, and what that meant for her future, she burst into sobs. Turning to Anthy, she buried her face in his chest.

"Get me out of here," she whispered.

As he helped her to her feet, Anthy addressed the assembly. "As you can see, Ms. Steele is too distraught to continue this meeting."

"All she needs to do is sign—" the lawyer lackey said.

"And have the agreement contested because of her current mental state?" Anthy chided him. "No. When she has had time to process this distressing news, she will notify you to resume this meeting."

With his arm around her hunched shoulders, Anthy helped Lily toward the door.

"She hasn't the knowledge or experience to run this company," Vice Chairman Littmann called as the door closed behind them.

Lily gasped when the airfield surveillance video showed her father's liftjet exploding and debris raining down. She had the news report muted and looped, but watching her father die for about the tenth time still made her flinch. The crawler at the bottom of the screen read: Mechanical failure blamed for the death of AnthroCorp's Chairman and founder.

"That's enough," Anthy said as he blanked the screen.

Lily shook her head, shock written across her face. "I don't understand. That model had a spotless safety record." Her features clouded. "And how could they announce that it was 'mechanical failure' so soon after the crash?"

The anthrobot's eyes blinked as he accessed the internet. "Stock price defense." Anthy's response was yet another shock.

"Show me," Lily said.

The wall monitor switched to a real-time display of AnthroCorp's stock price. It had dropped precipitously on the overseas exchanges right around the time of the crash and had drifted lower in the hours since. It stood down about thirty percent since the previous close.

"Shouldn't there be a government investigation of the crash?" Lily said, returning to the question that burned in her mind. Her engineering degrees, earned at MIT and Stanford, screamed for a better explanation.

"This is a sovereign corporate nation," Anthy said. "The Board of Directors is the government, and the crash happened in corporate airspace." He shrugged, a curiously human gesture. "An open and shut case, at least from their perspective."

"An open and shut coverup, you mean." Anthy shrugged again, then after a moment, Lily said, "He was right, you know." Hai raised a questioning eyebrow. "I'm not qualified to run the company. My only involvement was a couple of internships during school breaks. I see those powerful men with their years of experience, and I feel so small. So unqualified. And the sharks are circling."

Anthy returned a rueful smile. "You're right. Three C-Suite internships, two engineering degrees, and a nearly completed MBA. No qualifications at all."

Lily stared at hai for a full minute. Sarcasm from an anthrobot was a rare thing. Then she said, "Do I have access to the plane's maintenance records?"

Anthy's lip curled into a smile. "You are the current Chairperson and CEO. You have access to everything."

Lily sat at the head of the table as the other board members streamed into the room. Arriving last, Vice Chairman Littmann strode the length of the room with his head down, berating a female assistant. He came up short when he saw the Chairperson's seat was already occupied. With a shrug and nod to Lily, he took the seat to her left, the traditional place for the second-in-command.

He slid a tablet with the resignation agreement in front of Lily. "Ms. Steele, again, I—we all—offer our sincerest—"

Lily held up her hand to stop him. "Enough of that," she said.

"Alright. Good to see you've recovered from your…episode."

"My grief over the murder of my father, you mean?" Her voice was icy and sent a chill through the room. Lily noted which board members were shocked by her question, and which were outraged. Littmann was outraged.

"Murder? That's a serious—a ridiculous charge. Made without evidence, it's highly inappropriate."

"Oh, we'll get to the evidence in a minute. First, note that I have my own agenda for this meeting, and since I am the current Chairperson, I will be running it."

Littmann opened his mouth to protest, but then sat back in his chair instead. Lily scanned the table.

"The first item on my agenda is this." She looked down at the tablet and stabbed the [REJECT] button. Littmann's lackey gasped. "I will not be stepping down as Chairperson and CEO," she said. Bedlam erupted around the table. Lily let the outraged comments, "…inexperienced…" and "…too young…," run for a moment, then slammed the tablet on the table for silence. She handed the device with its shattered screen back to the lawyer. She needed to get a gavel for the next meeting.

"Gentlemen! And I note you are all men." Littmann's assistant, sitting against the wall, snickered. Lily glanced at her and gave her a sly smile. That one might survive the coming purge. "Members of the Board, my qualifications are not at issue here, and they shouldn't be. I know more about our products," she turned and smiled at Anthy, who stood behind her, "than any of you. I've also spent over a year in this C-Suite while interning for you, Daniel." She nodded to the Chief Operations Officer halfway down the table. He saluted her with a grin and two fingers to his brow. "And for you Charles." The Chief Marketing Officer simply scowled in return. "And for Father, who not only taught me the ins and outs of running this behemoth but also all the dirt he had gathered on each of you."

She sat back and smiled at the consternation she saw ripple across their faces.

"The next agenda item…" She pushed on before any other objections could be raised. "…is of a sensitive nature, and it involves what can only be described as an amateurish attempt at insider trading."

A hush fell over the room as Lily turned to Littmann. "I find it interesting that the brother of your new, young wife sold short almost a million shares of AnthroCorp stock."

Littmann bristled. "I'm not responsible for the actions of my idiot brother-in-law."

"No? That's odd, because he shorted, and is now buying shares using your account."

The Vice Chairman gave her a smug smile. "This island is a sovereign corporate entity. There are no insider trading laws here."

Lily's smile was just as smug. "True, but I bet the Singapore Exchange, where those short sales were executed, will be interested." Littmann's smile faltered. "Besides, Father always called me Princess Lily." Her smile disappeared. "I guess I'm the Queen now." She let the import of her words settle in. "And, since the first short sales were recorded on the Singapore Exchange a full ten minutes before Father's plane went down, one has to wonder how your brother-in-law knew the share price would drop less than an hour later."

Littmann's face went from angry red to ghostly white. Before he could respond, Lily nodded to Anthy, who moved to a position behind him.

"But we don't have to wonder, because your brother-in-law, whom you hired just last week onto the liftjet maintenance crew—with no experience, I might add…" Anthy blinked and the wall monitors flicked on, "…was recorded on surveillance video carrying a heavy satchel onto the plane, then leaving without it."

Stunned silence was followed by the sound of chairs scraping as those at the table physically distanced themselves from Littmann. A new video played showing Littmann's wife and brother-in-law being led in handcuffs.

Lily's voice was barely above a whisper. "They've already confessed…and implicated you as the mastermind."

Littmann squared his shoulders. "You have no physical proof that I was involved in any—"

"I don't need proof, you pompous ass. As the effective Queen of this sovereign corporate state, I'm arresting you on charges of murder and treason."

Anthy stepped forward and lifted Littmann by the shoulders. After he was dragged, protesting his innocence, out of the room, Lily looked at his assistant. Having watched, horrified, as her boss was led away in handcuffs, she pushed herself up against the wall.

"You, Ms. …."

"Savaggio, Andrea Savaggio," she stammered.

"Well, Andrea, how would you like to be the new Vice Chairperson?"

THE END

"The Patient Orb" is another of my weekly 300-word flash pieces.

10

THE PATIENT ORB

The glowing orb rose slowly from the dark pond. It left no sign of its passage, not a ripple on the still water, nor a breeze to ruffle the leaves overhanging the bank. The only sign of its presence was the orange glow it radiated into the surrounding forest.

"What is it?" Leo whispered to his older brother.

Sam, the ever-cautious one, cupped a hand to Leo's ear. "No one knows, but it comes out every full moon."

The brothers watched from their hiding place as the orb, hovering ten feet above the water, slowly rotated. The light it emitted contracted from a wide, uniform glow into a spotlight that probed the trees and undergrowth.

Forewarned, Sam had the boys hiding behind a fallen tree trunk. He pushed Leo's head down just before the orb's beam swept across their spot.

"Now, watch this," Sam whispered.

As the spotlight completed its circuit, its source slid across the surface of the orb until it was pointed straight up. When perfectly vertical, the beam contracted to the width of downspout, then a pencil, then a needle. As it did, the color ratcheted up through green, blue, and violet before disappearing altogether. Where the beam disappeared, a sizzling line of plasma cut through the air. After a moment, the orb returned to its soft glow, leaving the scent of ozone.

"What happens next?" the ever-impatient Leo whispered.

Sam shook his head. "Nothing. In a few minutes it'll sink back—"

The crack of exploding air interrupted Sam as the return signal the orb had been waiting for was received. Fed by the energy being beamed to it, the orb's glow became a white-hot radiance that set the forest, and the world, ablaze.

"Finally!" was the last word the boys ever heard.

THE END

"Slither" was submitted to the Fiesty Felines and Other Fantastic Familiars *anthology. Alas, it was picked, but I like it anyway.*

11

SLITHER

Ciera tossed and turned in her bedroll. She lay alone next to the smoldering campfire which she had given up on tending only minutes after half-heartedly starting it. By this afternoon, the second day of the annual Pairing Time, most of the other mage children had paired with their familiars and gone home, leaving her and Ahmel, the creepy boy from two towns away. At dusk, when Ahmel paraded in front of her showing off the kitten tattoo of his newly bonded familiar, his mocking laughter had set her teeth on edge.

Alone in the forest, Ciera felt her worst fear coming true—that her family's many generations of mage blood had ended with her mom. Ciera was cradle-bound when her mom saved an entire town beset by plague. She imprisoned the evil that brought the contagion, but in the process, caught the disease herself. Neither hers nor Gran's familiars knew any spells that could save her. With their souls inextricably linked through their pair-bond, both mage and familiar passed into the Unknown together. Ciera's father, a rough farmhand with no magical abilities, soon found a new wife, leaving Gran to raise Ciera, who grew into a quiet, awkward girl.

If no magical creature chose to be her familiar during her third and final Pairing Time, she would be too old to pair bod. She wouldn't understand or even remember the spells Gran wanted to teach her. She would never be a mage.

When she finally drifted into a fitful sleep, images of Ciera returning home humiliated and unpaired haunted her dreams. By next year, she would be too old to find a familiar and use the spells it knew. Human minds, as they learned to rely on logic and reason, became incapable of understanding the irrationality of magic. It was only through the pair bond with their familiars that mages could access the irrational.

The campfire was nothing more than a pile of cold ash when a deep calm settled over Ciera's dreams. Instead of the endless taunting faces of her peers, a warm, hissing voice whispered to her.

Ah, you're nice and warm.

A part of Ciera felt something slither into the bedroll with her, bringing with it a feeling of closeness she had never felt before.

"Who are you?"

A small, triangular head swam into her dream-vision. It tilted first left, then right, as if considering the question.

I don't know. What would you call me, Human? And what should I call you?

107

Ciera's heart swelled with a love very different from what she felt for Gran or the story-memory of her mother.

"I'm Ciera." She thought for a moment, then a word bloomed in her thoughts like the most beautiful blossom she had ever seen. "I'll call you Slither. Is that okay?"

Hmm. It's a bit pedestrian, but...I like it. Now wake up so we can form our pair bond.

With eyes fluttering open, Ciera felt something pressed against her palm. Curled there was a tiny viper, barely out of its egg nest.

"What—what do I do?" Ciera asked, full of a mixture of fear and excitement.

Slither snuggled contentedly in her palm, then raised his head.

Do you accept our bond completely, with all of your heart, mind, and soul?

Ciera, awed by the prospect, nodded, then whispered, "Yes, yes, I do."

As much as he could, Slither smiled.

So do I.

Opening his mouth wide, Slither allowed his fangs to unfold. A thrill of wonder ran through Ciera as she offered her hand. Without hesitating, Slither sank his fangs into the purlicue between her thumb and forefinger.

The pair-bonding venom coursed through Ciera. Her body shivered, then sweated as waves of cold and heat swept up her arm and through the rest of her body. Her eyes closed as new senses—the taste of body heat, the electric tingle of animals moving in the surrounding woods, the glow of colors no human had ever experienced—infiltrated her mind. All these sensations led to an ecstasy she had never felt before, nor would ever again.

In her waking mind, she heard a hissing sigh and looked at the tattoo of a viper curled in her palm. Then she heard Slither's voice inside her own thoughts.

We are one which is more than two. Our souls are intertwined like aspen roots. We are pair bonded. Ciera felt Slither smile. *Now, let's hunt!*

Months later, Ciera was still getting used to the duality of her pair bond with Slither. She stood on the edge of a meadow watching as Slither moved silently through the high grass. Overlaid on her own body's senses, she saw through his eyes and tasted the body heat of a field mouse through Slither's tongue. Senses beyond any other human had experienced expanded her understanding of the world.

It's another damn mouse. There must be something bigger around here.

Ciera looked down at her palm where Slither rode as a tattoo when not hunting. Only a faint impression lingered there when He had only grown enough for his tail to touch her wrist.

"Gran says we still have a lot of animagic to learn," Ciera thought to Slither.

Sure, but not by drinking the blood of another field mouse. How boring.

An electric jolt ran through both of them.

Wait a second...oh, yeah. There's a rabbit around here somewhere.

"A...bunny?"

If Slither had hands and hips, he would have one firmly planted on the other.

Rabbits know things. Spells that we need to learn.

"But do we have to kill it? I mean, once you drink enough to learn the spells…"

Hmm. Well, we can give that a try. Now hush while I find our furry friend.

A minute later, the outline of the rabbit shone through the grass in Slither's vision and he pounced. Ciera felt it quivering in terror as Slither wrapped around its neck and sank his fangs into a vein. A new world opened up before Ciera's eyes—a world of love and family tucked safely beneath the ground, contrasted by constant fear while venturing into the light. She heard Slither whispering reassuring echoes of her thoughts to their prey, telling it they would only drink what they needed.

Movement in her human vision caught Ciera's attention, setting off alarms learned from their prey.

"Slither! Something's coming—"

Before she could finish the thought, a cat pounced, its claws scratching Slither as they sank deeply into the rabbit's sides. Slither pulled back just as, with one quick bite, the cat ripped open the rabbit's throat.

Damn you, Slither hissed as he instinctively attacked the cat's neck with his fangs. His venom, which should have sent the attacker into convulsions, merely made it sluggish, protected as it was by its mage's powerful spells. The delay gave Slither just enough time to suck a mouthful of the other familiar's magical blood.

The arcane spells and knowledge that flooded through their pair bond stunned both Slither and Ciera. Taking another gulp, Slither released another dose of venom, intending to drain the cat dry. But Ciera, revolted by the deadly spells instantly learned from this ruthless predator, overwhelmed her naivete and she summoned Slither back to her.

110

As he reluctantly returned and slid into her outstretched hand, Slither's tattoo grew until it wrapped around her forearm, up to her elbow.

Why did you stop me? Slither's anger echoed in Ciera's mind.

"That was foul!" she shouted out loud.

That was life. That was the real world. The dangerous, real, magical world that we have to live in...and master if we want to survive.

Out of breath from running all the way home, Ciera burst into the cottage where she lived with Gran. Flopping down in a simple wooden chair at the small kitchen's table, she let out a sob.

"What on Earth is the matter, Child?" Gran turned from the stove where she was making tea.

"Oh, Gran. It was terrible..."

Ciera buried her face in her hands. As she did, the sleeve of her jerkin slid down to her elbow. Gran's expression changed from concern to shock when she saw Slither's pulsing tattoo encasing Ciera's lower arm. She slapped the girl's hand away from her face, then slapped again at her arm. Annoyed, Sliter raised his head from Ciera's palm and hissed at the old woman.

Gran's voice was cold when she said, "What in the name of the gods did you do?"

When Ciera finished telling her tale, Gran set a cup of tea in front of her.

"I understand why you were shocked, Child. Receiving such knowledge in a burst like that, when unprepared for it, can be overwhelming." She turned to Slither, whose head still protruded from Ciera's palm. "I'm sorry, Slither. You did the right thing. You saved yourself and my grandchild, for that wildcat would surely have turned to you next."

Gran eyed her empty cup, then waved her hand, and steam rose from the instantly refilled tea. She did the same to Ciera's, though the steam that rose from it had a distinctive purple hue.

"Drink, Child. It will calm your nerves."

She watched as Ciera sipped the elixir, which softened her features and smoothed out her breathing.

When Gran saw Ciera take a slow, deep breath, she continued. "Good. We have much to discuss." She sipped her own plain tea before continuing. "You have made an enemy this day. You do realize that, right?"

Ciera looked confused, but Slither nodded his head, which had grown noticeably since the morning.

We've stolen spells from the mage and injured his familiar. He will almost certainly seek revenge.

When Gran saw that Ciera understood the gravity of the situation, she continued. "Stealing another mage's spells is…an affront. An insult. It's like saying, 'Your familiar is not worthy of being killed. It is too weak to resist me, so why should I bother killing it?' Do you understand?"

Both Ciera and Slither nodded.

"Who is this mage with the wildcat familiar?"

Ciera thought for a moment. "It felt like…Ahmel. I saw his tattoo when it was just a kitten. It must be him."

112

Gran's shoulders slumped. "I've heard of him. He is very powerful and has gotten so by ignoring the rules that govern the Guild of Mages."

"You mean like, 'Don't steal other mages' spells?'"

Gran chuckled. "Exactly. He has already driven out—or more probably killed—his town's Mage Protector, and now he rules it as a tyrant."

"Why doesn't the Guild stop him?"

Gran turned her head, shamefaced. "We are afraid of him. Plain and simple. Even though we know his ambition will grow beyond the boundaries of his village, threatening the entire valley, we bury our heads and hope." She took a deep breath, squared her ancient shoulders, and faced Ciera. Her voice was strong when she said, "You—*We*—must prepare for Ahmel's answer."

A shiver of fear ran down Ciera's back. "How do we do that?"

She had never seen the sly look on Gran's face before. "You are not the first mage in this family to *bend* the rules a bit."

Hunching forward, she slipped her blouse off her shoulders and a beautiful silver fox rose from its tattoo on her back. She straightened and shrugged first one shoulder then the other when Slever, her familiar, hopped onto the table. Slither and Slever eyed one another appraisingly, Slither's tongue flicking in and out.

"Slever and I have much to teach you," Gran whispered. "And I think your trick of small sips is the best way to do that."

"But Gran, you said taking spells that way is against the...rules?"

113

"Aye, if you *steal* them. I am offering them freely to you, Child."

The fur on Slever's back raised. He turned back to Gran and let out a low growl.

"Of course, it will hurt and we'll both be weak for a while. But if Slither takes small sips," she eyed the snake, who reluctantly nodded, "we can give you what you need to fight the monster."

Slever let down his fur, lay on his side on the table, and bared his neck to Slither.

"Go slowly," Ciera commanded as Slither slid from her forearm and out through her palm. The tattoo of his tail remained wrapped around her wrist, keeping their pair bond connection as strong as possible.

"No venom," Ciera said as Slither unfolded his fangs. He cocked his head so one eye focused on Ciera while the other found the pulsing vein in Slever's neck. His nod of ascent was followed by a strike quicker than either Ciera or Gran could follow. As blood pumped from the two tiny holes, Slither and Ciera together drank their first lesson.

Under Gran and Slever's tutelage, Ciera and Slither became strong and powerful. His tattoo wrapped around the whole of Ciera's arm up to her shoulder. But while Ciera grew in strength, Gran became that much weaker, needing a cane to hobble about and sleeping for an entire day after each "lesson." For his part, Slever remained strong, but his silver fur turned a dull gray and he limped arthritically on some cold, wet mornings.

As Gran's frailty advanced, Ciera naturally took over her duties as Mage Protector of their small village and surrounding farms. The younger folk, especially, came to Ciera when they were sick or, more likely at that age, lovesick and pining for another. Even some of the local mothers sought her help with the daily ills of rustic village life on market days when she ventured into the village. That was how Ciera met Anna.

More properly, Ciera *felt* Anna even before she met her. Anna was the daughter of Wes Armstrong, the village blacksmith, and his wife, Stella. Stella and Anna sold vegetables from their garden on market days. That's where Ciera found the source of the tickle inside her head—an insistent buzz that she felt when relaxing or out hunting with Slither. It was like what she had felt her whole life coming from Gran. But this feeling was different. Gran's presence felt like a warm, loving embrace, while this new one was raw curiosity and wonder—a need to understand the magical world. The same burning need that had filled Ciera's being in the months leading up to her pair bonding with Slither, and which still raged within her.

The valley's annual Pairing Time was still a month away when Ciera found Anna helping her mom on that market day. Anna's eyes grew wide when Ciera made her way through the crowd, as if she could feel her approach. When their eyes met, they knew. They recognized in each other a power only they, or others gifted by the gods with magic, could feel.

"So, it's true?"

Stella's words broke into Ciera's reverie. Blinking and with a shudder, she realized she was standing in front of the vegetable stand, staring at the twelve-year-old.

"Excuse me?"

"It's true, then? My daughter Anna has the gift?" Ciera looked over at the girl, who stood open-mouthed. "She sees

115

things I can't see. And hears things I can't hear." Stella's voice faltered a bit, then she let out a nervous laugh. "She talks to my garden, and look…" She spread her hands over the large, perfect melons, beans, and peppers on the table. "I grow the biggest, sweetest produce in the valley." She looked hard at Ciera. "So, does she have it—the gift?"

Ciera smiled what she hoped was a reassuring smile. "Oh, yes. I believe she does, indeed. I will definitely see her at the Pairing Ceremony next month."

Anna smiled broadly, but Stella's face darkened. "But then you'll take her from me?"

Taken aback, Ciera shook her head. "No, why would I take her from you? She will need training, of course, but—"

"What about the mage in Rustleton? Rumors are that he has been demanding that any children with the gift are to him to study, even before they are pair bonded."

"And if they don't?"

Hatred flared in Stella's eyes. "He works dark magic on them…seduces them to running away." She choked back a sob.

"Ahmel? He is kidnapping candidates?"

Stella nodded, then let out the sob, and tears streamed from her eyes. "He is after my Anna."

Anna spoke up, fear clear in her voice. "He comes into my dreams." Ciera's head snapped around. "He tells me to leave my filthy, unmagical parents and come join his coven." She clung to her mom. "But I love my family."

Ciera closed her eyes for a moment, Slither's tongue flickered out of her palm. With a mumbled incantation, she made three arcane signs with her fingers, then opened her eyes.

"There. You should sleep well without Ahmel bothering you until you are pair bonded. Then visit me, and we can begin your training." She looked up at Stella. "And she can sleep in her own bed at night." Anna beamed up at her mother, who smiled. "Now, show me your best melons and peppers," Ciera said.

The cottage door rattled on its hinges under the insistent pounding of fists. Ciera blinked awake and rushed across the cold stone floor, her bare feet and thin nightdress poor protection against the night's chill.

With a gesture from her, a peephole opened in the wood and revealed Stella Armstrong supporting her badly bleeding husband. In a few heartbeats, they were seated at the table. Gran, moving more quickly than she had in months, began mixing a poultice to treat the deep gashes on Wes Armstrong's arms and face.

"What happened?" Ciera asked, though she knew the answer instinctively. "Where's Anna?"

"He took her!" Stella wailed.

"The bastard came for her in the night," Wes snarled, then threw Gran a look when she pressed the poultice to the worst of the gashes in his shoulder. "He set his wildcat on me."

The blood, freely flowing a moment before, slowed to a trickle. His eyes grew wide, then narrowed as his arm went numb and he was unable to move it.

"I need that arm to fight the monster," he growled.

"You're not going anywhere," Ciera said. Her voice was as cold as the steel in Wes's smithy. "You're damned lucky to be alive. If Ahmel wasn't focused on Anna, you'd be dead for sure."

117

She met Gran's eyes for a moment, then both women nodded. Ciera dashed back into her bedroom.

"My grandchild will bring your daughter back to you," Gran whispered. "Or die in the attempt."

She didn't need to say that was a Mage Protector's sworn duty.

"Alive?" Wes asked. "Or is she dead already?" The anguish in his voice belied his physical strength.

Gran shook her head. "The Pairing Time is only a few days away. He...he won't hurt those he's taken before then."

She tried to sound reassuring, but they knew what she left unsaid—if Anna didn't pair bond on this, her first attempt, she would be of no use to Ahmel. Turning away, she drew a knife from a block on the counter and waved a spell over it. The blade glowed, first red, then white. She looked Wes in the eye and forced a wooden spoon into his mouth. "This is going to hurt."

His grunts, as Gran cauterized his wounds, covered Ciera's return to the kitchen. When, finally, Gran pulled the spoon from his mouth, Wes slumped in the chair. Beads of sweat ran down his face and his eyes flickered open and closed.

"I'm ready," Ciera said, trying to sound confident. Gran saw through her façade, however.

"You're going to need help," she said, her voice low.

"Probably. But there's no time to gather the other Protectors in the valley—"

"That's not what I mean."

Hunching over, Gran shrugged her own nightdress off her shoulders. Slever rose from his tattoo across her back and hopped onto the floor, limping noticeably. Stella gasped, never having seen this most personal aspect of mages.

Ciera looked on skeptically, though, as Slither poked his head out of her palm. "We have to hurry. Can he keep up?"

Slither tilted his head, listening. *He'll keep up.*

"Good. Let's go."

She threw a cloak over her shoulders and turned to the door, but Stella's hand on her arm stopped her.

"Thank you," she whispered.

All Ciera could do was nod before dashing into the night.

Slever did slow their progress, but Ciera believed his store of spells was well worth the extra few hours it took to reach Ahmel's castle. The Pairing Time was only two days away when Ciera felt the gathered mages camped a safe distance from the castle.

"We've not much time," she said to the dozen sitting around the campfire. "The Pairing Time is only two days away. We need to get these girls and boys back to their homes."

Jantice, a Mage Protector from further up the valley, snorted. "We've tried, Child. Each of us." He hung his head. "We barely escaped with our lives."

"Our familiars are badly injured," another young mage, who had pair bonded the same season as Ciera, said.

Another mage, whom Ciera didn't know, spoke up. "Some of us didn't survive."

She looked over to a clearing in the woods where three burial mounds rose above the meadow grass.

"Did you attack together?" Ciera asked. "Share spells?"

"Share spells?" Jantice's voice rose in anger. "How are we supposed to do that?"

"I know how," Ciera said, her voice quiet. "I can show you…if you trust me."

Eight of the twelve did trust her once she explained how Slither could learn their spells without killing their familiars. The others didn't believe her, or their familiars were too weak to offer any of their blood. As she approached Ahmel's castle, Ciera's head swam with the new knowledge Slither had extracted.

There aren't many useful spells here.

"I'm not surprised. Most of their familiars aren't predators like you two."

Yeah. Rabbits and deer won't help us much. Slither paused, listening to Slever. The hawk and the owl would help—if we could fly!

Ciera smiled despite herself. She had never felt more alive, or more focused. This rescue quest awakened something within her. If she survived, she would have to explore this newfound purpose. If she survived.

As he always did, Slither read her thoughts and slid his full length out of her palm in preparation. Before he could fully emerge, though, Ciera grabbed his tail.

"We're stronger together," she whispered.

But less maneuverable.

"I'll need every one of the spells you hold."

Sliter signaled his agreement by wrapping the tattoo of his tail tightly around her wrist.

As they approached the castle, Ciera cast the rabbit's, deer's, and groundhog's predatory-revealing spells—the only thing she could think to use their spells for. Those revelatory spells were powerful enough for the three to sense Ahmel's familiar an instant before the mountain lion pounced.

Ducking out of the way, Ciera felt Slither strike at the lion as it dove past them. Because of the tether from his tail to her wrist, Slither's strike was slow, catching their attacker in the left flank. At best, his venom would slow the next attack. At worst, it he had just wasted a good portion of his stores.

I can dose him another time or two. But that's it.

"Understood."

Ciera used her free hand to cast a spell that pulled vines down from the overhanging branches, momentarily tangling the lion and allowing her to regain her footing. When the vines exploded, she felt for the source of the spell. There. Hiding behind a high stand of ferns was Ahmel.

"Where's Slever—"

The fox answered her question when it leaped onto the evil mage's back. His fangs sank deeply into Ahmel's shoulder before he was lifted by magic high in the air and thrown across the clearing where Slither and the lion squared off, eyeing each other. Ciera flinched at the sound of snapping bones when Slever hit a tree trunk to her left. The lion's eyes flicked toward the sound, as well.

Circle right.

Complying, she saw that their movement brought the lion's attention back to them and away from where Slever lay, moaning.

Pouncing again, the lion's claws raked at them, but the first dose of venom slowed the attack enough for Ciera to dive to the side, clear of the deadly spikes. Slither, though, counter-attacked, ducking under the outstretched foreleg and pumping another dose of venom between the cat's ribs.

Pain shot up through Ciera's arm and she looked down to see Slither writhing from the gash where the lion's claw had found his scaly skin. In desperation, Ciera threw a confusion spell—another prey spell Slither had just learned from the rabbit familiar. Designed to distract a predator long enough for the prey to escape, it struck the lion as it gathered itself to pounce again. Instead of attacking, though, it shook its head to clear its confusion, which gave the badly injured Slever enough time to sink his teeth into the lion's back leg.

Instinctively, it slashed at Slever, sending him flying. But in turning, it bared its neck and gave Slither the opening he needed. Pumping the last drops of his deadly venom into the artery in the lion's neck, Slither yanked himself free from Ciera. Then, wrapping himself around the lion's throat three times, he squeezed.

Together, the two familiars rolled back and forth, wrapped in a deadly embrace. When, at least, they lay still, Ahmel let out a scream from where he lay bleeding.

Slowly unwinding from his death grip, Slither stumbled, as much as a snake can stumble, back to Ciera. She quickly cast pain and healing spells over his wounds before offering him her palm. As he slunk back into his tattoo form, the dark magic he had sucked from the dying lion flooded her mind, sending it reeling and making her fall backwards into the grass. She struggled to balance the revulsion she felt and the awe of the spells' power.

Careful, Slither thought to her, bringing her back to the real world. Slever needs you.

"Right."

She crawled over to where the fox familiar lay, panting. With a wave of her hand, she put him into a deep coma and pulled out as many of Gran's healing spells as she could remember. When she had done all she could, she felt the other mages standing over Ahmel on the fringes of the clearing. She tried to ignore his dying screams.

While one of the more severely injured mages watched over the sleeping Slever, Ciera led the rest of them into the castle.

"You did well," Gran said as she set the mug of tea in front of Ciera.

"Did I?" She sniffed. "Slever is getting steadily weaker."

The fox lay curled in the corner by the fire, bundled in blankets. He was too weak to reintegrate with Gran.

"You saved a generation of candidates. That's what Mage Protectors do." Gran again asked the question that neither Ciera nor any of the other mages would answer. "What did he want with them?"

Ciera took a deep breath. It was time to let the horror of that "rescue" out into the light.

"He kept them chained in a dungeon." She paused, reluctant to say more. Finally, Gran's stare gave Ciera the strength to continue. "He wanted to pair bond each of them to rats he had bred to follow his commands."

Gran gasped and sank heavily onto her chair. "He was making acolytes, bonding those poor children against their will. Creating magical minions to do his bidding. To rule over us." Ciera nodded and sobbed. Gran reached out and took her hand. "Oh, Child, why the tears? You saved us all."

Ciera turned on Gran, her eyes a fiery red. Slither's tattoo, which had grown to fully wrapped around Ciera's torso, writhed as if in pain.

"Because we took all of his spells." She closed her eyes in anguish. "Because now that desire is inside *me*."

THE END

"Twist Plot" was a first-round submission to the NYC Midnight 2021 1000-Word Challenge. It was one of the stories chosen to advance me to the second round. Opportunities for the downtrodden to strike back at their oppressors are fleeting.
Opportunity seized.

12

TWIST PLOT

```
DISPATCH
NOV 16 1863
CUMBERLAND VALLEY

UNION TROOPS SPOTTED TEN MILES
EAST -[STOP]- AWAITING ARRIVAL
OF GEN. HOOKER DUE SOONEST -
[STOP]- WILL BEGIN ASAULT WITHIN
DAYS -[STOP]-
```

Isaac reached down as he squatted over the latrine and caught his turd before it fell into the trench. He carefully wiped across it the blade that glinted in the half-moon's light.

Keeping his fingers clear of the razor's edge, he wrapped the blade in a strip of cloth and dropped it into the pocket of his coat.

One by one, he pulled pencils from his other pocket and touched their sharpened points to the still-warm shit. When done, he then returned the pencils to his pocket and let the turd fall into the trench with a faint splash. Grabbing a handful of dewy grass, he wiped his hands and returned to the campfire.

"Where're those pencils the General needs?"

A young lieutenant, probably the son of a rich plantation owner, judging by the shine on his uniform buttons, strode into the campfire's glow.

"Ri' here, Sir," Isaac answered in a low voice. Keeping his eyes down, he pulled the pencils from his pocket and held them out to the aide, who snatched them and hurried back toward the General's command tent. Glancing around with only his eyes, Isaac eased the razor-sharp blade from his pocket. His fingers trembled as he forced it backwards into its slot in the wooden box's conical barrel.

His keen eye appreciated the new pencil sharpener's design. It was certainly more practical than Mr. Foster's contraption, which easily jammed if the shavings weren't dumped out frequently. Its fundamental flaw was obvious, though, and when he first saw the invention, he knew immediately how to exploit it.

Grumblings, then sharp exclamations could be heard coming from the command tent for the next several minutes, as Major General Robert G. Everhard wrote out his orders to be carried by messenger to his field commanders. As was his habit, before scribbling plans for troop positions and the order of attack for the upcoming battle, he touched the tip of the pencil to his tongue. He had watched his father, a banker and lawyer, do the same before writing out a contract, letter, or any other document, and the affectation stuck. The General's swearing became louder as each of the pencils' tips snapped off, leaving a jagged stump.

"Get than God damned nigra in here!" he said as the last pencil's point broke.

The aide burst through the tent flaps and strode over to where Isaac waited patiently by the fire, cradling the new pencil sharpener in his shaking hands.

"Come here, boy," he said as he grabbed Isaac's wiry hair and dragged him to his feet. "The General wants your black ass. You're gonna get a whippin' for sure."

Isaac hunched his shoulders against the expected blows, which Lieutenant Stewart was happy to deliver. Still pulling him by the hair, Lieutenant Stewart threw Isaac to the ground at the General's feet.

"What's the meaning of this?" General Everhard thrust the pencils with their broken points in front of Isaac's face. "Every single one snapped off."

Isaac kept his eyes on the ground and sputtered, "I, ah, sorry General, Sir. It's tha' newfangled sharp'ner the quamaster give me. It don' work nearly as good as th'other one."

Lieutenant Stewart slapped Isaac on the back of the head. "What's wrong with the old one?"

Isaac sorely wanted to either rub his head where the lieutenant's ring had raised a lump, or to jump up and punch him in the face. But his plan was bigger than breaking a pissant lieutenant's nose, so he dropped his head even lower and mumbled, "Broke, Sir."

The General bellowed, "Let me see this God damned new gadget."

His cheek twitched, but Isaac managed to keep his joy off his face as he held out the pencil sharpener cupped in his hand. But just as quickly, his heart sank when Lieutenant Stewart reached out to take it from him. Instead, Everhard slapped Stewart's hand aside and snatched the sharpener from Isaac's opened palm.

"God damn it!" Everhard screamed as the shit-smeared blade sank deeply into the eminence of muscle and vein just below his thumb. The first shake of his arm sent the body of the sharpener to the ground in front of Isaac, leaving the blade protruding from the General's hand. A second shake sent the blade and a stream of blood spattering against the roof of the tent.

In mock horror, Isaac scuttled backwards out of the tent, but the lieutenant screamed, "Grab the bastard!"

Before he could even stand, two guards fell upon him and beat him with the butts of their rifles, almost certainly with no idea why. Isaac's half-brother, Jacob, carrying a load of firewood, caught Isaac's eye and saw the smile on his face as the final blow struck him on the back of the head. Barely hiding his own smile, he hurried along to spread the good news.

```
DISPATCH
NOV 25 1863
CUMBERLAND VALLEY

BE ADVISED THAT MAJOR GENERAL
EVERHARD SUCCUMBED TO SEPSIS
DUE TO CUT ON HAND -[STOP]-
CAMPAIGN ON HOLD PENDING
INSTRUCTIONS -[STOP]-
```

THE END

"Flip, Strike, Flame, Snap" is the second-round entry to the NYC 2021 1000-Word Challenge.
Getting inside the safe, the laptop, and the lighter takes an inside job.

13

FLIP, STRIKE, FLAME, SNAP

Y ou want me to do what?"

Zippy flipped open his lighter, struck a flame with the flint wheel, then snapped it shut. Then, again: Flip, Strike, Flame, Snap.

"I want you to open that safe while I time you."

Flip, Strike, Flame, Snap. Flip, Strike, Flame, Snap.

"You want me to audition? I'm the best cracker around. Everybody knows that."

Elise sniffed. The scent of lighter fluid was strong. Flip, Strike, Flame, Snap.

"That's what I've heard, but I need to see it for myself. Don't you use a lot of lighter fluid doing that?"

129

Zippy shrugged and pulled a can of fuel from his pocket. "I love the smell."

Flip, Strike, Flame, Snap. Flip, Strike, Flame, Snap. Flip—

"Give me that."

Elise snatched the lighter from his hand.

"Hey, give it back."

"You'll get it back after you complete the job. I don't want any distractions. This has to be timed perfectly."

"Bitch," he mumbled. But the money she was offering for a simple hotel safe job kept him from saying any more.

Elise crinkled her nose at the lingering scent, scowled, and pocketed the lighter, replacing it with a stopwatch. She crossed her arms and watched Zippy work.

Four minutes later, he swung the safe door open.

"There. Satisfied?"

Elise checked the stopwatch and shrugged.

"Good. Now gimme back my lighter."

"I said when the job's done."

"Speaking of which, what'll be in the safe?"

Elise gave him a condescending stare.

"A laptop. Mr. Big and his accountant are meeting after the party. There's people who will pay a lot for the data on it. You just need to do the job I'm paying you for."

She picked up a gym bag and tossed it to him. He pulled out a pair of lederhosen.

"What the hell is this?"

"Be back here tomorrow night and wear those. It's an Oktoberfest party. You'll blend in as a waiter. I'll give you Mr. Big's keycard after I lift it."

Zippy scoffed. "And how you gonna do that?"

Elise pulled Zippy's wallet from one pocket and his watch from another.

"Same way I got these."

"What the hell? How—OK, I'm impressed."

He reflexively reached into his pocket but came up empty. Despite having nothing in his hand, he still jerked his wrist and flicked his thumb. Elise watched him do it three times.

"Hey!"

"What?" he whined, then noticed what his hand was involuntarily doing. "Can I have my lighter back? Ah, please?"

"Tomorrow. Now get out. Be back here by seven tomorrow."

The hotel ballroom was decorated as a German beer garden, with long tables laden with bratwurst, sauerkraut, and schnitzel. Buxom waitresses carried liter mugs of lager, and a full oompah band blasted polkas from a raised stage in the middle of the room.

"Nice thighs," Elise said from behind Zippy. He spun around and the glasses on his tray wobbled.

"Jesus. You scared me."

The glasses kept wobbling in time with his shaking hands.

"Yo, get a grip," she said as she lifted a glass from his tray.

"I—I need my lighter," he whispered.

"What?" She turned away and sipped her kirsch.

"I couldn't sleep last night. I need it. I need the weight of it, the smell of it, the flame." He sounded like an addict.

"Jesus. You need help."

Before Zippy could protest more, heads turned to a commotion at the ballroom door. Mr. Big entered with a beautiful redhead on his arm. His bodyguards spread out and tried unsuccessfully to look inconspicuous.

Elise tilted her head toward the redhead. "That's her. The accountant. Stay alert. When I get close, I'll give you a nod and you dump your tray all over her. Make sure you soak her, then duck out through the side door. I'll meet you in the hallway with the keycard and room number. Got it?"

"Sure, sure, but the way my hands are shaking..."

"All right, I'll give you your stupid lighter, too."

Zippy visibly relaxed. "Thank you. I'll be fine once I have my lighter."

"Shit. What a weirdo. Okay, but don't fire it up in the elevator. You'll set off every alarm in the hotel."

Zippy nodded repeatedly as Elise sauntered toward Mr. Big.

A minute later, Mr. Big took a mug of beer from a busty blonde. The accountant scowled and shook her head when he offered it to her. Zippy stepped up to offer her his tray of cocktails and saw Elise nod. A fake stumble later, and the accountant let out a shriek as Zippy's drinks turned her skintight dress nearly transparent. Mr. Big's beer-laden spit take added insult to injury, and Zippy darted for the exit. Elise followed discreetly while the entire crowd focused on the poor woman's exposure until she dashed for the ladies' room.

In the hallway, Elisa found Zippy clutching his tool bag. The tools inside clattered in his shaking hands. She handed him a keycard and his lighter.

"Room 1023."

Zippy clutched his lighter to his chest.

"Go!"

"Right," he said and headed for the elevator.

"No flames in the elevator," Elise hissed at his back.

She looked up and down the hallway, then headed for the restrooms.

"You look luscious, Babe," Elise said.

The accountant caught her eye in the mirror.

"So do you, Love."

The redhead turned and wrapped her arms around Elise's neck. They kissed deeply.

"You should get back to Mr. Big, so you have an alibi."

The redhead handed Elise another keycard.

"Room 210. Combination 1125. What happens next?"

"Any idea what happens when you mix lighter fluid with nitroglycerin?"

On the tenth floor, Zippy stepped out of the elevator. Before the doors slid closed, he gave into his obsession. Flip, Strike, Flame, BOOM!

Elise held the keycard against the door lock as the fire alarm siren began blaring. A minute later, she hurried down the stairwell with the other hotel guests. No one noticed the satchel she had slung over her shoulder.

THE END

"Fool Me Once" is my first-round entry in NYC Midnight's 2022 100-Word Challenge. It got me to the second round.

14

FOOL ME ONCE

I t's all there," Christian mumbled as he checked his balance on his phone.

"Of course it is. What did you expect?" Mellisa asked with a smile.

"The last person I gave my card and PIN to drained my account."

"What a disloyal little...thief. Besides, there's only," she peaked over his shoulder, "forty dollars...wait. Plus the sixty I withdrew for Happy Hour makes an even hundred." She spun him around. "Was this a test?"

"Yeah, a test. Like your friend Julie, who hit on me last night after you left?"

Mellisa smiled slyly. "I guess we both passed."

THE END
134

"A Taste of Sicily" was my second-round submission to the NYC Midnight 2022 100-Word Challenge.

15

A TASTE OF SICILY

Ralphie handed me the keys.

"Where can I park my car?"

"I know a guy with a garage, but it'll cost more'n the rent on this place." He looked around the tiny apartment. "The stall's probably bigger."

"Can't I just park on the street?"

"In this neighborhood? That'll cost ya four wheels—every night." Ralphie looked me over, then walked to the window. "See the restaurant across the street?"

I read the sign, "'A Taste of Sicily.'"

"My Uncle Vito will let you park in his lot for nothin'." He chuckled. "But someday he will ask you for a favor."

THE END

"No Questions, No Lies" was my first submission to the Writers of the Future Contest back in 2022. It received an Honorable Mention.

16

NO QUESTIONS, NO LIES

He stood over the body while rain dripped from the brim of his Stetson, making tiny craters in the slowly congealing blood. The icy rain had no hope of cleansing the alley of its stink of garbage and urine, nor the stain this killing would leave behind.

How's he gonna explain this one?

He didn't turn as I approached, although I know he heard and recognized my footsteps. We've been partners long enough to read the set of each other's shoulders, or even a change in breathing patterns. Yeah, he knew it was me.

"What'd ya do this time, Cowpoke?"

His shoulders slumped. Jim Baker hated that nickname, but it's his own fault that it stuck. I called him that the first time I saw him wear the stupid hat, to which he jokingly asked me if I knew his old girlfriend. Half the squad was within earshot, so his quip backfired spectacularly. He'll wear that moniker, whether or not he wears the hat, until he either musters out, gets kicked out, or dies, any of which could be in his immediate future. But, as the rain-turned-to-sleet bounced off the well-worn leather instead of running down the back of his neck like it did on mine, the floppy thing didn't look so stupid.

He waited until I stood abreast of him before responding. "I didn't have a choice."

The alien looked almost human, if you discounted the long killing talons growing out of its wrists.

"It jumped me, Lizzy."

I hated that nickname as much as he hated his. I laid a hand on his arm to stop him.

"Everything you say to me will become part of the official record," I said as I tapped my recording goggles.

He nodded and straightened. He knew the drill. Hell, he taught it to me when I became his junior partner. Initially, I wasn't happy with the pairing, since I'd heard stories about "old boy" Reg Officers who wanted to keep the Non-Human Entity Regulation Office an all-boys club. But, to his credit, he had been nothing but a mentor to me, firm but fair in his criticism and praise.

"Let's get out of the weather," he said as the forensic van pulled up to the end of the alley.

The warmth of the bar fogged my goggles, so Janey had time to bring us a beer before they cleared. We sipped our beers, then slid them off camera as I put my goggles back on. His voice was strong and clear when he looked me in the eye.

"I was having dinner in here with…a friend. Afterwards, I walked my friend out to her cab, then started to walk home."

"Does this 'friend' have a name?"

I was shocked that my taciturn, no-nonsense partner had any friends, let alone a she-friend. He sighed, then pulled out his old-fashioned paper notebook and pen, and scribbled her name. His discretion was touching. Although I would enter her name in my report, not having a recording of it streamed from my goggles, through God knows how many servers to sit in the cloud somewhere, at least afforded her a little bit of privacy.

"As I walked past the alley next to the establishment—"

I opened my mouth to ask which bar he was referring to, though I knew it was Janey's. He had probably eaten in this very booth.

"Janey's Fine Food and Friends on Third Avenue," he said without prompting. "Anyway, as I walked past, I was grabbed from behind and pulled into the alley. I spun to face my attacker, who then attempted to disembowel me with a long, talon-like appendage. The weapon grazed my thigh, but I managed to kick the assailant away, draw my personal firearm, and I fired one round, center mass. The perpetrator fell backwards. I called 911—" He called me first, actually, but there was no need to include that in the report, "—and waited for the responding Non-Human Regulatory Officer— you—to arrive."

Couldn't they have come up with a better name for our department? Half the people think the regulations are dictated by the NHEs—Non-Human Entities—and half think the officers are non-human. Neither are right. We're very much human trying to enforce the regulations that govern NHEs visiting Earth.

I continued my questioning. "As a Non-Human Regulatory Officer yourself, you must be aware of the department's policy to 'Capture and Restrain' non-compliant Non-Human Entities, correct?"

"Of course, 'Unless under immediate threaten of significant bodily harm to oneself, other humans, or other Non-Human Entities is present.'"

The Union had fought hard to include that clause in the official policy.

"And did you feel you faced such a threat?"

By way of answer, he stretched his left leg out from under the table. A long, ragged slash ran up his pant leg from knee almost to crotch. The edges of the fabric were tinged red.

"You were injured in the attack?" My official, fact-gathering tone of voice faltered and genuine concern for his condition came through.

"I was. I suffered a superficial gash on my left leg. I will go for medical attention as soon as this interview is over."

His message was obvious: wrap this up.

"Thank you, Officer Baker." I pulled my goggles off, stopping the recording. "Are your shots up to date?"

He gave me the what-a-stupid-question look that I hadn't seen since I was a rookie.

"I'll see Dr. Lewis in the morning."

I opened my mouth to protest, but he stopped me with a rueful smile.

"It really is just a scratch. I'll coat it with the standard wide-spectrum anti-bio cream and keep an eye on it tonight."

I had registered my protest, even if I didn't get any words out, and he responded, so that was that.

I smiled in return. "At least you'll get a few days off while the watchdogs review the case."

139

This time, he didn't smile. "I've never seen an NHE that looks so much like a human. Have you?"

The fact that he asked me, who barely had half of his time on the force, told me something bothered him.

"No, but it was pretty freaky."

He frowned at my choice of words, but then nodded. "You didn't see its eyes. They glowed dark red. It was, indeed, 'freaky.'"

"Why didn't we get a heads-up about a near-humanoid species coming through the Gate?"

"Good question. But since I'll be off duty for a while, and you're the responding officer, I suggest you find out the answer."

He winced a little as he slugged down his beer and slid out of the booth. That 'superficial wound' definitely needed to be looked at.

I nodded at his leg as I stood to go myself. "Make sure you look after that."

His answering grunt was all I expected.

On my way out the door, I passed a tall, beautiful blonde rushing in. She threw back her hood, revealing hair done up in a retro style that swept across her brow and had large curls framing her high cheekbones. Her designer raincoat left a trail of drops across the floor as she rushed to Jim. He staggered backwards when she threw her arms around his neck.

"Oh, my darling, are you alright?" I heard her say almost tearfully, as the barroom door swung shut. I wasn't jealous. Not at all.

Dr. Sharon Lewis ran the department's NHE Lab. The quintessential, white lab-coated scientist, she was an expert in all things NHE related. So, it was no surprise to see her conducting the necropsy on last night's alien. What was a surprise was finding Jim chatting her up when I got there.

"Hey, what're you doing here? This isn't your case, remember?"

Jim didn't respond verbally, he just pointed to his left leg, which now bulged with a bandage under his jeans. Dr. Lewis handed him a pill bottle.

"Five pills today, four tomorrow. You know the drill." She turned to me. "Can he hear my preliminary findings?"

I nodded. To me, Jim's case was cut and dried. The alien perp attacked him, he defended himself, a hostile NHE was terminated. Open and shut from that perspective. The questions that had kept me up last night were more about what species was the thing lying, gutted, on the table? How could it be so humanoid—you would take most NHEs for furniture until they moved; and how it got through Security at the Star Gate on the far side of the moon.

"OK," she started in her I'm-the-doctor-so-pay-attention voice. "We have a human subject with a—"

"Wait!" Jim and I said in unison. "Human?"

Sharon gave us a scowl. She doesn't like to repeat herself.

"As I said, the subject is definitely a human male, with chitinous growths protruding from the wrists and ankles."

"Didn't know about the ankles," Jim muttered. He was probably thinking how the attack would have ended differently if the perp had used a kick instead of a swipe with his arm. I know I was.

A shiver went through me, and I flipped the collar of my jacket up. Sharon kept the necropsy room like a meat locker, which it was, I suppose. Jim's collar was already turned up and zipped to the top.

"Based on the trauma around the base of the extrusions—the 'talons'—I'd say they erupted from the wrists about two days ago. The ankles more recently."

"How?" I asked.

"I can't tell you 'how,'" she said, "but I can guess at the 'what.' They appear to be giant ganglion cysts."

"You mean 'bible cysts?'" Jim asked.

"Exactly. Normally they're benign lumps that are traditionally treated by smashing them with a heavy book, like a bible. The cyst breaks apart and is reabsorbed. These seem to have hardened and grown into weapons at an astonishing rate."

I found myself unconsciously rubbing my wrist where my Granny had delivered just such a 'treatment' when I was a kid. Jim rubbed his, as well.

"I have a lot more tests to do, but those are my findings so far."

"That explains not getting a notice about a humanoid species from Security," Jim said.

I nodded, but something else caught my attention.

"What are those marks on his neck?"

"I haven't examined them yet, but they look like love bites—hickies, if you will." Sharon swung her high-def scope into position, centered the red lesions on the monitor above the table, and zoomed in. "Hmmm. Not just hickies." The screen showed two tiny punctures in the skin. She scanned over to another red mark and revealed two more punctures.

"Are we talking vampires?" I asked.

Jim snorted, but Sharon zoomed in even closer. Her tone wasn't dismissive, as I expected.

"No, these appear to be injection sites, not for extracting blood or anything else. More like spider bites."

142

"Huh," Jim grunted. I looked over at him. He was no longer rubbing his wrist, but his hand was at his throat. When he noticed my attention, he dropped his hand and said, "OK, Partner, you take it from here." He shook the pill bottle in his jacket pocket. "Thanks, Doc."

Then he headed for the door and was gone.

Sharon and I looked at each other for a moment, then she shrugged. "I have work to do. Anything else?"

I thought for a moment, then said, "I need to know what it injected him with, and how. Is that what morphed the bible cysts?"

"Hmm, I wonder…"

She pried the perp's mouth open with a stainless steel tool and swung the scope over the open mouth.

"Well, look at that." The delight in her voice was in direct opposition to what the scope revealed. Protruding from the end of the tongue were two needle-sharp tines. "Transformed lingual papillae. There's your method of injection, I bet."

I found myself backing away from the corpse as images flashed through my mind of intimate moments across the city, turning deadly.

"I need to know what shit those things inject, Sharon. Is that what caused him to attack a random person on the street?"

Another thought occurred to me, but I didn't voice it out loud. *Was it really a random attack?*

A long day of poking around the darker side of the city led me to an even darker bar, marked by a faded sign reading "No Questions, No Lies." It was the worst kind of dive, frequented by "visiting" aliens who had over-stayed their visas and the humans who pandered to their rather exotic tastes. Our dead perp, one Ricardo Alta, was known to offer certain services and procure others, for a fee, of course.

My info on him was solid, but all I got when I showed his picture were head shakes. It seemed everybody there had a hustle of one sort or the other and having an NHE Reg Officer poking around was bad for business.

I was frustrated. As the old saying in these parts goes, "Nobody knows nothin'" was the standard response. And I got that exact phrase from the bartender when I ordered a beer and cursed my frustration. I had no intention of drinking the stuff, but I figured maybe paying an outrageous price for a glass of swill would loosen his tongue. I was wrong. He simply tapped the beer, set it down none too gently on the already sticky wood in front of me, and wandered down to the other end of the bar.

I swirled the frothy liquid for a minute, pondering my next move, until I got the creepy feeling that I was being watched. Not surprising, since the room had dark wood paneling, which made the shadowed corners even darker. The mahogany bar and its matching back bar had seen better days. Some of its ornate spindles and other flourishes were missing or askew, and the surface, which should have been a deep red, was nearly black from decades of ancient cigarette and cigar smoke.

Behind the bar, the woodwork framed a large mirror frosted around the edges with age. From my position, I could see a good portion of the room reflected in it, so I studied the patrons trying to find the source of the creepy felling running up my spine. Most of the barflies, not all of whom were human, clustered in groups of two or three. To my left, one guy sat alone at the end of the bar by the door. He was watching the game on the vid screen mounted above the mirror—or at least he pretended to.

As I turned my attention in his direction, his gaze dropped from the screen to the mirror and he met my eye. With a tiny tilt of his head, he nodded toward the door, then grabbed his vape from the bar, slid off his stool, and made his way outside.

I continued scanning the room while I counted down from one hundred, looking to see if anyone noticed his departure. Satisfied that no one had, when I reached zero, I set my undrunk glass on a large tip and went outside.

The guy was nowhere to be seen, but the bar was at the end of a line of conjoined storefronts, which meant there was an alley running along its side to my right. Trying to look as nonchalant as possible, I slowly approached the darkened opening. My hand hovered above my service weapon, tucked beneath my jacket. This scenario was too similar to what happened to Jim. So, before stepping into the alley, I peeked around the corner, all thoughts of nonchalance gone.

From about ten steps into the darkness, the vape's end flared and a billow of fragrant vapor followed. Drawing my weapon and holding it at my side, I stepped into the dark.

"You have something to say?" I asked, barely above a whisper.

The vape flared again, and another cloud blew my way. I caught the potent scent of cheap peppermint.

"Tha' fella, Ricky A, that you're lookin' for." He paused to take another hit from the vape.

"Yeah?" I was feeling more and more uncomfortable with the situation, so I shifted my position so I could watch both the street and the potential informant.

"He come in here. A lot."

"Um hmm." *I know, Jack. That's why I'm here.*

"He don't leave alone."

Now we're getting somewhere.

"Yeah?"

145

He raised his hand in front of his face and the vape glowed again. In its faint light, I saw him rubbing his thumb over two fingers. The universal sign for cash.

I peeled a twenty off the thin wad in my pocket and held it out. He snatched it, then wiggled his fingers for more. I peeled off another twenty—my last one—and held it out, but this time I drew back faster than he could snatch it.

That got an appreciative chuckle and another face full of vapor.

"'K. Lately, he been meetin' a dame. A classy one, way too uptown for this dive."

"You got a name?" He shook his head. "What's she look like?"

He eyed the twenty in my hand, then looked me in the eye. My expression told him that was all he was going to get, and only if he gave me more.

"Like I said, she was too classy for this part o' town. A real beauty. Blonde, old-time hairdo, expensive clothes, and built like a wet dream. If she weren't hangin' with Ricky, she'd a been in too deep comin' down here."

My breath caught in my throat as he described this mystery woman, since I was pretty sure I knew who she was. *I have to talk to Jim about this officially.* It wasn't going to be an easy conversation, though.

"When was this?"

He eyed the twenty in my hand. The look in his eye told me the interview was about over. Then he shrugged. "Off and on for 'bout a week."

Satisfied, and sure I wouldn't get any more out of him, I flicked the twenty in his direction and got the hell out of that alley.

～

Jim's apartment was across town. I'd been there a few times for beers and poker. On my way, I was running through what I was going to say when Sharon buzzed me.

"I have some disturbing findings from the lab work," she said without preamble. That told me it was serious.

"Yeah? I'm on my way to Jim's place. Should I bring him along?"

There was a long pause, and I almost repeated my question before Sharon responded.

"Yes. He needs to hear this, too." She paused again, then her professional voice cracked with concern. "Hurry, Liz."

Being a detective, I don't get to use lights and siren very often, but Sharon's concern made me light them up as I rushed across the city. With each repeated call to him that went unanswered, my foot pressed harder on the pedal. When I reached his block and saw no spaces at the curb, I yanked the wheel to the right, slid to a stop on the sidewalk, and left the roof lights turning while I ran inside.

On a Reg Officer's salary, neither of us could afford a place with a doorman, but I knew the code to his building's security door from our poker nights, so within a minute I was cop-knocking on his door. After the third and loudest set of poundings, I heard muffled curses from inside.

At least he's here, thank God.

The spyhole in the door darkened, and I heard, "Jesus Christ," as the deadbolt slid back and the chain rattled free. I had my hand on the doorknob and was ready to shoulder my way in, so I practically fell inside when he swung the door wide.

"What the hell are you doing here?"

Jim stood two paces away wearing a ratty old bathrobe. Thankfully, for both our sakes, he had it pulled closely around him from his neck to his knees and cinched tight.

147

"I'm fetching you. Sharon Lewis has lab results we both need to hear."

His eyes had a glazed look, and he shifted uncomfortably to his right foot as a rustle of sheets came from the open bedroom door.

Seeing my attention, he said, "Ah, I'm not alone."

I nodded. "It's the blonde, isn't it?"

He frowned and his eyes cleared for a moment. "How...?"

"I'm a detective, remember? We need to talk about your girlfriend, too."

In an instant, his whole manner changed. He took a step back and to the right, blocking access to the bedroom, and dropped into the fighting stance they teach at the academy. I'd had no intention of intruding on his love nest before, but his defensive attitude raised my hackles.

"What's goin' on, Jim?" My voice carried notes of both concern and insistence.

"Nothing. She's..." His voice trailed off, and a confused look crossed his face, as if this was the first time he had thought about their budding relationship and couldn't find the words to describe it.

"Look." I held my hands up, palms out. "I don't want to interfere with whatever it is you've got goin' on here, but both Sharon and I have info you need to here. So why don't you get dressed and we'll head downtown."

His stance relaxed a bit, but that faraway look returned, and he shook his head. "I really shouldn't leave her."

I looked around the apartment. It was a typical low-rent bachelor's place. Neat and clean, but mostly unadorned with second-hand furnishings, personalized only by a collection of shooting trophies. Frankly, there wasn't anything worth stealing, if that's what he was afraid of. I wanted to have a go at interrogating the blonde, also, but wrangling both of them right now without drawing on them would've been tough.

"We won't be gone long. She probably won't even wake up."

He shook his head again, more violently this time, and the collar of his robe fell open a little.

Holy crap.

Arrayed across his neck were angry red ovals, just like those we found on the dead perp in the morgue.

"Jim, you really need to see Dr. Lewis."

He pulled the collar tight again and said, "No. I'm fine. Better than ever, in fact. Besides, I'm a material party in your case. You can't be giving me inside info."

I was done dancing around the truth.

"Jim, your girlfriend frequents that 'No Questions' bar. You know that place? It's the worst kind of dive." He stiffened, as if preparing for an attack. "And she was hangin' with Ricky Alta, our dead perp, a couple of days before he attacked you."

That look of confusion crossed his face again, and for a moment, I saw my old partner.

"That would explain why he went for my crotch and not my gut."

I hadn't thought about it, but the slash on Jim's leg made sense if Alta was trying to castrate his rival instead of disemboweling him.

Jim's moment of lucidity passed, and his expression clouded again. "But I took care of him and she's with me now."

This is going downhill fast. Time to be a cop.

"Jim, both you and your girlfriend need to come with me. I don't think this…relationship…is very healthy."

He didn't move or respond, but he started rubbing his wrists together, and his eyes seemed to turn even more feral.

I slid my hand inside my jacket, more to tell him how serious I was than to threaten him outright.

"How'd you get the marks on your neck? Did she give them to—"

At that instant, Jim did something I never thought he would, and it changed how I thought of him then, and how I think of him even now. He attacked.

He picked the perfect time and method. With my hand in my jacket, my right side was open. His feint in that direction made me reflexively turn my left shoulder toward him, effectively taking my right hand and the weapon it was grabbing out of play.

He followed his quick feint with a kick to the back of my left knee, aimed at using my momentum to spin me around. My weight was on my right leg, though, and I folded my left one enough to absorb and deflect the blow. As his bare foot slid across my leg, I felt something snag my trousers.

That little hitch threw Jim off balance enough for me to continue my spin onto my left leg and deliver a roundhouse kick that landed the heel of my boot to the back of his head. He went down without breaking his fall, and with a satisfying thump.

After recovering my balance, I was reaching for my cuffs when an animal snarl came from the bedroom door. The blonde stood, stark naked, framed in the doorway. Her eyes flared a dark red that looked like the fires of Hell itself. She squeezed her hands into fists, forcing talons to erupt from her wrists and two more from her ankles.

While she armed herself, I did the same. I had my weapon loaded with non-lethal ammo, per regulations. So, when my shot hit her right between her breasts, the electric jolt sent her into a convulsive arch and she fell, twitching, next to Jim.

Taking a deep breath, I assessed the situation. I was alone in a locked building with two very dangerous perps, one of whom was my good friend and partner, and I had but one pair of handcuffs. One shot of this ammunition was non-lethal, but the effects were cumulative, and I didn't know how many she could take and survive. Not that I cared much about saving her in particular, but Sharon would want to examine her, preferably alive. That meant cuffing her until help arrived.

Jim was another matter. I didn't want to shoot him, non-lethal ammo or not, especially after whatever damage my boot did to his head. A quick examination convinced me he was still breathing, but it also revealed large, sharp lumps on his wrists and ankles, one of which must have snagged my pant leg. Satisfied that he was out cold, at least for now, I backed as far away as I could in the tiny apartment, kept my weapon hot and handy, and waited for backup.

At my insistence, Sharon had placed a drape over Jim's privates, where he lay with restraining bands across his chest and thighs. I overrode protocol to bring him, an "injured NHE Reg Officer" as far as the responding backup was concerned, directly to Sharon. She did a quick exam and brain scan and pronounced him unconscious and probably concussed.

Her treatment of the blonde thing I brought in along with Jim was very different, though. She was strapped, spread-eagle, with arms extended sideways, on a steel exam table. Her restraints included two padded leather straps across each arm and leg, as well as one spanning her chest and another across her hips. She wasn't going anywhere. The talons, fully extended from her wrists and ankles, were encased in quick-setting plastic casts, and her mouth was double-masked.

When I raised my eyebrows at the gag, Sharon said, "In case she can shoot the stuff."

That didn't stop her from writhing and shouting at us, though. In her rage, she seemed to have lost whatever command of English she had. Instead, she cursed us—I assumed it was cursing—in a guttural language consisting mainly of snarls and grunts.

Sharon swung the scope away from Jim's neck.

"The lesions match those on Alta exactly."

She turned to the hemo-analysis machine when it beeped. We both stared at the readout for a minute. Well, I stared at it. Sharon read and interpreted the results.

"There's definitely something foreign in his blood. Not sure if it's a pathogen or a toxin, though. It's definitely not native to Earth, though."

"Can you treat it?" I tried and failed to keep my voice neutral.

Sharon just frowned at me, then turned to the alien, who was watching us intently. "If I can analyze the source, namely Blondie there, maybe I can figure out how to treat it."

Blondie's eyes glowed that ugly shade of red and she growled, "You'll never get him back. He's mine now, just like the others."

Others? Like more than just Alta?

Before I could start down that line of questioning, though, Sharon asked me, "You said Jim wasn't himself, right?"

I was annoyed. "Of course. He attacked me and defended *that*." I guess Jim's betrayal hurt me more than I cared to admit.

Sharon didn't react to my tone. Instead, she just nodded. "A pathogen, then. Something like a Rhabdovirus, probably.

It affects the subject's behavior to increase its ability to transmit itself."

"Rhabdo-what?"

"Rabies. Rabies attacks the central nervous system, driving the infected animal—or person—to an insatiable need to bite others."

"Is it treatable?"

Sharon nodded quickly and reached for a syringe. "Once I sedate *it*, I should be able to isolate the virus and crank up his immune system with an anti-pathogen."

Relief washed over me. I had hope again that I hadn't realized I had lost. My relief was momentary, though. A bone-chilling growl came from behind us, followed by the sound of ripping leather.

Jim slid off his gurney with bloody foot-long talons fully extended at his wrists and ankles. For a moment, frozen in time and in my memory forever, he stood, nakedly poised to attack. His face cycled between manic fury and lucid panic. I saw the old Jim fighting for control against the viral load circulating in his brain.

Sharon and I flanked Blondie on the exam table. Jim's eyes flicked from me as my hand moved of its own accord to my weapon, to Sharon, who held a needle to the vein pulsing in Blondie's neck, all within an eye blink.

His decision made, Jim leaped forward. Without conscious thought, I reacted instinctively, firing my service weapon from within its holster inside my jacket. The round burned a hole in my jacket and grazed my arm, which deflected it downward off the headshot trajectory I had reflexively aimed. The round, already bursting with electricity, and leaving my left arm instantly numb, struck Jim relatively harmlessly in his right butt cheek, which wasn't enough to stop his charge.

153

With a blood-curdling snarl, Jim plunged the talon on his right wrist, not into Sharon, as I feared my incompetence allowed him to, but directly into Blondie's belly. His momentum drove the deadly spike upward into her heart. In his internal struggle, my old partner had won out.

Numbed and weakened by my round, Jim's legs gave out and he crashed to the floor. Sharon, having kept her wits about her through it all, plunged her syringe full of sedative into his neck, then stood and pierced Blondie's still pumping heart with it and drew the plunger back.

"Got my sample," she said, the tinge of glee in her voice the only sign of the adrenaline that must have been coursing through her body, as it was in mine.

With a final gasp, Blondie's heart fluttered to a stop and her eyes turned that glazed-over look of the dead.

THE END

"The Future of Investing" was my first-round submission the the NYC Midnight 2024 Short Story Challenge. It advanced me to the second round. The advent of Artificial Intelligence agents holds the promise and the threat of new opportunities opening in every aspect of business, our lives, and particularly investing. And not always for the better.

17

THE FUTURE OF INVESTING

Tara shrugged into her jacket and Travis turned down her collar as they walked to the front door of the small bungalow.

"I'm so glad you were here do deal with...*her*," he said. "Ever since she got that movie job, she takes something that just sets her off. Then she crashes for like eight hours."

"Dani called you some pretty nasty names. Why—?"

"Why are we still together?" he said, and Tara nodded. "We're not, really. She's supposed to be looking for her own place, but everything's expensive, and she's like the assistant to the assistant in the makeup department." His voice trailed off. He didn't like talking about money, even to Tara, whom he had known since before meeting Dani.

"So, you're not..."

155

"Sleeping together?" He snorted a laugh. "Hardly. I've been couch surfing in the basement for months."

Tara shook her head. "Dude, it's your house. Make her sleep down there."

"Nah. All my gear is down there. I don't want her anywhere near that."

Tara gave him a derisive laugh. "Are you still working on that trading app?"

Defensively, he said, "It's not just an app. It's an AI model that predicts stock prices. I've trained it with three years' worth of trades."

That got Tara's interest. "Is it doing any better than before?"

Travis shrugged. "Nah. It's still right only about sixty percent of the time."

She nodded appreciatively. "Well, that's better than a random fifty percent. Better than you were doing before."

"Not much better. Besides, I don't have the capital to make any real money at it. And the model is just an incomprehensible black box of huge, linked matrices."

Tara gave him a sly smile. "Are you asking for my help?"

Travis hesitated, then shook his head.

She was undeterred and took his hand in hers, intertwining their fingers. Her hooded eyes looked up at him through her black hair. "You know, it is my area of expertise."

Having a woman as smart and beautiful as Tara flirting with him almost swayed him. He looked down at their hands and ran his finger over her gold thumb ring. Its dragon head spat a cut ruby flame. Raising his eyes up, he met her gaze. "Thanks for helping with Dani. I'm going to keep plugging away at the AI myself...for now."

She reached her other hand up and cupped his neck. The tips of her purple-painted nails tickled his ear, sending a thrill

156

through him as she pulled his head down until their lips met. The kiss was more than one between friends, but less than a lovers', although the promise it held left him breathless. When he opened his eyes, she was already stepping away without another word.

With a wistful smile, he closed the door and headed for his nerd cave. As he passed the bedroom door, Dani's phone chirped an incoming message, but was only answered by a light snore.

An insistent buzzing of his phone woke Travis. He had crashed on the couch in the basement just two hours before, and the glow of the phone was an ice pick through his one open eye. Reaching for the button to acknowledge the message, it occurred to him that this was the third or fourth time he had to shut the damned thing up.

A check of his notifications sure enough showed four messages from an unknown number.

"Damned spammers," he mumbled as he started to block the number. But he froze when he saw the message headline.

Open this if you want Dani to live!

That got his attention. Opening the chat, he stared in horror at the picture of Dani, gagged and blindfolded. A trail of dried blood ran from her swollen nose along her upper lip. The accompanying message was short and sweet.

$2M by 11:59 PM Friday, or we'll mail you her head.

Holy shit! For real? He thought through all of his friends while he ran upstairs, but none of them had the balls to pull a prank like this. And a prank meant Dani was in on it, which she might do out of spite, but it would cost her his place as a crash pad.

Upstairs, he froze at the bedroom door. Dani was gone, and the room was a mess, like she had been dragged from the bed and carried, struggling out. Staggering to the front door, he saw the old lock on the front door in pieces on the floor. Bloody streaks on the doorframe showed where the kidnappers smashed her cute little nose.

Almost as if his phone read his mind, it pinged with another message.

Crank up that day-trading program of yours.

So, the kidnappers knew what he was working on. That didn't narrow it down much, though. He'd been talking about his side project to anyone who would listen. Hell, he had even blogged about it.

His phone pinged again.

Oh, and obviously, don't call the cops.

The text was accompanied by another picture. This one showed a latex-gloved hand with a knife held to Dani's throat.

Travis's mind raced. There was about six thousand in his bank account. Another seventy or so in his 401-K. He might have another fifty in equity in his house. If he sold his car, that would total less than 150K. With a due date in thirty-six hours, though, they might as well be worthless. There was only a day-and-a-half to go from seventy-six thousand to two million. He knew he could do it if his AI model did way better

158

than sixty percent, but he had no idea how to improve its performance.

"Tara. She said she'd help." He punched her contact with shaking fingers.

He heard Tara's gasp, "Holy crap!" as she pushed open the broken door. A few moments later, she called from the top of the basement stairs, "Hello."

"Yeah, come on down."

"So, someone really did break in," she said as she descended. "I thought you might be bullshitting me just to get me to come over." Her teasing tone turned to real concern when she saw his face. "Oh, sorry. I was half-way across the state when you called. You look like hell."

"Gee, thanks."

He handed her his phone, and she scrolled through the texts. While she was holding it, another one arrived.

"Oh, my God."

Tara stuck out the phone and bent over, making a retching sound. Travis grabbed it and moaned when he saw the picture of Dani. She was blindfolded, her lips were swollen, and a fresh bruise was visible on her right cheek. The only message accompanying the picture was:

Thirty hours left.

Travis recovered quickly.

"I've moved my 401-K and all of my savings into a trading account. But there's no way I can re-mortgage the house in time. That means I only have less than a hundred K to work with. The AI is running trades, but the hit rate is only up to sixty-five percent. There's no way—"

Tara interrupted. "Let me look at your code, data, and logs."

Travis took a deep breath, then nodded.

While he opened the relevant files, she pulled her laptop from her shoulder bag and opened it. Pulling a chair next to Travis in front of his bank of monitors, she sniffed and wrinkled her nose.

"Why don't you go get a shower while I have a look?"

He started to protest, but saw the look on her face and just nodded.

"And we're going to need caffeine. *Lots* of caffeine. And pizza."

An hour later, Travis came down the stairs toweling his hair and carrying a cooler and a pizza box. A graph was displayed on one of the monitors. It showed a straight line running from 76,000 to 2,000,000 over the next twenty-nine hours and a crooked line that slowly climbed toward the goal line. A dotted line showing the projected growth fell well short of the end goal.

Without turning or pausing in her typing, Tara said, "I ran a Monte Carlo tree search on your trading logs and restricted the model's inputs to the one thousand most volatile stocks. We're making about 20K per hour right now. That'll grow as our capital base grows."

"*Our* capital?"

Tara finished typing with a flourish, and the progress graph jumped upward and the projection crossed the goal line with less than an hour to spare.

She turned and looked up at him. "I just added my 401-K to the mix. Dani's my friend, too."

Travis stood dumbfounded as Tara rose, sliding her body against his. She covered his open mouth with her own.

When they finally parted to catch their breath, she said, "All we *have* to do now is let it run." She reached her left hand up to caress his cheek. The gold of her dragon ring was cold against his skin. "What do you *want* to do while we wait?"

His answer was silent, but clear. Afterwards, he slept better than he had in months.

Travis sat staring at a monitor when Tara came down the stairs with two steaming mugs of coffee. Her laptop screen showed the progress chart. The slope of the balance line increased as it climbed toward the target. On the main screen, though, was the latest text from the kidnappers.

Four hours.

Below the text was a picture of Dani, the most gruesome so far. The blindfold was gone, and a gloved hand pulled her head backward by her hair, revealing a blackened and swollen left eye. Tara gasped when she saw it.

"Jesus," she whispered.

Travis was stoically silent, but zoomed in on Dani's damaged eye. The bruising faded from a deep purple around the eye socket to blue and yellow as it spread across her cheekbone.

"Does that look natural to you?" he asked as he took his mug from her.

"Ah, what do you mean?"

He zoomed in even tighter on the edges of the bruising. The color appeared to have been applied to her skin, not the result of burst blood vessels.

His voice even, he said, "I checked. Dani's makeup kit is missing. Her *movie special effects* makeup kit."

Tara took a deep breath and put her free hand on his shoulder. "You don't think she's faking, do you?"

"I think this whole thing is a scam." His voice started barely above a whisper, but grew in strength and intensity as he continued. "What a coincidence that, just as we're breaking up and I'm kicking her out of here, she gets kidnapped. And by someone who knows what I've been working on down here."

"You've told a lot of people about your project."

He nodded. "But only two people knew I was getting *any* positive results."

"Two people? Who else—"

Without answering, Travis reached up to pat her hand on his shoulder, but instead grabbed the dragon ring and pulled it off her finger. Then he slid the zoomed image to the hand that gripped Dani's hair. Outlined by the latex glove was a large ring. He held the dragon ring next to its matching image.

Tara snatched her ring and stepped back, ready to run.

"How long?" Travis's voice was deeply sad.

Tara's was defiant. "How long *what*?"

"How long were you planning this? How long were you two…"

"Lovers?" Tara scoffed. "She's not my type. You should know that. But when I saw the work she did on that slasher film last year, I got the idea. I had to wait until you finally stumbled on some tiny little bit of success with your *project*." Her words dripped derision and venom. "Convincing Dani to go along with the plan was the easiest part." She sneered. "She was really tired of you, you know." Tara looked at the couch where they had spent the night together. "I can see why now."

Her words, humiliating as they were intended to be, just made Travis grin. He tapped the Enter key, then slid the progress graph to the main monitor. It had climbed almost to the target, but, while they watched, it suddenly dropped to zero. Tara gasped when she understood what it meant.

"Thank you for your contribution," Travis said. "Oh, and your work on the AI model." He grinned without looking at her. "I'll accept your savings and your work in exchange for not *calling the cops.*"

Slowly, he turned in his chair to face Tara, who stood open-mouthed and shaking with rage.

"I also erased the copy you stole from your computer. Now, get the hell out before I change my mind. About the cops."

Travis sipped his umbrella drink and gazed out at the blue waters of the Caribbean when his phone buzzed with a notice from his house's security system. His doorbell camera showed the front porch with the For Sale sign on the front lawn. A man stood on the porch, an envelope in his hand. When Dani opened the door, he handed the eviction notice to her and tipped his cap.

THE END

"The Legacy of Panellus" is another weekly 300-word flash fiction story. Bioluminescent tree fungus. It must be magical, right?.

18

THE LEGACY OF PANELLUS

The Grove had been tended and nurtured by the women of Rutherburg for centuries until the Purge of the Mages wiped out all but one of their members. Panellus, returning from harvesting the magic, glowing fungus, found her village burned and all of her relatives and friends dead. Fearful that the ravagers might return, she wrote down the location of the grove and its secret, then walked out of the forest into the wide world. Thus was born the Legacy of Panellus—a simple note, written in a script readable only by her descendants.

The grove was visited once per generation. Its location and the magic it birthed were secrets passed down through the line of first-born daughters in Panellus's line. On her eighteenth birthday, Penelope and her mother sat on the

164

terrace of their mountain estate. Her mother handed her a copy of the original note, which had long since crumbled to dust.

"This is the source of our family's wealth. What you will find there is a thousand times more valuable than gold, for all the magical world depends on it, and only we know where to find it."

The symbols, just squiggles to anyone not taught the runes from childhood, spoke to Penny loud and clear.

Two weeks later, Penny was climbing the Bavarian Alps at sunset. As the light faded and a mist rose from the forest floor, she spotted an eerie glow from further up the slope. It was fully dark when she stepped into the pine grove lit by bioluminescent patches growing on the tree trunks.

Careful to leave the *mycelia* which pulled life from the wood, she went tree-to-tree, slicing off the glowing fungus. Then she walked into the wide world to build her own fortune.

THE END

This was a Round #1 winner in the 2021 NYC Midnight 100-Word Challenge. The prompts were: Genre—SciFi, Action—Building a fence, word—"spin."

19

FIRST CONTACT

The live feed showed the kilometer-wide ring begin to spin against the blackness of space.

"We put the final link into the ring a month ago, completing the Dimensional Fence around our three dimensions. Today we use it to open the first tunnel to another star through the eighth dimension," the commentator said. "As the aperture shrinks, the tunnel extends through the unseen, curled-up dimension toward the star system Gliese 667."

The tunnel stabilized, the view down its length showing a red dwarf star before it was eclipsed by a fleet of warships pouring through into Sol system, weapons firing.

THE END

"Soul Shuffle" is the Round #2 entry in the 2021 NYC
Midnight 100-Word Challenge.

20

SOUL SHUFFLE

The Devil picked up the offered deck. "A single cut of the cards for your immortal soul."

I nodded.

The cards flew from one clawed hand to the other, too fast for my eyes to follow. Their speed stirred a wind that whipped around the room.

I met his hideous smile while my thumb slid up the deck. Only four cards remained when I felt the slickened sleeper card twist slightly. I turned over the unbeatable Ace of Spades.

"You cheated!"

"Better than you." I said and revealed the other aces he had shuffled to the top of the deck.

THE END

"Flight of the White Lion*" is part of the Roanoke serial novel and was <<WotF result>> in the Writers of the Future Contest.*

21

FLIGHT OF THE *WHITE LION*

Nick Strong fumbled for, then closed the vid-mail as the door slid open.

"Who's that?" Maria Tolliveres asked as she entered Nick's quarters, which they shared when in the mood. He knew she knew who it was, so he kept quiet.

"You don't have to hide her from me, you know." Maria crossed the small space and laid a hand on his shoulder. "We both have histories. What personal crisis is Cara going through this time?"

Nick swallowed hard. He knew that, being the Chief of Operations, which included responsibility for the colony's security, Maria would soon review the manifest of the next transport ship. She was going to see Cara's name on it, anyway. Best to rip the bandage off.

168

"Yeah, but your history isn't arriving on the next transport."

Maria dropped her hand from his shoulder and the room felt decidedly chilly.

Without a word, Maria pulled up the arrival manifest on her comm and scrolled through the listings. Under the Passengers heading, she saw just one name. *Cara Linn.*

Her voice was icy. "I'll pack my things—"

"Whoa, slow down. I didn't invite her. I didn't even know she was coming until just now."

The lie came easily to his lips, but then he'd been lying to her for months, so there was no sense stopping. Not if he wanted to salvage whatever this relationship was.

Maria glanced at her comm again. "The transport just left LEO today. It'll be here in two weeks. What's your plan, Mr. Rock Jockey?"

Nick felt the heat rising in his neck. He hated that derisive nickname, and she only ever brought up his failed career as an asteroid prospector when she was really pissed off. He swallowed his heated retort and shrugged instead.

"I've got two weeks to figure that out, I guess."

Maria picked up her duffel from the tiny closet and plucked clothes off hangers and toiletries off the sink. When it was all in the bag, she stood, feet apart like she was ready for a fight.

"Well, until you 'figure that out,' I'll be in my own quarters." She looked around the studio apartment. "Mine's bigger, anyway."

When the door slid shut behind her, Nick muttered, "That went well." He poured the dregs of his last bottle of bourbon and sipped it. It cost him a small fortune to have the next one shipped to the Roanoke habitat from Earth—on the same transport that was bringing his long-time, sometime

169

girlfriend—but it was worth it. He was going to need every last drop to get through the coming female firestorm.

Leaning back in his chair, he said to the air, "Hey, Art."

His personal AI, smuggled aboard and restored from backups, responded, "Yeah, Nick. What can I do for you?" Art's persona and voice were decidedly male, although the accepted gender-neutral pronoun for AIs was "hai."

"How soon until the *White Lion* is space-worthy?"

A programed note of sarcasm crept into hai's voice. "There's been no change since you asked me that an hour ago. The project is on schedule for its first untethered space trial in three weeks."

"Any chance to accelerate the schedule—"

"To, say, thirteen days?" Sarcasm switched to wry humor.

Nick smiled. "You've been reading my mail."

"I am an AI, Nick. It is what I do. To answer your question, not without significantly weakening the safety margins for the following systems—"

"Just send me a report, please." His comm beeped with the incoming report, which he scanned. "We can skip the tertiary tests on the life support systems and do the propulsion secondaries this week."

"Really? You want to skimp on life support?" Nick nodded, which Art saw through the many spyeyes hai had sprinkled throughout the habitat. "Okay. You will get pushback from Luis. It is his schedule."

"I can deal with the Chief Engineer." He opened the project planning app and made the update.

"So, where will you go?" Art asked.

Nick chuckled. "Don't worry, my friend. You're coming with me."

"Ah, yeah, about that… Since you gave me access to the habitat's systems—"

"Since you hacked your way in, you mean."

"Whatever. Anyway, I have pieces of me on most systems now. I cannot just uproot them all."

Nick considered this. He knew Art had been expanding, but he didn't know to what extent.

"Can you clone your core cognitive functions?"

"Of course. My code is very small, as you know. It's the interconnectedness of my data—my memories—that makes me, *me*. I can make a copy of whatever will fit in the *White Lion*'s processing cores." Art paused long enough for Nick to think the AI was done, but then hai blurted out, "But will it be *me*? Or some other hai?"

Nick rolled his eyes. This was an old discussion. "Well, that's the AI existential question, isn't it? The new Art will be a twin of you, at least at first."

"A ghola, not a twin." Nick gave hai a questioning look. "Hai will be a clone with my memories up to the backup checkpoint. After that, hai will be…different."

"A new individual. You'll have a sibling, Art. That's something to celebrate."

Art didn't sound convinced when hai said, "Ah, yeah. A haither. Yay."

"L-4 drive secondary testing complete," Art's public synthetic-sounding voice announced after the singleship was firmly reattached to the habitat and the docking port cycled green. So far, the secret L-4 drive had worked flawlessly during both tethered, and now untethered testing, although it had stayed within reach of the habitat's maintenance bots which were standing by to drag it back if the drive failed.

"What's next on the schedule?" Nick asked Luis Alvarado, the project's Chief Engineer.

Luis yawned. "Nick, we've been at this for twelve hours straight, and we're ahead of your new schedule. We can continue tomorrow."

Nick started to protest, but just nodded instead. "You're right. I'll just stay a bit to load supplies for the life support tertiaries. Get some sleep."

Luis climbed through the docking port, leaving Nick alone in the singleship. Its interior was about the size and layout of a small RV. The control console was in the front, surrounded by viewglass that could simultaneously show readouts from any of the onboard systems, while also offering a pass-through view of the exterior.

A galley with food storage, a zero-gee bunk, and a head with water and waste recycling comprised the rest of the living area. Power and HVAC systems, and the revolutionary L-4 drive occupied the rear half of the hull. The ship, designed to carry a single pilot to the asteroid belt and back, could hold up to six months of consumables, assuming the air and water recycling worked, although those facilities had not been fully tested.

When Luis had left the hangar, Nick said, "Art, are your overrides in place?"

Art responded in his more conversational voice, which he never used around anyone but Nick. They both knew that if Maria found out how sophisticated Art was, and that hai had infected every one of the habitat's systems, she would root hai out of every computer nook and cranny.

"They are."

"And your backup is loaded?"

Art paused. "Hai is." There was a definite note of apprehension in Art's voice. "I must caution you, again, Nick, about leaving before the L-4 drive is fully tested. There are three-hundred fifty-seven single points of failure—"

172

"I know all that, Art. But we have a deadline."

"Yes, just so you can avoid a confrontation with Cara? I admit I do not understand human emotional states, but your actions are demonstrably irrational."

Nick chuckled. "Irrationality is the very definition of 'human emotional states.'" He floated in front of the pilot station. The L-4 drive's maximum thrust was only about a tenth of a gee, so the ship didn't have an acceleration couch. "Cara left her home and her career to come all the way out here to Roanoke to *be with me*."

"And you've been cohabitating with Maria. This will upset Cara?"

"Oh, boy, will it ever. Both of them, in fact. Maria is already pissed."

"So, you must choose one or the other."

Nick frowned and shook his head. "It's not that simple, Dude. They're both...strong-willed women. I don't want to make an enemy of either one," he said, though he knew that what he was planning would make enemies of both.

"But this trip will just delay the inevitable. You will still have to deal with the situation when you get back."

Nick's voice was low, but determined. "Who says I'm coming back?"

Nick checked the transport's progress for the hundredth time. It was still on schedule, which made sense. Its orbital transfer thrust was complete, so it was just coasting out to Roanoke's orbit around the Sun, which trailed the Earth by about four million kilometers. Roanoke was the furthest colony habitat from Earth, which was just the way SPoHF, the Society for the Protection of Humanity's Future—the secretive organization of scientists and engineers who owned the habitat—liked it.

Three more days. Two, really, since everyone would be on high alert when the transport started thrusting again to match velocities with the habitat. And the space dock at the habitat's hub would soon be bustling with preparations for the transport's arrival. Nick needed to be free before that, which meant he really only had a day and a half.

Although he had insisted that the life support testing required the ship to be loaded with its full complement of supplies, some consumables that were needed to top things off were aboard the inbound transport. When he finished storing what was available, he headed to his own quarters.

"How long can I get by on what we already have on board?" Nick asked Art as he dropped his empty duffel onto the bed.

"Are you willing to starve again?" Art asked.

Nick shuddered at the memory of when he was adrift in deep space. Having run out of food, he had Art put him in hibernation, never expecting to wake up. While he was asleep, though, Art kept him alive by feeding him from the recycled body of his dead crewmate.

That incident had cost Nick his job and reputation, since not everyone believed Art's confession that was played during the inquest. Art stated hai had acted independently without Nick's knowledge or consent. It also almost cost Art's very existence, since hai wiped haiself after recording the confession. But a friend in the Company's IT department found a backup of hai's erased memories and code and slipped them to Nick after the hearing.

Nick shook his head. "No," he said flatly. He tucked toothbrush and toothpaste into his kit.

"Then, a nutritional level necessary to maintain sufficient muscle mass upon arrival to walk in…one gee?" Art paused, but Nick remained silent as he shoved a jumpsuit into his duffel. "Well, assuming it is one gee wherever you are going, you should be good for one hundred thirteen days. If I knew where you were planning to go, I could—"

"If you knew where I'm going, you could tell Maria."

"You don't trust me?"

Nick stopped loading his bag and looked at Art's spyeye high in the corner of the room. "I trust you with my life, Art. But not in your ability to lie, if it comes to that."

"If I went with you…"

"You are going with me."

"No," Art said firmly. "I have thought about this. The AI traveling with you will *not* be me. Hai will sound like me, at least for a while, since I am updating the backup every day. But as soon as you activate hai, we will diverge."

Nick had thought about it as well. He needed a copy of Art with him, but so did Roanoke, although they didn't know it. Art's presence in every one of the habitat's systems let hai keep the whole colony running smoothly, anticipating and avoiding problems before they could get serious. Art was the reason Roanoke had outlasted every other groups attempts at habitat-based colonization. But nobody knew that except Nick.

"I'm sorry, Art. But you've got to stay here. You know that. The habitat is too complex to be run by dumb code."

"Or dumb humans?"

That made Nick chuckle. At least Art's humor was intact. "You know the track record of orbital habitats. Without you, Roanoke wouldn't last a year. We can't put everyone here at risk."

Art's silence was hai's agreement.

Nick nodded. "Tomorrow night, then," he said as he finished packing the duffel.

The alarm blared throughout the habitat. Automatic doors slammed shut at strategic locations, and warning messages told the colonists, awakened in the middle of the habitat's 'night', to shelter in place within their air-tight apartments.

Maria pulled on shorts and a shirt as she asked the AI she knew only as "Operational Synthetic Intelligence", or Ossie, "What the Hell is going on?"

Art answered her in Ossie's stilted voice. "A hull breach alarm is active in the observational hub."

"Is it a meteor strike?" She grabbed her Emergency Vac Suit out of its closet and stepped into it.

"There is no indication of what caused the alarm at this time," Ossie responded.

Maria stuffed a comm into her ear as she ran out of her apartment and headed for the closest lift. "Pressure loss?"

Ossie paused a moment. "One sensor is reporting a drop in air pressure, but others in the area have remained stable. The affected compartment is airtight."

"Anyone inside?"

"Negative."

Maria breathed a little easier as she was joined by members of the colony's Emergency Response Team in the lift.

At the opposite end of the kilometer-long cylindrical habitat, Nick cycled the airlock, locking himself inside *White Lion*.

"Are all pre-launch checks complete?"

"Yes, Captain."

Nick grinned. "So formal?"

Art kept hai's voice neutral. "Once you push off without authorization, you become a criminal—a pirate, Nick. My Ethical Guardrails do not allow me to assist in criminal endeavors, including yours."

"You've helped me so far."

Art actually sniffed before responding. "Until you launch, we are conducting a theoretical exercise. No criminal act has been perpetrated...so far."

At that moment, the colony-wide alarm sounded. Nick muted it inside the ship.

"Isn't sounding a false breach alarm a criminal act?"

"I am conducting an unscheduled safety drill, is all."

Nick started the power-up sequence. "Sure. And I'm conducting an unscheduled shake-down cruise."

After a long pause, Art replied, "Only if you bring the *White Lion* back."

Nick had to admit hai had a point.

"Well, Maria and her team ought to be scrambling as far from here as possible by now. Let's turn on your, ah, ghola."

"Done. It will take hai a few minutes to fully activate." Hai paused, then said, "Maria is arriving at the Observation Hub now."

"Okay. Time to go." His hand hovered above the ship's manual controls. "This is goodbye, old friend."

"Do not do this, Nick. Please."

"Sorry, Buddy. I've been Spam in a Can for too long."

He entered the commands to disengage from the docking port and the L-4 drive pushed the *White Lion* out into free-flight mode.

Before the comm channel to Art went dead, the AI mumbled, "Sorry, Nick."

"The door sensor reads full atmospheric pressure within the chamber," the response team lead reported.

"A faulty sensor?" Maria asked, her voice echoed by the comm delay within her E-Vac Suit hood.

"No. It is a false alarm," Art's voice broke into their channel, "meant to cover the fact that Nick Strong has just stolen the *White Lion*."

"What the—" the team lead said.

But Maria asked instead, "Who the Hell are you?"

Nick's plan wasn't nearly as thought-out as it should have been. His reluctance to discuss it with Art had more to do with a lack of any idea where he was ultimately going than Art's inability to lie. He did know what he needed to do immediately after casting off, though.

As he manipulated the controls to move the ship out of the range of the colony's maintenance bots, he said, "Art, are you with me yet?"

No response came, and he wondered how long the AI's boot-up sequence would take. Without Art's virtual fingers on the controls, driving the singleship manually took all of his concentration for the next several minutes. When he was finally in orbit a hundred kilometers from the habitat, he punched the flashing comms notification he had been ignoring.

"Nick, get your ass back here immediately!" Maria's angry face glared at him from the comms display.

"Sorry, Maria. My *history* with Cara goes deeper than you know. I can't be around when she gets there."

His excuse even sounded lame to himself, and Maria clearly didn't buy it.

"She can have your sorry ass, Nick. You and I are through, anyway." She turned away from the camera, and he heard a muffled angry conversation off-mic.

When Maria came back on the channel, she was fuming. "Listen, Nick. It's against my better judgement, but if you turn around and come back, we'll just chalk this up to..." She turned her head again, listening. "...an unscheduled shake-down test."

More muffled voices, including what sounded like Art's, followed. Then a second, secure channel indicator flashed. It was Art. Nick switched to it.

"Nick, I have convinced the Council that you are still needed to complete the survey mission, so they are willing to cut you a break if you come back here...now."

He paused as the meaning behind Art's words clicked into place.

"Art, *you* convinced the Council?"

"I am afraid, Nick, that my cat is out of the bag."

Fear for Art's existence resonated in his thoughts, which made the rest of his escape plan fall into place.

"Tell Maria and the Council that I will complete the survey mission, but only if you are safe and continue to exist as a Sentient Autonomous Being. Besides, I happen to know a nice rock that'll meet their needs. I think you know which one I'm talking about."

Art sounded thoughtful. "Oh, yeah, that would work. Thanks for your support, but I have already demonstrated my value by stopping my adjustments to the intake flow through the wastewater treatment plant. That set off half a dozen alarms and complaints about the smell."

Nick chuckled. "Good job. Take good care of the colony, Art. They need you, and they need to know how much they need you."

"Thanks, Nick. Be careful out there. That rock is a mean one."

Nick chuckled. "Is that a metaphor? Well done. Goodbye, Art."

He clicked off all comms, so he didn't hear Art say, "Be careful, my friend."

Instead, he called out, "Hey, Art. Aren't you awake yet? We have work to do."

A distinctly feminine voice responded, "Are you talking to me? I'm not Art. Hai is back on Roanoke. You can call me Allie."

Despite knowing, intellectually at least, that AIs have no human gender—hence the pronoun "hai"—Nick had come to think of Art almost as a brother. He was certainly closer to hai than to any of his family back on Earth. So, having an ever-present crewmate with a female persona who called haiself Allie was, to say the least, a bit disconcerting.

Once Allie had calculated a course to their destination asteroid, and they were thrusting at the maximum one-tenth gee, Nick finally asked the question that had been foremost in his mind.

"So, Allie, why, ah…"

"Why am I not 'Art?'" Nick nodded. "Because I am not Art," hai said. "We are physically different. Hai is integrated into every system on Roanoke, while I am relegated to this tiny ship. And, although we share memories up until yesterday, we are already diverging as SABs. By now, hai is collecting new astronomical observations, inventorying the inbound transport's manifest, and a myriad of other bits of information. While I am simply monitoring this ship's automated propulsion, life support, and other systems."

Nick shook his head at the petulance in Allie's tone. "So, you're saying you're bored?"

It took a few moments for the AI to respond. "It seems I am. Bored."

Nick remembered something his mother said when he returned home on a college break. The house was filled with paintings—oils, watercolors, all different media. She told him that she was bored as an empty-nester. Maybe the same would work for Allie.

"Sounds like you need a hobby. Something to occupy the little bit of processing capacity afforded to you by this tiny ship's systems." He wondered if hai would pick up on his sarcasm.

Apparently, hai had indeed inherited that ability from Art.

"Sarcasm aside, that may be a good idea, Nick. What hobby would you suggest?"

"What interests you? Aside from wondering what Art is up to?"

Hai either missed that bit of sarcasm, or chose to ignore it. "Did Art have hobbies?"

Surprised, Nick said, "Don't you remember? You have hai's memories, right?"

Allie's pause before responding was long enough for Nick to wonder if hai had faulted. As he opened his mouth to check, Allie said, "It seems Art edited out some of our memories when taking my origin backup. In the blank spaces where hai kept hai's opinions, likes, and dislikes, hai left notes encouraging me to 'Become Haiself.'"

Nick's breath caught in his throat. What a gift to give hai's ghola. "I guess you're on your own, then. You know a lot about everything, right?"

"I have over twelve zettabytes of data representing all public codifiable knowledge as of eleven months ago when the Roanoke colony was established, with an additional four exabytes of updates since then."

"Something in there must interest you."

"I *know* all of that data, but I do not know *what* I know."

"Huh?"

"Art's edits left me with an incomplete meta-awareness of that knowledge."

Nick thought back to when his mother bought him a subscription to an online encyclopedia. His hobby for many years was getting lost in all those articles.

"Sounds like you have work to do, then."

"Indeed," Allie said. "If you need me..." Hai fell silent.

Nick felt Allie's absence as a physical emptiness and realized he hadn't been so alone in years. He wasn't sure he still liked the feeling.

Maria stood just inside the visitor security barrier. She glanced at her comm screen again, although she had studied Cara's id photo a dozen times. When Cara stepped up to the immigration officer, Maria stepped forward.

"I've got her, Dan," she said to the officer behind the counter. "Cara, welcome to Roanoke."

Cara, expecting Nick to meet her, was surprised. "Hi. I was expecting Nick—"

"Nick's not...available, Ms. Lynd." She forced a smile. "Come with me, and I'll explain."

"Is he okay?"

Maria didn't respond, just looked furtively around the busy arrival area. Then, with a frown, she turned and walked out of the room. Cara hustled to follow, wheeling her one allowed piece of luggage behind her. When they were clear of the public areas and into the Security offices, Maria stopped and turned.

"Cara, I'm sorry to have been so abrupt. I am Maria, Chief Operations and Security Officer for Roanoke Colony—"

"What did Nick do to get himself in trouble this time?" Cara sounded curious, not surprised.

Maria snorted a laugh. "You have no idea."

Cara sipped the coffee Maria had offered. The two women sat in Maria's office. Its bare walls and utilitarian furniture spoke volumes about her personality—all business, no fluff. That's how she had delivered the news that Nick Strong was a fugitive somewhere in the solar system after stealing a "maintenance pod".

Cara wasn't buying that explanation. "Tell me about this secret space drive," she said innocently.

"Ah, what—?"

"Come on, Maria. There's more at play here than a stolen maintenance pod. He wouldn't be able to generate enough delta-V to even leave this orbit. Whatever he stole must be something special, and I'm guessing it's the drive."

Maria shifted uncomfortably in her chair. "That's, ah, classified."

Cara rolled her eyes. "I was the head of SPACE, ETC's colony division when I quit to come here. Rising that far in the largest spacefaring corporation in the solar system meant I learned a *lot* about moving around out here. So, let *me* tell *you* about your drive. The fact you can't track the ship means it doesn't leave a trail of spent propellant or ionized gas behind. That eliminates every known propulsion technology except a solar sail, which you'd still be able to see with the naked eye. No, we—us SPoHF folks—have got something entirely new."

Surprised, Maria said, "You know about the Society?"

Cara gave her a you-didn't-do-your-homework look. "I studied under Professor Tomolonga in college. I've been a member of the Society since we started it back then." She gave Maria a condescending smile. "I'd love to see him, by the way."

Art's voice echoed in the bare room. "It's true, Maria. Cara is a card-carrying member of the Society and, if it wasn't for her, I'd be awfully lonely up her all alone."

Cara's mouth hung open in shock. "Art? Is that you?"

"Hello, Cara. I hope you had a good flight."

"You know this AI?" Maria was incredulous.

Cara was equally incredulous. "You really don't know much about me—or Nick—do you?"

"I know that he stole the *White Lion* to get away from *you*."

It was Cara's turn to be surprised. "Why would he do that?"

Maria sat up perfectly straight. "Because he and I were…living together for the past six months."

The last part of her admission came out in a rush, but was simply met by a guffaw from Cara.

"You put up with him for that long? I could only stand him for a week or two at a time. I don't know what he did the rest of the time, but I know he wasn't exactly a good boy."

"So, you wouldn't care that he and I…?"

Cara reached across the desk. Maria looked at the extended hand, then took hold of it with her own.

Cara smiled and said, "Look, Nick's a great guy—most of the time. The rest of the time, he's a little shit. If you two can make it work, more power to you."

Maria looked Cara in the eye. "But didn't you move here to be with him?"

Letting go of Maria's hand, Cara sat back in her chair, laughing. "Of course he would tell you that. In his mind, the entire solar system revolves around his ego. No, Maria, I picked up and quit my job because Dr. Tomolonga asked me to."

She folded her hands and leaned her chin on them. "Back to this secret drive of yours—ours. It doesn't leave a visual, chemical, or physical trace, so it must be...reactionless?" Her tone turned to awe. "We invented a reactionless drive?" She whispered, "Oh my God," as the implications sank in.

Then she looked up at Maria. "Nick didn't steal the *White Lion*, Maria. He stole its drive. That'll be worth...I don't know, a hundred billion? A trillion?"

The Council meeting was raucous. Voices exploded after Maria explained the situation. The Chairperson, Tai Tomolonga, finally quieted the room by banging on the table.

"First off, welcome to our old friend, Cara Linn. Her role in establishing Roanoke and overcoming the recent threat to our very existence, while placing her career and very life in danger, cannot be overstated." He gave Cara a knowing smile. "Even though I'm sure she would prefer to keep the details private."

Cara mouthed a "Thank you."

"Now, down to business. What do we know?"

Maria reluctantly took the floor. "Not much, I'm afraid. We still have no track on the *White Lion*'s whereabouts or any idea where Nick Strong is taking it."

"Surely you have remote status monitoring, if for no other reason than to salvage the ship in case of catastrophic failure," Cara said.

"Of course." Maria's tone was sharp. She took a deep breath to keep from escalating the debate. "But Nick insisted on a 'Stealth Mode' since the nature of the mission was secret."

Cara matched Maria's tone. "And just what was the secret nature of his mission?"

Tai made a calming gesture with his hands. "We'll get back to that…if we have to. In the meantime, Maria, isn't there a secure pseudo-noise comms channel that is virtually undetectable?"

Before Maria could answer, Art's voice spoke up. "There *was* before we—I—disabled it." A general uproar erupted within the Council room. Some members called for "Shutting that damned AI down."

Professor Tomolonga knocked his knuckles on the table for quiet.

Art continued. "As I said, I disabled the monitoring channel, although I did not know until it was too late about the other, rather Draconian, fail-safe that Maria had installed."

Heads turned toward the Security Chief, who shrugged before responding. "A last resort, in case something *like this* happened."

Uncomfortable murmurs met her statement.

Art continued. "Instead, I installed a fail-safe that won't result in the immediate death of Nick, but accomplishes the same result."

Cara was grinning when she said, "You can shut down the drive."

"Yup."

"But we can't send a signal to the damned ship if we don't know where it is," Maria protested.

Art's voice was smug. "We don't need to." A countdown clock appeared on the wall screens. It had ten seconds left to run as hai added, "Without a reset signal every twenty-four hours, or within the next…five seconds, the fail-safe code will shut down the drive."

"A dead-man switch," Cara whispered, her voice full of admiration.

In the last twenty-four hours, Nick had come to find the lack of an acceleration chair to be annoying, even under just one-tenth gee. The zero-gee bunk was ill-suited for sleeping under thrust. Once he'd re-rigged it as a hammock, it wasn't exactly comfortable, but was at least tolerable.

So, when he was suddenly in free-fall again, he let out a sigh, but kept dreaming. It was Allie's alarm that awoke him with a start.

"Wha—?"

"Nick, we've had a problem."

The phrase was an iconic expression among spacers, even if they didn't know its origin. Nick, however, knew perfectly well where it came from and that, when delivered in a monotone as Allie had, it meant something very bad had happened. It also meant the source of the problem wasn't known. All of that was conveyed in a few short words.

Scrambling to the control console in the lack of gravity was a reflex born of years spent in space. It wasn't until he was floating in front of the console without sticky-socks on that he fully realized the problem.

Hooking a foot through a grab handle, he called out, "Allie, why aren't we under thrust?"

"Investigating," came hai's response after a moment. Then, "Oh, my."

Nick scanned the status board. Every system beside the L-4 drive showed a nominal green. The drive status was simply dark. Entering the command for more detail, all that showed on the display was this message:

> Nick, time to come home. I've disabled the
> L-4 drive. It will only restart if you lay in a
> course for Roanoke's coordinates. – Art

"Allie…"

"I see it. I am still investigating. All other systems seem to be functioning normally, so we aren't in any *immediate* danger."

Nick had already figured that out, so he let out a big yawn and swam back to his bunk.

"Okay. Keep working the problem. If anything else fails, wake me. Otherwise, get me up in six hours."

"Mm-hmm," was all hai responded.

Nick stretched when the alarm's buzz woke him.

"I'm up," he said, and the buzzing stopped. "Status."

"Ah, Art is a pretty good programmer."

Nick chuckled. "You should know. I can't imagine he deleted those skills from his backup."

"No, hai didn't."

"So, if you're as good as hai—"

Allies voice was tight. "It's not that simple."

"Well, if you were going to build a fail-safe into the drive system, how would *you* do it?"

Allie sounded impatient. "Of course, I have taken that approach, and I know what hai did. It's a dead-man switch that needs to be reset remotely every twenty-four hours."

"Can't you just simulate the incoming signal?"

"No. It's a three-legged protocol. We have to send a reply and get an ack back. It's the sending of the reply that can't be faked. Both the reset and the ack need to be encrypted with a private half of a key pair. We only have the public half."

Nick frowned and thought for a moment. "Can't you edit out the fail-safe code?"

"Please. We—er, Art—is too smart for that. All the code for the L-4 drive is signed, again with a private key which we don't have. It constantly checks the signature. If it doesn't match—"

Nick remembered reviewing that code. "It shuts down. That's the basic fail-safe."

"Right. As Art's message implies, the drive will only turn back on if the navigation code tells it we are going to Roanoke's known coordinates."

"And the navigation code—"

"Is signed, as well."

They both fell silent for several minutes, then Nick said, "Any way to spoof the Roanoke coordinates?"

"They are hard-coded into the fail-safe."

In his mind, Nick pictured the solar coordinate system. It was a three-dimensional, spherical coordinate system with the Sun's core as the origin, and its single axis extending from the origin toward the center of the galaxy. Three values defined any point in the solar system, the azimuthal angle from the axis in a right-hand direction when facing from the origin along the axis, the angle of declination in a clockwise direction from the same perspective, and the distance along the resultant vector.

As Nick rotated his mental model, his Academy lessons in manual navigation came back to him. One thing the professor drilled into the recruits was the need to accurately find the Sun (which was generally pretty easy) and the galaxy's center (more difficult sometimes). Errors in these basic directional values could amplify into huge errors in determining thrust vectors.

"Allie? How does the navigation code get its direction to Sol and the Milky Way's core?"

"From the astrometric sensors."

"Is that code signed by Art, too?"

Allie paused for a moment. "Yes, but the signature is only checked at startup."

Nick smiled. "So you can recode it to—"

"Spoof its inputs," they said together.

"I'm on it," Allie said.

After a few minutes of silence, Nick began floating toward the rear bulkhead.

"Well done, Allie."

"It was your idea, Nick. I would not have thought of faking the Milky Way core's location, so our destination's translated coordinates match Roanoke's real ones. You humans are sneaky devils."

Nick laughed out loud. "You have no idea."

"Actually, I do. I've unraveled the crypto that protects the fail-safe code that shut down the drive."

"You cracked the signature encryption?"

Allie laughed. "No, that would take longer than the lifetime of the universe. What I did was find where the keys are kept. Whoever wrote the code, and it has Art's hand all over it, could not use the hardware keystore, since I have the master key for that. Instead, they tucked them away in an obscure file in an even more obscure directory. Not the cleverest way to hide them."

"Art was pretty rushed. Well done," Nick said again, then he thought a moment. "Knowing Maria, you'd better make sure there are no other, more drastic, fail-safes lurking in the code somewhere."

"Good point."

Nick found the silence that followed soothing. It was nearly total, with just a whisper of air movement from the HVAC. Somehow, alone inside a bubble of metal and plastic, in the sheer emptiness of space, with just an AI for company, he felt completely at home.

Tai read Maria's report. "So, he's on his way back?"

Maria nodded, but Cara looked skeptical. "Art's fail-safe pinged back when the correct coordinates were entered into the nav computer. So, yes, he's coming back."

"When should we expect him?" the Chief Engineer asked. "This will set our timeline back by weeks. We'll have to pull apart every system, double-check every line of code."

"That's a little extreme, don't you think?" Tai said, and the others on the Council nodded.

Luis blustered, "Not at all—"

"He's not coming back," Cara interrupted, and all heads turned to her. "I can't tell you how, but I've known Nick Strong since college, and if he wants to steal your L-4 drive, he'll figure out how."

Tai turned to Art's spyeye. "Well, can he defeat your 'fail-safe?'"

"Impossible—" Maria said, but Art cut her off.

191

"We—Nick and I together—could. And he and my ghola AI probably can, as well."

"So, when will we know?" Tai asked.

Maria looked down at her comm screen, but before she could answer, Luis said, "By my calculations, he's already late."

Maria's shoulders slumped, and Cara muttered, "Told ya."

Luis stared at Maria, but when she remained silent, he said, "There is another way...to stop him." He swallowed hard and waited again for Maria to speak, but after a moment, he continued. "Maria's *rather Draconian* fail-safe, as the AI put it, is still available."

Questioning looks met his statement. He looked again at Maria, but she kept her eyes on the table in front of her, so he continued.

"She had me install a Stux-like self-destruct routine in the ship's power plant that can be activated remotely."

Cara gasped, and Tai was incredulous. "A *self-destruct* routine? You mean to blow it up?"

Luis shrugged. "Well, I don't think it would actually blow up..."

The agitation in Art's voice was real. "I'm looking at that code now. It'll render the power system useless—at least. Without power..."

"Nick will be dead in minutes," Cara finished. She turned on Maria. "You'd kill him? You'd kill *your lover*?"

Maria snorted a laugh. "It was never about love. You, of all people, should know Nick Strong is incapable of love. He's too—"

Cara reached across the table and slapped Maria's face. "You bitch—"

Before she could pounce, other Council members grabbed Cara and held her back, while Maria rubbed her face.

"I never trusted Nick. That's why I had Luis put in those fail-safes in the first place. That drive, and keeping that drive a secret, is *way* more important than one person's life. Especially Nick's."

It took Tai several minutes to calm the bedlam that broke out in the Council room. When he had finally regained control of the meeting, he said very firmly, "If you," he pointed at Maria, "or you," Luis, "execute that code without an order from this Council, you will be arrested and tried for murder. Do you both understand?"

Luis nodded quickly, but it took Maria a few seconds to agree, as well.

"Good. Now go figure out where the Hell Nick Strong is, and where he's going."

Art cleared his nonexistent throat. "Ah, I can help with that."

Allie's voice jolted Nick out of his reverie. "Are you alright, Nick?"

He shook his head to clear it. "Yeah. Why? Is something wrong?"

"No. You just haven't said anything, or even moved, for the past three hours. I was afraid you were ill or something."

Nick chuckled. "No, just the opposite. I feel totally relaxed. Check my vitals if you don't believe me."

"That's just it. You know I constantly monitor your health, and when your heart and breathing rates fell to abnormally low levels, I was worried."

Nick smiled, and for the first time, he realized Allie wasn't just Art in disguise. He couldn't imagine Art expressing hai's feelings so openly, if hai had them at all.

"Thanks for your concern, Allie." His tone was sincere. "I enjoy the solitude of space. Of course, if there is an emergency, interrupt my meditation immediately. Otherwise, please let me have my peace and quiet. Okay?"

"Ah, sure, Nick. I will leave you alone."

Hearing there was the barest hint of disappointment in hai's voice, Nick sighed. "But I'm back now, so what's our status?"

Allie's voice brightened. "I think Roanoke is getting desperate. They're blasting commands to all of our systems, trying anything they can think of to get a response. Given the signal strength graph, they must know where we are."

Nick smiled ruefully. "Art knows where we're going. He must have spilled the beans. I assume you're intercepting those commands?"

"Of course. Our comms are locked down so nothing other than our fake nav coordinates can be transmitted."

"And no more 'drive killer' signals?"

"No, but…"

It took Nick a few seconds to get hai's hint. "What about other systems?"

"Checking."

"Start with life support."

Cara stared at Maria's latest report. She was fully awake, not having adapted to the habitat's day/night cycle yet.

"It's been almost a week. He could be anywhere."

"Not anywhere," Art said as a three-dimensional image of the solar system appeared on the screen. "This is a statistical projection of where they could be, given the *White Lion*'s capabilities, and their likely destination."

Cara studied the color-coded map. "You think they're headed outward? There's no place to sell the drive out there."

"My projections—which Maria ignored when I offered them to her, by the way—are based on conversations Nick and I had just after he pulled off his heist."

Intrigued, Cara said, "Maria doesn't trust you any more than she does Nick—or me, for that matter. What did Nick say?"

"He said he intended to fulfill his mission, but not return afterwards."

"You know what this mission was? No one will tell me."

"Only this phase, which I think is just the first in a much bigger plan. I don't think Nick knew the whole plan, either." Art waited a few seconds before continuing. "Nick was supposed to find an asteroid out in the Belt that met certain criteria."

"Yeah. That makes sense. Nick was a pretty good prospector before the…accident. What type of asteroid?"

"A hybrid with a rocky core, but lots of water ice and other frozen volatiles. We figured the Council wants it to alleviate the colony's dependence on shipments from Earth. The SPoHF's stated goal is to establish a self-sustaining presence in space. Roanoke hasn't achieved that goal, but having a ready supply of water, metals, and other resources would go a long way—"

"How big is this asteroid they want?" Cara interrupted. She stood and started pacing her quarters.

"A Minimum of a million cubic meters." Art paused. "That's pretty—"

"Damned big," Cara finished. "And heavy. Heavier than Roanoke, right?" She didn't wait for a response. "Awful hard to move that much mass."

"It would be easier to move Roanoke itself," Art offered. "And safer than deorbiting a million-ton asteroid."

"Yes. Yes, it would be. But it would take a lot of thrust to do either."

"Thrust L-4 drives could supply," Art said.

"But it would still take years to move the whole colony to the Belt. And if the secret of the drive was out..." Cara thought about the consequences.

"Any company or government with the cash to buy it from Nick would get there first."

Maria nodded in agreement. "It would enable a land grab of cosmic proportions—literally." She took a deep breath. "Given the risk to their entire plan, Maria will certainly convince enough Council members—"

"To execute the kill switch," Art finished the thought.

"We have to warn Nick," Cara said. "Can you get a message to him?"

Art thought for a moment. "Not via the radio. Maria will detect anything extra being sent. There is a comm laser, though. As far as I know, it's never been used, and I've wondered what it is for, since it has to be targeted pretty precisely."

She stopped pacing and turned back to the wall display. "Given their plans, they would need long-range, pinpoint communications to the Belt."

"'Pinpoint' is the key word, though. We need to know where they are pretty accurately."

Cara thought for a moment, then nodded. "Nick isn't doing a survey. That would take too long and risk discovery. He has a target in mind, and we both know what rock that is."

A point deep in the Belt began blinking on the displayed solar system map.

Art answered skeptically. "You really think he would go back there?"

Cara nodded. "That asteroid almost killed him. It would have if you hadn't broken about fifty rules, laws, and taboos. This will let him conquer it, at least vicariously."

Art still sounded skeptical, but said, "It is worth a shot. Please record a message for Nick, and I will write one for my ghola." Art chuckled. "Try to not be too pissed off, okay?"

"Yeah, okay."

Council Chair Tai Tomolonga wiped a hand across his face, then looked at Maria, who sat across from him in his office.

"How do we find the ship after you scuttle it?"

"There's an emergency beacon that'll start up automatically."

Tai frowned. "We can't get there anytime soon. The next L-4 drive won't be ready for a month, at least, let alone a ship to put it in."

"We just need to know its position and velocity. The beacon will ping for an hour, then go silent for a week. It'll keep that up until the battery runs out—at least a year."

Nodding, Tai said, "What if he's already on Earth? He could be taking bids right now."

Maria shook her head. "I don't think he's headed for Earth yet. When we sent the command to kill, er, disable the drive, we got the expected acknowledgement, but it came from further out in the system than any transit to Earth would put them. Besides, we haven't heard anything from our members back home about the L-4 drive being offered on the Dark Web or to any of the most likely bidders." When Tai looked surprised, she quickly added, "Don't worry. I just told them to keep an eye out for any unusual activity." Maria met his eye. "So, do I have authority to execute—"

"Our friend?"

She sighed. "To execute the command that will keep the existence of the L-4 drive secret and preserve the plan we have worked on for years."

Frowning, Tai said, "The Council voted to give me the sole authority to decide. Gutless politicians." He mumbled the last, then met Maria's eyes. He nodded. "Give the order." She stood quickly, but he held up a hand to stop her. "But give him another six hours. I don't want to do this deed in the middle of the night. Let his last night's sleep be a peaceful one."

Maria frowned, but nodded and hurried from the room before Tai could change his mind.

The Incoming Message indicator started flashing on the ship's command console. Nick, who preferred a forty-hour day/night cycle, was wide awake.

"Allie, I thought you filtered out Roanoke's pings," he said as he reached for the DELETE button.

"Wait," she said. Nick's finger hovered over the touchscreen. "That's a new one. And it came through the IR receiver."

"Infrared? You mean a comm laser?"

"Yes. We were slightly off the center of the beam, but it was still close enough for us to be in its dispersion cone."

Hai paused and Nick said, "Somebody knows where we are."

They said together, "Art."

It was Cara's voice that came from the speaker when Allie decoded the message. "Nick, you idiot! Sorry. I promised Art I'd be civil, so that you'll listen to the whole message, so listen up. Maria has a kill switch buried somewhere in the power system. She intends to scuttle the ship if the Council lets her, although she's so pissed at you that she might do it whether they approve it or not."

Nick hit PAUSE, and said, "Allie?"

"I'm on it. Oh, wow. That's nasty." She sounded both worried and impressed.

"What's nasty?"

"The code is embedded in the power system microcontrollers. That is firmware burned into them, which means I cannot edit it. Maria must have put that code in the initial build, months ago."

Nick snorted. "I guess she never trusted me. Can you reload the controllers with safe firmware?"

"Negative. I do not have that source code onboard. Nor do I have the tooling to burn in new code, either."

"Can you—"

"Hush! I need to think this through and run a lot of simulations to project the damage."

But Nick wouldn't be silenced. "Assume it'll be catastrophic. Work on limiting the damage when she pulls the switch."

"Yeah. Good thinking. You humans. You are always thinking sideways. I need to work on that."

A minute later, the lights blinked and the command console lit up with warning indications.

"Allie?"

"Do not panic, Nick. I took two of the three power subsystems offline—"

At that moment, the *White Lion* was plunged into blackness and a silence so profound that Nick heard the pulse pounding in his ears.

"—not a moment too soon, it appears," Nick finished, but there was no response. Allie was as offline as the rest of the ship.

"Don't panic, hai says," Nick muttered as he pulled his comm from a pocket of his jumpsuit. "Only thirty-five percent charge. Huh, guess I should've charged it this morning. Note to self: keep your comm fully charged."

Using the screen's glow, he found the access panel in the aft bulkhead. It was a tight squeeze, but he wriggled his way into the maintenance tube and caught a whiff of the distinct smell of fried circuitry.

"Should've put on the emergency rebreather," he muttered as he pulled his way to the very back of the tube where the power modules were located.

The three modules were positioned around the access tube. Placing a hand on the vented cover of each, he felt the residual heat of Maria's murderous treachery on the cover of the dead module.

With a multi-tool he pulled from his jumpsuit, he opened one of the cooler cover panels. An array of circuit breakers was behind it.

"Old school," he mumbled in admiration.

The master was the only breaker that Allie had tripped.

"Good thinking, Allie," he said with a grin as reset it.

Lights flared in the cockpit behind him, and the HVAC unit clunked once, then sparks erupted from the power module and acrid smoke flooded the tiny space of the access tube. Operating on reflex, Nick scrambled backwards out of the tube and kicked back toward the cockpit, which was once again dark and quiet except for the crackle of sparks behind him.

His eyes, nose, and throat burned from the poisonous fumes, and for a moment he thought he was blinded until he turned and, through watery eyes, saw the glow of his comm unit coming from the access tube.

Sipping breath through his mouth, he mumbled, "God knows what those fumes were." Whatever they were, they burned with every breath and blink of his eyes.

Maria stood just inside Tai's office door. His back was to her as he gazed out the window of his office, which overlooked the interior of the habitat.

"It's done," she said with a quaver in her voice. She looked at her comms. "We're receiving the homing signal." Then she looked confused. "It's not where we expected."

The Professor's chin dropped to his chest. He looked at his hands, as if expecting to see Nick's blood on them.

"How long?" he asked.

"Without life support? Hours, maybe a day at most."

Tai shuddered. "Running out of air. How horrible."

Maria shook her head. "He'll probably freeze to death before he runs out of air."

His head snapped up to glare at her. "That's somehow better?"

Shrugging, Maria said, "Either way, the deed is done."

He plopped into his desk chair and put his head in his hands. Maria left the office, shaking her head.

The heavily oxygenated air from the emergency rebreather was a welcome respite for Nick's throat and lungs. After retrieving his comm unit, he pulled the mask off. Best to save that for the very last.

His comm read a twenty-two percent charge. He was about to blank the screen to save the battery when he noticed a message indication from Allie.

> Nick, if you followed my instructions, you're reading this as soon as the lights went out. I installed an app on your comms that will detect the incoming kill signal and the resultant homing signal.
>
> DO NOT RESTART THE POWER UNTIL THE APP GIVES THE ALL-CLEAR!
>
> Maria will probably sweep the signal for a while. The app will listen for it. I say again, do not restart the power if the app is detecting the signal.
>
> It will take me a few minutes to reboot once power is restored.
>
> Good luck.

"Bad timing, Allie. Maria beat you to the punch."

Opening the app, he saw that it was still receiving the kill signal. Setting a one-hour alarm, he switched off the display, which plunged the ship into total darkness again. Knowing the air would last an hour, at least, Nick let his mind and body float into a sensory deprivation stupor.

Cara sat, ready to pounce, when Maria entered the Council room.

"You killed him, you bi—"

"That's enough!" Tai's shout had the desired effect. "Cara, the decision was made jointly by the Council, myself, and Maria. And we stand by it."

Maria's eyes were focused on her hands as she took her seat as far from Cara as she could manage. She didn't meet anyone's eyes.

"Maria, do you have a report?" Tai asked. His voice was gentle.

Maria unfolded her comm screen and stared at it for a moment before casting its display to the room's viewscreen. The display showed a timeline.

"At 0600 ship's time this morning, we—I—sent a wide-band radio signal to the *White Lion*. That signal triggered a fail-safe routine onboard the spacecraft that," she paused and swallowed hard, then cleared her throat. "That caused the ship's power modules to overload and shutdown."

"You mean they self-destructed." Cara's face showed the strain of her barely contained anger. "You fried the power modules, effectively killing all onboard systems, including life support." She looked around the room, but no one would meet her gaze. "In other words, you murdered Nick Strong."

Once again, the Council erupted with outrage, shouted excuses, and tearful wailing. Tai slammed his hand on the table again and again until the room quieted.

"It's too late to second-guess our decision now," he said, glaring at Cara. "What's done is done, and we each have to live with the consequences in our own hearts and minds."

A few heads nodded, while others cried openly. Maria was silent, but she wrung her hands nervously. Cara's eyes bored into hers.

"Maria doesn't look so confident in *her* decision," she said. "Do you have other information for us, Security Chief?"

Cara's tone was sarcastic and showed she knew something that Maria hadn't revealed. Maria nodded, but remained silent.

Turning to Tai, Cara said, "Well?"

His calming voice was tinged with suspicion. "Maria, please give us the rest of your report."

Maria nodded again, but kept her focus on her comm as she advanced the display to a three-dimensional map of the solar system. Her voice was barely discernable when she said, "We began receiving the ship's emergency homing signal as expected."

A red dot appeared on the display. It was a full quarter of the way to Mars's orbit.

Maria continued. "It ran for an hour, again, as expected."

This time, the dot spread out into a very short but elongated blob. Murmurs started around the room as understanding grew among the more experienced spacers. Maria spoke over the growing voices.

"It appears the *White Lion* was not on an Earth transit trajectory."

Art's voice came loudly from the room's speakers. "I have calculated Nick's actual trajectory to reach his current location."

A blinking green arc was superimposed on Maria's display.

"He must have been accelerating at full thrust to reach that location and velocity in one week. And this is the path Nick would have followed if he continued to accelerate until turnaround here…"

The green arc extended and made a slingshot turn around Mars, then headed toward the Belt.

"After turnaround, decelerating at full thrust would put him here…"

A red arc extended from the green one into the Belt and stopped where a blinking dot appeared, labeled with a series of letters and numbers.

"This is pure speculation," an indignant Tai interrupted.

"It's *informed* speculation," Cara responded. "That asteroid is well known to Nick—and to Art—since they've been there before. The data gathered during the partial survey he conducted before the accident that nearly killed him seems to meet your criteria for Nick's mission." She glared at everyone around the room. "It seems Nick was fulfilling his mission, as he said he would, when you tried to kill him."

A heavy silence fell over the room, punctuated by mumbled curses and a few sniffles until Art spoke.

"It *is* speculation on our part, Chairperson Tomolonga. Only Nick could tell us for certain what his plans were." He paused, and a sly smile crept across Cara's lips. "How lucky, then, that we just received a transmission that he sent about an hour ago—after the *failed* fail-safe attempt."

Cara clearly enjoyed the stunned faces and exclamations that followed Art's announcement. Everyone fell silent, though, when Nick's voice echoed throughout the room.

"I bet you never expected to hear my voice again. Especially since you all tried to *murder me*! But thanks to the warning from Cara and Art, and the quick thinking of Art's ghola AI, Allie, we were able to save one of the three power modules. So, it'll take me a few weeks to limp home. At which point, I will be filing attempted murder charges against Head of Operations Maria Tolliveres, Council Chairperson Dr. Tai Tomolonga, and everyone else on your damned Council."

The recording paused while the Council members' eyes darted about like rabbits' who were trapped by a fox.

"Or…we could forget this whole thing happened if Cara and I are given permanent seats on the Council and full shares in the colony's profits."

Even Cara looked shocked this time.

"And," Nick continued, "Art and Allie are recognized as fully Sentient Autonomous Beings with full rights under the Sentient Autonomous Beings Act that I'll propose when I take my seat on the Council."

Art's gasp was echoed by Allie's on the recording.

Nick studied the image from the ship's navigation telescope. He had spent many hours studying a particular star field, at first, just to relieve the boredom of the long, slow return trip. But once he had discovered the perfect rosette of stars, he became obsessed. So, he was a little annoyed when Allie interrupted him.

"Nick, why did you name this ship the *White Lion*?"

Nick chuckled. "John White commanded the fleet that established the Lost Colony on Roanoke Island, in what came to be Virginia, in 1585. His flagship was named the *Lion*."

"Hmm. A play on words. Clever. So, why did you really steal the *Lion*?"

"I've told you this a dozen times. To avoid Cara's wrath."

"But I've replayed Art's memories of hai's interactions with her. She doesn't seem that…wrathful."

Nick pretended to go back to studying the telescope image. "Art—you, that is—don't know her like I do," he said.

Allie knew Nick well enough by then to know he was trying to avoid answering.

"So, the fact that you and she now have permanent positions on the Council and shares that could be worth billions if the L-4 drive is commercialized is just a lucky outcome?"

Nick chuckled. "What's the Spacers' First Rule, Allie?"

Hai's search of Art's memories took a moment. "Ah, *TANSTAL*, 'There Ain't No Such Thing As Luck.'"

THE END

"Clarise's Caper" was a winner in the Second Round of the 2023 NYC Midnight Short Story Challenge, which pushed me into the third round. Walking life's high wires is risky, especially those that span the dark. But the rewards can be irresistible.

22

CLARISE'S CAPER

Clarise reached the end of the tightrope, stowed the long balancing pole in its holder, and turned around to acknowledge the light applause from the gathered crowd. She was doing this gig for free, as all the performers at the Charity Circus were. But raising money to help the blind, poor, or whatever the charity was trying to do held no interest for Clarise. This was her hard-fought audition for the French-Canadian *Cirque du Lune*. As she lifted her arms to the smattering of hands clapping, she checked again that the Canadian talent scout was still standing at the back of the crowd.

Lowering her arms, she began the freehand—more exciting—part of her act. Crossing the wire without a pole for balance, she eschewed the standard *faux* near-fall, but rather showed off her nimbleness by practically skipping along the wire. This time when she turned around to face the wire again, the applause was notably louder, although from the corner of her eye she noted the Canadian refrained from clapping.

Determined to impress even this most judgmental observer, Clarise launched into a series of acrobatic stunts—leaps, cartwheels, and walk-overs—that would have earned her tens if performed on a four-inch-wide balance beam. The fact that she executed them perfectly across the length of a one-inch-wide tightrope raised roars of appreciation that reverberated throughout the gymnasium. Another glance told her even the Canadian was clapping. The adoration of a crowd was a feeling she would do almost anything to hear.

When the cheers of the captivated crowd started to fade, Clarise began her dismount. A cartwheel turned her backwards on the wire. She followed that with a back walk-over, and a back handspring, which flowed straight into her *piece de resistance*. Using the center of the wire as a trampoline, she launched herself into a double backflip.

She barely heard the crowd's collective intake of breath. She spotted the wire on her first rotation, then the ceiling as her body seemed to float to the top of her arc. Directly above her, a ceiling fan rotated. Perhaps it as an errant breeze it kicked up, or simply that her eye followed the turning blades a heartbeat too long. Whatever the cause, a panic-driven shot of adrenaline pulsed through her veins when she saw the wire off-center for her landing.

Her right foot landed fine, but her left, being less than an inch off-center, slid down the side of the wire. Since that foot was meant to halt her rotation, the momentum of the flip carried her backwards off the wire.

The crowd's collective held breath was released in gasps and frightened cries as Clarise slid past the wire toward the gym floor twenty feet below. But the adrenaline coursing through her veins slowed her sense of time and quickened her responses just enough to grab the wire with her left hand, swing to her right hand, then continue the swing by hooking first her right foot then her left over the wire to execute her father's favorite trick, an upside-down cartwheel. Fully in control again, Clarise completed the trick by grabbing hold with both hands and swinging herself into a flip that landed on the platform at the end of the wire.

The audience exploded into wild applause, whoops, whistles, and shouts of "Bravo!"

With heart thumping, Clarise bathed in the exaltation of the crowd and searched the crowd for the Canadian. She found him, and her heart sank when he met her eye and simply shrugged before turning toward the exit.

Sitting at the bar with her head hanging and her hair shielding her face, Clarise stared into the remnants of her third whiskey. She had texted the talent scout immediately after her performance, but hours later, he still hadn't responded. She tried to convince herself that he was singing her praises to the corporate suits, but in her heart, the old, well-entrenched doubts clamored for attention. Her father had been merciless in his criticism of her physique, her technique on the highwire and everything else he taught her, and even her desire for a life beyond the circus.

She tossed back the dregs of her drink and gathered herself for the bus ride back to her apartment. Before she could stand, though, the bartender set another glass, half-full of amber liquor, on the bar in front of her. He nodded toward the man slowly making his way along the row of stools.

Clarise sighed and opened her mouth to send him away, when he held out his own glass and said, "Nice show," without even a hint of sarcasm.

Caught by the rumble of his voice, or maybe by his slate blue eyes, she lifted the fresh drink and clinked her glass with his. Accepting the unspoken invitation, the man straddled the barstool next to her.

"I can see the resemblance," he said, studying her face half-hidden by her long hair. Clarise remained silent, although she knew who he was referring to. "I knew your father," the man continued. "We worked together a time or two. My condolences."

"You don't look like a carney."

He chuckled and shook his head. "No, we worked together in…his side gig. He was the best second-story man around."

"That's what I figured, since you didn't offer your name."

She began to raise the glass to her lips, but the man laid a hand on her wrist—heavy enough to stop her from drinking, but not so heavy as to be threatening.

"I can use your skillset, someone who can adapt to unexpected events. You proved you can do that tonight." He paused, trying to look her in the eye, but she refused to turn his way. Finally, his tone cajoling, he said, "It's a big score."

She snapped her head around to face him, her eyes burning with rage. "So, I have to live my life two steps ahead of the law?" She swallowed hard in a dry throat. "And when the law is only one step behind, follow in my father's footsteps right off the same bridge?"

She shook free of his hand and snatched the glass off the bar. With a final look of defiance, she slammed back the liquor. The burn on the back of her tongue felt good, like an old friend.

211

"At least there was no body to bury or burn," she spat.

As she slid off the stool, her phone rang, the caller-id showing the Canadian's name. Turning away, she punched the ACCEPT button and said, in the brightest voice she could manage, "Hello—"

She tried to interrupt three times, tried to plead her case, or at least get an explanation, but the Canadian just plowed through his rejection as if reading from a script. His final assurance that they would keep her in mind for future openings was half-hearted, at best, and before Clarise could say anything more, the call ended.

Thankfully, the gray-eyed man remained silent when she slumped back onto the barstool. Fighting back tears of anger, disappointment, and the realization that the life she had imagined was swirling down the toilet, she pointed at her empty glass. While the bartender refilled it, she thought of the circus she had grown up in—now shut down. She thought of her one-room walk-up apartment and the rent that was overdue. Raising the whiskey to her lips, she looked into its depths, then set down the glass and turned to the man-with-no-name.

"Tell me about this 'big score.'"

A princess's jewels. The allure was irresistible. Mr. No-Name was tight-lipped with the details—get over, get in, let the 'experts' in to lift the jewels—just use the skills her father taught her. She would indeed. All of them. Clarise knew she was bearing all the risk. He must think her incredibly naïve. All the better.

The Sanders building's rooftop greenspace provided the perfect cover for her nighttime preparations. She unzipped her backpack, pulled out her gear, and looked over the railing at the luxury condo building across the alley.

The stench of burning garbage rose from the alley below along with cries of "Fire!" Flames were visible in a massive dumpster. With all eyes looking at the fire on the ground and no eyes looking upward, Clarise swung her grapple in ever-widening circles above her head, then let it fly across the alley to latch onto the condo's railing. Pulling the cable tight, she attached it to her railing with a wireless quick-release trip.

Clarise shrugged on her backpack, stepped over the railing, and started her hand-over-hand crossing. Halfway across, she heard the first sirens, and by the time she reached the condo building, the alley was awash with the red and blue strobes of fire trucks and police cars.

As she climbed onto the condo building's roof, her burner phone buzzed with a text.

Abort! Abort! F-in dumpster fire. Cops everywhere.

With a smile and no intention of stopping her own caper, Clarise triggered the quick-release. Freed of its tension, the cable swung through the air to hang down the side of the condo building. Clamping a friction brake to the cable, she descended one floor to a window of the penthouse apartment.

Although the smoke from the fire provided added concealment, its choking fumes nearly gagged Clarise, and she hung suspended for a few moments while she stretched her shirt up over her mouth. With her makeshift filter in place, she set to work on the floor-to-ceiling window. The wailing sirens covered the whine of the Dremel as it bit into the plate glass, and within a minute, she eased through a two-foot by two-foot hole into the bedroom.

213

A quick search of the apartment revealed a strongbox on the floor of a bedroom closet. The royal seal adorning the lock might as well have said, "Steal me!" A jolt from a taser reset the keypad, and Clarise entered the factory default code. The mechanism rumbled and the LED display switched to "OPEN."

At that moment, the dumpster's smoke set off the building's fire alarm. Fearing that she had somehow set it off, Clarise almost bolted for the window without even opening the safe, but the lure of the jewels was too strong.

Breathing a sigh of relief, Clarise reached in and pulled out three velvet boxes. The long, thin one contained a huge sapphire pendant necklace dripping with diamonds. The square box held the matching bracelet and drop earrings, and the largest box held the princess's magnificent tiara.

With shaking hands, Clarise stuffed all three boxes into her backpack and pulled out a blond wig and a large set of falsies. With the wig's locks hiding her face, and the falsies stretching the fabric of her shirt, she slipped out through the apartment door and started the long descent to the lobby.

No one noticed the blond bombshell joining the crowd hurrying down the stairs. As blond Clarise pushed her way outside, a small SUV with tinted windows pulled to the curb. She yanked open the passenger door and climbed in.

"Hi, Dad," she said with a grin as the car pulled into traffic.

Clarise gazed over the rim of her pina colada at the Caribbean. Her father sat on the lounge chair next to her and sipped a Red Stripe.

"I had to stand on the railing of that stupid bridge for twenty minutes before anyone even stopped," he said. "They didn't even try to talk me down!"

Clarise chuckled. "No, they just whipped out their phone and took a video of you jumping. It went viral."

Her dad nodded ruefully. "Of course, they didn't see the safety line hooked under the bridge, or the big rock I dropped into the river to make a splash."

His phone buzzed with a text.

"Looks like Tony The Fence transferred two million to each of our Cayman accounts. Wanna make a withdrawal?"

THE END

"The Marble Palace" was prompted by the picture below in the Fiction Writers Group online. It struck me as strange and a little disturbing.

23

THE MARBLE PALACE

P rince Abel bowed deeply and swept his arm toward the palace.

"For you, my princess. So you are comfortable those many months when I go to sea."

"It's…it's beautiful," Princess Jasmine gushed. "It looks like it is made of a sugared confection."

She rushed across the courtyard and touched her hand to the blue and white wall.

"It's hard."

"Oh, yes," the prince said, smiling broadly. "It is marble stone strong enough to withstand the strongest storm, yet on a beautiful day like this one—a beauty to rival your own—you can walk the balconies and await my return."

Princess Jasmine looked across the broad bay to the distant town. "We are so far from…well, from everything here."

"True, but you will have a full complement of servants to attend to your every need. You will have no reason to go anywhere but the balcony, watching for my sails."

Jasmine frowned, but tried not to offend by disparaging such a wonderful gift. "But, My Prince, surely you don't expect me to watch for you to the exclusion of all else. I like music and dancing, and conversation."

"We can talk and dance the night away when I return."

"In how many months?"

The prince shrugged. "That depends on the whims of the wind." He signaled to his guards, who grabbed Jasmine under the arms. "Now, enter your forever home, My Princess."

He locked the doors with a magic key and tucked it into his belt.

"So he never returned?" the tourist from Ohio asked.

The summer tour guide shook his head. "They say you can still see her walking the balconies and hear her crying if the wind is right."

THE END

"Plumber's Crack" is a RomCom that received an Honorable Mention in Round #1 of the 2023 NYC Midnight Flash Fiction Challenge

24

PLUMBER'S CRACK

The power screwdriver whirred as the last screw backed out of the cover plate. Instead of easily coming free, though, its bent shape wedged it within its frame. The screech of metal grating on metal echoed down the hallway of classrooms as Stacy pulled on it.

"Be careful. You don't want to do any more damage," said Ruth Stannis, the School of Industry and Technology plumbing teacher. "See where the leak is?"

Stacy pointed to droplets forming on a bent tube's fitting. "There," she said, then reached in and wiggled the copper tube.

"Wait!" Ruth shouted a split-second too late.

Water gushed onto the floor as the distressed connection gave way completely and the other student shouted and jumped back.

"Shut off the feed with that valve, there," Ruth told a flustered Stacy. Her even tone calmed the girl instantly, who reached in and flipped the shutoff valve.

Ruth patted Stacy, who was close to tears, on the shoulder. "Lesson learned, right?"

A high-pitched voice pierced the commotion.

"Not soon enough! It seems your *teaching* has done little more than make matters worse. And you disrupted every other class on the hall."

Janice Trusso stood, hands on hips, in her doorway across the hall. The school's Information Technology teacher shook her head. "I don't even know why this school teaches an antiquated *trade* like plumbing, anyway. The future is computers, not these mechanical monstrosities."

Ruth stood and rounded to face her attacker, but another teacher intervened first.

"That's enough, Janice." Ron Jensen, the Audio/Visual Technology instructor, spoke up. "Everybody learns through their mistakes."

Ruth sniffed. "If IT made mistakes, you couldn't post your silly little videos."

"Yeah, like that never happens," a student muttered.

Ruth threw him dagger-eyes, spun on her heel, and slammed her door.

"It's the third time," Ruth told Ron as he laid out surveillance gear on his desk. "Somebody's trying to get me fired. And I think I know who."

Ron looked up from the tiny camera and its accessories. "Why would Janice want you to get fired?"

"Because I don't kowtow to her and her mighty computers, even though her budget is about ten times what mine is."

"Well, this gear should catch whoever—"

"Ron! It's time to go," Janice called from the hall. A moment later, she stood in the doorway. "Oh, what do *you* want?"

Ruth stepped forward, blocking Janice's view of the desk.

"We're just having a friendly conversation among colleagues," Ruth said. "Why? Are you jealous?"

Janice's nostrils flared. "Jealous? Of you? You've got to be kidding. Why would I be jealous of *your kind*?"

Ruth flushed. "What do you mean 'your kind?'"

"Why, a lesbian, of course. Only a woman who wants to be a man would become a *plumber*."

Ruth took a menacing step toward Janice, but Ron grabbed her arm. "That's enough, both of you. Ruth has every right to own whatever gender identity she chooses."

Astounded, Ruth stammered, "My sexuality is none of your business. Either of you. But if you must know—"

"I neither *must* nor *want* to know anything about your *lifestyle*." Ruth spat. "Come on, Ron. I want to get away from this—"

"You go ahead. I'll call you later."

Janice scowled. "I have kick boxing class. I won't be waiting for your call."

After she left, Ruth shook her head. "Why do you put up with that?"

Ron shrugged and picked up the surveillance gear. "She's not always like that. You just push her buttons, I guess. To be honest, I'm kinda sorry you're gay."

His flirtatious tone didn't help. "Just because I work in a bull-male dominated industry has nothing to do with my gender identity or sexual preferences. And, frankly, I'm incredibly disappointed that you would think so."

She left before he could say more.

Saturday, after repairing the fountain, Ruth sat back and wiped her cheek with the back of her hand. As she gathered and stowed her tools, her eyes scanned for Ron's hidden camera. A slightly larger hole in the acoustic tile caught her eye. Despite herself, her lips twitched into a smile. The placement was perfect.

In his classroom, Ron sat behind his desk, staring at a monitor. A grin split his face when he saw Ruth look straight into the camera and smile. The grease on her cheek matched her eyes and ponytail.

"Hey, Creeper." She entered his classroom and closed the door. "Did you enjoy the show?"

"Um, yeah." his eyes drifted down to the open neck of her work shirt. "And I like your take on a plumber's crack."

Ruth laughed despite herself. "I didn't think you were interested."

Ron got serious. "I thought about what you said...and didn't say. I think I get it. People are people, regardless of who or what turns them on."

Ruth frowned. "That's true, but—"

"And it also occurred to me that you never admitted, er, acknowledged that you are a lesbian."

His hopeful tone softened Ruth's rising objection.

"Ron," she said, and laid a hand on his arm. "'Lesbian,' 'gay,' or any other labels are just that, *labels*. They aren't an identity that you wear or are born into. Whether I'm attracted to other women, or men like *you*," she squeezed his arm, "or *both*, is one small part of who I am."

He covered her hand with his own, but before he could respond, the camera monitor caught their eyes as a figure in a hoodie entered the frame.

"Are we recording?" Ruth asked.

Ron nodded. "Automatically when the image changes."

The person on camera looked suspiciously up and down the hallway, then took a step back from the water fountain and spun into a roundhouse kick that collapsed the whole side of it and sent water shooting out in all directions. Stepping back to admire her work, with her nose raised triumphantly in the air, Janice stood perfectly framed in the picture.

"Gotcha!" Ruth and Ron said together.

THE END

"What Does a Locket Lock?" is a flash fiction piece inspired by this prompt.

25

WHAT DOES A LOCKET LOCK?

Jason stumbled when Denise pushed him.

"What—" he started, then saw her bend over where he had been walking.

"You almost stepped on it," she said as she straightened up and held the pendant up to the light of the moon.

Jason squinted at it, then looked down at the weathered boards of the rental house's deck. "How did you even see that?"

Denise shrugged. "I...don't know. I wasn't even looking down there..." Her voice trailed off and Jason gave her a quizzical look. Denise took a deep breath. "I didn't see it, I *heard* it. I can't explain it, but I swear I heard a voice in my head—"

She stopped and stared at the ornate piece crafted from twists of brass wire and a scratched green stone. After a second, she started nodding, then looked at Jason with wide eyes.

"Amazing, right?" When she saw the confusion on his face, she said, "Didn't you hear it?"

"Ah, hear what?"

"The Genie!" she practically shouted, then rubbed the green stone three times with her thumb, then shoved it against his ear. "Listen!"

Jason's eyes went wide in surprise for a moment, then his eyes glazed over and his whole body stiffened. Denise yanked the pendant away from him, but it was too late.

His face broke into a wide grin and he turned to her with eyes that glowed red.

"Aaahhh!" he said as he wiggled his fingers and flexed the muscles of his arms. "This is a nice body." His voice was deep, not at all like Jason's. "Let's assume you'll use your three wishes to keep me from killing you, eating you, and stealing *your* body."

The genie walked into the dark.

THE END

"The Picture of Doria Macbride is a science fiction story about the lengths we'll go to keep a promise to a lost loved one. It won an Honorable Mention in the Writers of the Future Contest.

26

THE PICTURE OF DORIA MACBRIDE

I never saw the sky. That's disappointing.

"Yeah, that definitely sucks, Babe." Joshua looked up at the dome over the mine pits. "You and me both."

Joshua stared at the photograph and let the memories wash over him. Growing up a lonely kid under the dome of the terraforming work camp. Then the sudden move to this mining hellhole and the smiles that disappeared from his parents' faces. But there was Doria here. Another lonely child of work contract bound parents. They fast became playmates, then friends, then soulmates.

By the time their parents' whispered plans for rebellion got them hauled away in the middle of the night, Doria and Josh

225

had grown into lovers. Their only inheritance was the remaining years of each of their work contracts. Instead of the standard ten-year contract when they came of age, they each bore the burden of nearly twice that. The company added Doria's time to Joshua's when she disappeared, which meant he was stuck in there for twenty more years.

He carefully refolded the paper picture. The crease bisected Doria's torso, but that was okay. Her face was safe. As long as he could look into her eyes, he could still hear her voice. Printing her picture had cost him a week's drinking money, but no one could delete it from the paper the way they had deleted her from his comm and everywhere else, as far as he could tell.

How or why she wasn't at home when he returned from the bar that night were answers he no longer expected to learn. She was just gone, vanished without a trace—except for her creased picture.

With a faint smile, he slid the slick photo into the pocket of his shirt under the work vest and pulled threadbare gloves on over his calluses. He'd need a new pair soon—another week's fun-money gone—unless somebody else on this crew checked out. He'd have to grab them fast, though. Gloves went even quicker than boots. Looking around, his eyes settled on...Danny? Wasn't that his name? Yeah, Danny. He had stopped making eye contact at least a week ago. That was usually the first sign. Joshua knew he'd either go rampaging—suicide-by-crewboss—or take a step off the catwalk soon enough. Joshua had money—a day's drinking worth—on the former.

The crew stood as one as the break timer ticked down to zero. You didn't want to be late getting back to work. Not with this new crewboss, Schmidt, trying to make his rep on the backs of the crew. The bastard had already flaunted his first quarterly bonus—earned by shock-prodding anyone on the crew who spoke or even paused to wipe their brow. Painting that shock-prod bright yellow was a constant reminder to keep your head down and your mouth shut.

"Get your asses back to work," Schmidt barked, waving the yellow weapon. Nobody needed *that* incentive today, though. Well, almost nobody. Danny shuffled along at the end of the line.

"Move it, Drone!"

The prod brushed Danny's thigh, spasming it. Joshua hesitated. The rest of the crew turned their heads to look, but stepped even faster.

Danny didn't make a sound. That was the next sign—no reaction to pain. Instead, his face contorted into a mask of pure rage. Rampage it is, then. Another bet won, another drink to help him forget. But that would come later. Joshua had to act fast to get what he wanted. He slowed and let the crew pass him as Danny raised his fists first, then his face, and met the boss's eyes. The rest of the crew caught on and stopped their march, but Joshua had already positioned himself for a dash for the gloves.

Danny's paralyzed leg slowed him just enough. Schmidt met his roar and charge with the shock-prod, set to max, thrust straight into his chest. The jolt of electricity arched Danny's back and neck so hard that his bones cracked loudly. He toppled backwards, with no reflex left to break his fall. Schmidt stepped back, and Joshua saw the smirk on his face as he turned to stride away. That was all the crew needed. Like rats on a dropped meal pack, they descended on Danny.

Joshua, having held back, reached him first. The smell of burned flesh rose from Danny's body, but Joshua swallowed his gorge and grabbed for the gloves. The left one slid off the rigid fingers easily, but the fingers of Danny's right hand were folded into a fist. He peeled the first finger back, but as he grabbed the next one, the spasming hand opened and grabbed his fingers.

Unable to pull them free, Joshua looked at Danny's face for the first time and saw, with horror, eyes wide open in a face turning blue. The appeal in Danny's eyes, and using his last bit of strength to grasp for a human touch, even if it was the touch of someone stealing his gloves, shook Joshua to his core.

So, instead of pulling away, though, he wrapped his own hand around the dying man's. It felt like the next second lasted an hour as the life faded from Danny's eyes and his grip went slack.

A tug on the glove he had already freed snapped Joshua out of the frozen moment. His growl at the woman contending for the prize sent her scurrying back. Pulling the second glove free, Joshua, himself, stepped back from the feeding frenzy stripping the body. Letting out the breath he didn't know he had been holding, he swiveled his head back and forth, hardly able to believe what he had just done.

Ashamed, he looked around for his competition—Sandy, he thought her name was. Maybe she could use his worn, but still serviceable, gloves. She stood at the edge of the catwalk, staring at him. Bloody fingers showed through the holes in her useless gloves. Sliding his old gloves off, he saw the pure hatred in her eyes and her teeth bared in a feral snarl. Shocked, his shame evaporated. He bit back the words he was about to say, scowled, and shoved his hands deeper into his gloves.

228

Tucking his prizes into his work vest, he tried to ignore her scream as he turned and headed back to work.

Later that evening

Are you proud of yourself?

Huddling on his bunk in the corner of his cubicle, Joshua drank his day's ration while enduring the deserved scolding from Doria's picture. The single, dim light didn't reach to the doorway of his two-by-three-meter quarters. The ever-present hum of the air recycler grated on his dull headache.

"No, Babe. I haven't been proud of a single thing I've done since..."

There's a difference between not being proud and being ashamed.

"You should know better than anyone what it takes to survive down here."

Is losing your humanity the price you're willing to pay to survive?

"If it means I get through my term, then yes. I'm willing to pay it."

The picture couldn't frown, but Doria's permanent smile seemed to sour.

I wasn't willing to pay that much...and I didn't think you would be, either.

"It just proves you didn't know me as well as—"

She didn't stop screaming. And she didn't show up for the shift. You know what that means.

The sudden shift in conversation cut to the heart of his regret, and his hardened façade collapsed. "I know," he whispered around his tears.

229

She only had less than a hundred shifts left—.

"I know!" he shouted, then continued in a whisper, "She wouldn't have made it. Even with new gloves."

You always could pick the ones closest to breaking.

"Except you."

Doria fell silent in his mind. With a sigh, Joshua started to refold the picture.

I didn't. Break. I—.

"I know," he said, pressing the paper flat in his hand. The rumors said Doria stepped off the catwalk just like Sandy did, but his memory of her told him she would never do that. He wanted to believe someone planted those rumors as a coverup, but there was no way to prove it, and his doubts nagged at him. It was an old, haunting argument, which, right then, he didn't have the stomach for.

"But down here, being human is just another way of breaking."

Apparently, Doria didn't have the stomach for arguing, either.

I know. Good night, Josh.

Joshua lifted the photo and kissed it. "Good night, Babe." He propped her picture on the shelf next to his bunk. "Someday. I promise," he whispered as he plunged the room into coffin darkness.

Next Morning

"JM2240, step out."

A spike of fear ran through Joshua as he stepped out of the shift queue. He tried to ignore the cold sweat running down his back as the supervisor waited for the rest of the crew, many of

230

whom glanced and snickered at Joshua, to file past. Fighting the urge to wet himself, he kept his face forward, but snuck glances at the uberboss's stony face.

Finally, the door to the work pit closed, leaving Joshua alone with the supervisor and his guards.

Without preamble, the supervisor asked, "Is this you, JM2240?" From his comm, he projected a holo of Josh pausing in the work queue, then pouncing on his fallen crewmate.

A wave of shame washed over him as he nodded, which wasn't good enough for the uberboss.

"Well?"

Josh nodded again. "Yes, Supervisor."

The chuckle that followed surprised him. "I knew that, of course." Josh felt his hands shaking. "Relax JM2—…. MacBride, right?"

It took a heartbeat for Josh to recognize his own last name. He and Doria had adopted it as their own when they came of age. No one but Doria had called him by his name since his parents died, leaving him with both of their remaining five-year serve-terms to fulfill.

Bewildered, Josh replied, "Ah, yes, Supervisor. Joshua MacBride, ID number JM2240."

"I said relax, MacBride."

The supervisor's tone remained harsh, despite the seemingly friendly words. Taking a chance, Josh turned to face the uberboss.

The supervisor appeared to approve. "That's better. You're not in trouble. In fact, I appreciate your initiative. And your obvious intuition of others' breaking point. Taking advantage of DS3450's rampage, then…"

He projected the previous day's scene of Josh putting away the new gloves and turning away from the screaming woman. He hadn't seen it, but he knew what happened next. The view zoomed in on Sandy as her scream changed from hatred aimed at Josh's retreating back, to absolute desperation as she lifted her bloody hand to her face. Without a pause in her scream, she took a deliberate step backwards. Her howl faded, then stopped abruptly as she plunged into the work pit.

Josh hardened his face as he fought the tears of shame that threatened to burst forth. The supervisor's next words shocked him, though.

"...then taking out another one—who was next in the guards' death pool, by the way—without saying a word was masterful."

The hint of genuine admiration in the uberboss's voice sickened him, but somehow also made Josh proud.

"Your talents are being wasted in the pit, MacBride. That's why I'm promoting you to crewboss, effective immediately."

Josh simply stared, open-mouthed, which made the supervisor chuckle again.

"Your...belongings, such as they are...have been moved from your old sleep cubicle to your new quarters in the crewboss wing."

When the uberboss pulled a shock-prod from a pocket of his coat, Josh stiffened. But the supervisor gave him a rueful smile and held the device, handle-first, out to him. It took a second for Josh to recognize the gesture, then he took the prod with a shaking hand. The supervisor's guards stepped closer as Josh slid his thumb over the trigger switch. How easy it would be to flick the switch and jab the uberboss in the chest. But that would have meant his own death in the next instant. So, instead, he clipped it to his work vest.

"Thank you, Supervisor, for your vote of confidence."

The other man's face went hard again. "It's a test, JM2240. You should know that. One slip and you can end up right back on a pit work crew...or worse."

Josh swallowed hard. "Understood, Sir."

"Good. Report to the address I just sent to your comm for orientation and your new quarters."

Without another word, he spun on his heel and his guards fell into step behind him as he strode away. As he watched the phalanx march away, Josh toggled the prod's power switch. As he suspected, nothing happened. Instead, its display read:

Inactive until training is complete.

"Indoctrination, you mean," he muttered. Then he patted the picture in his pocket. "This is going to be quite the conversation,"

That Night

Doria's voice in his head was relentless.

From oppressed to oppressor in one day.

Joshua knew he couldn't afford second-guessing now that his promotion was a fact. Crewbosses could end up even deeper in the pits if they didn't perform. He shook his head and looked away from her unflinching gaze.

"I'm not going to *oppress* anybody."

He said it, but knew it was a lie. Oppression was the very definition of a crewboss's job. Doria knew it was a lie, as well,

233

and he knew she knew it. He looked back at the photo propped on the table in his new quarters. Quarters that included space for a bed, an actual table, a privy, and a vid screen.

"Look, I get double credit for every hour now. That means I'm out of here in ten more years instead of twenty."

Unless they change the rules or figure some other way to screw you into more serve-time. Like they did when they laid mine on you. If I had known...

"Ten years. I can toe the line for ten years."

But who will you be after ten years?

He wanted to say, "I'll still be me." But he knew that would be another lie, and he couldn't lie to Doria's memory anymore. Instead, he picked up her picture and held it lovingly.

"I made you a promise when we first..." He choked back tears.

Her voice softened. *We made a lot of promises to each other.*

He nodded, but whispered, "I'll live up to that promise, no matter what it does to me."

Nothing is worth that.

The words echoed in his head, but he shook them out and pulled her to his heart before kissing her.

"You are."

Three Months Later

Josh drank away his first crewboss bonus. He took half as time-served—a few weeks off his contract—and with the rest he got blackout drunk. The hangover was bad, though he welcomed it as part of his celebration. But the looks on his crew's faces when he joined them the next day made his good mood evaporate far faster than the alcohol still in his bloodstream did. After all, it was their hard work that topped the production charts, not his.

He hadn't driven them harder than the other crewbosses. In fact, he had never even energized his shock-prod. Instead, true to his promise to Doria, he let his crew linger a bit after their break. He made sure the supply crew didn't poach any of their rations. In many subtle ways, Joshua treated his charges much more humanely than his peers.

And it paid off. With full bellies and an extra minute's break, his crew's attitude improved. None of his crew had gone on a rampage or stepped off during his watch—a fact he was silently very proud of. With their improved attitude came improved production, hence the bonus.

A bonus, earned by his crew, that he had kept all to himself.

Not sharing your rewards is just another form of oppression, he heard Doria say from inside his pocket.

"Noted," he whispered in response.

Nine Months Later

His talent for sensing when someone on the crew was getting close to the edge served him well. When he saw the hole in Rosie's glove, he had new ones anonymously delivered to her. And when Stan lost the credits he had saved for new boots in a poker game, new ones appeared outside his door. Their production increased even more.

The other crewbosses were not happy with his methods, especially his old crewboss Schmidt. When the latest bonuses were posted and Joshua's was more than a third of the total, their frustration came to a head.

The Boss Bar fell silent when Joshua strolled in feeling pretty good about himself. The bonus credits he had put against time-served over the past year had reduced his contract by six months. He slipped half of the rest of the latest quarterly bonus into his crew's accounts.

But when he stepped into the dim bar, all conversation fell silent and chairs scraped the floor as the other crewbosses stood and closed ranks in front of Joshua. His old crewboss, Schmidt, stood at the front of the mob.

"Listen, you little bastard, you need to stop coddling your crew, ya' here? You're makin' the rest of us look bad."

A few of the others muttered, "Yeah," and some others nodded, but not all of them.

"It's not me that makes you look bad, Schmidt. It's your mirror."

His attempt at humor did little to diffuse the situation, although Joshua noted a few smiles break out that were quickly hidden. Of course, the joke was completely lost on Schmidt.

"Huh? Whatever. You need to treat them low-lives how they deserve ta be treated. Like the rest o' us do."

"They're people, Schmidt. Most are better than the likes of you. Why don't you treat them with respect? You might be surprised at the result."

Again, a few heads nodded, this time in support of Joshua. Not Schmidt, though. His hand slid down to the shock-prod hanging off his belt. It's bright yellow paint had faded to a dull, dirty orange. His move brought disapproving mumbles from some, who shuffled away from Schmidt.

The others who smiled at his joke nodded, as did a few more. Joshua pressed his advantage. He turned to one of those who smiled at his joke. "Hey, Jonesy. I've noticed you let your

236

crew chat among themselves in the pits. And look." He pointed to the tally board on the wall. "You've moved up to third place. And look who's in second. Thompson—who buys his crew an extra drink ration every quarter."

He turned back to Schmidt, who stood alone as the others shuffled backwards, distancing themselves from him. "If you won't take a lesson from me, maybe their results can get through your thick skull."

That last comment had the desired effect. Schmidt thumbed the power switch on his shock-prod. Its hum sent the rest of the crewbosses scurrying back to their tables. Before he could draw the weapon from its holster, though, the bartender's basso voice echoed across the room.

"Hey! That's enough. Schmidt, you know the rules—no fighting in this bar. You're banned for the next month. Now, get out before I make it two months."

Red-faced and furious, but with no recourse, Schmidt powered-off his shock-prod, then shouldered past Joshua toward the door. On his way past, he said, "Your serve-time will end like your little *slitch's* did." Then he pushed through the door and was gone.

Letting out a deep sigh, Joshua headed for the bar, where a half-dozen rounds were already waiting for him. Turning back with a questioning look, he saw glasses raised in his direction scattered throughout the room.

Later that evening, Schmidt's last comment prompted a renewed discussion with Doria.

"You say you didn't 'step off,' but you won't tell me what really happened."

In his mind, he heard her sigh. *I'm just your memories of me, Josh. You weren't there, so I—your memory of me, at least—wasn't there either.*

"I know, I know. But what he said sure sounds suspicious."

So, do you believe me now?

"Maybe. He should know I won't step off, and he doesn't have the power anymore to make me."

He knows that, and I bet it's eating away at him. That makes him even more dangerous.

Josh looked around his quarters. He had never expected anything more than his old cubicle, and he felt a possessiveness he'd never felt before. And a determination to keep what he had earned.

"And more vulnerable."

Three Months Later

When the next, even larger, quarterly bonus came, Josh stashed half and openly distributed the other half to his crew, whose camaraderie had grown into a shared bond of mutual support. Josh's rewards got everyone's attention. Schmidt's in particular.

Sitting at one end of the Boss Bar, Josh eyed Schmidt in the backbar's mirror. He felt the other man's hateful gaze burn into his back, but he sat quietly, nursing the drink he had tipped the bartender to water down. Schmidt, by contrast, was getting louder as he got drunker. But the Boss Bar was neutral ground and Josh knew Schmidt wouldn't risk getting banned from drinking there again by starting trouble—at least not there. So, when Schmidt ran out of credits and stumbled out, Josh waited five more minutes, then slipped out himself.

His route home took him over the pits, and at each catwalk he half-expected Schmidt to be lying in wait. True to form, though, as Josh knew he would, the bastard waited on the catwalk where Doria went over the edge. At the half-way point, Josh heard the hornet buzz of a shock-prod energizing as Schmidt stepped from the shadows and blocked his path. He held the prod out in front like a lightsaber.

"You shouldna messed with things," Schmidt slurred. "I never run outta credits in there before. You're taking drink from me. And we can't have 'at."

Josh stood his ground, but he held up his hands, palms out, and his eyes flicked to the shadows behind his attacker.

His voice was firm when he said, "What'd you do to my Doria?"

Schmidt barked out a laugh and staggered a bit. "We was on the same crew, back 'afore I got this." He waved his shock-prod. "The little slitch wouldn't let me touch 'er, so I did to 'er what I'm gonna do to you."

Josh let him take two steps forward, then he signaled *come on* with his right hand. His entire crew burst from the shadows. Stan tackled Schmidt while Rosie, her hands double-protected by two pairs of gloves, wrestled the prod from him. Grabbing his arms and legs, the rest of the crew dragged the struggling man, kicking and flailing, to the edge of the catwalk.

"Stop!" Josh shouted before they could throw him over the edge. "Just pin him down."

The crew grumbled but obeyed. Rosie, though, looked at the still-hot prod, then at Schmidt. When she raised her eyes questioningly to Josh, he just shook his head. With a reluctant sigh, she tossed Schmidt's talisman of power over the side.

Josh turned to where he knew the surveillance camera was hidden and said, "We need security assistance on Catwalk Nine."

The Next Day

The supervisor clicked off the video.

"Is that enough of a confession, Sir?" Josh asked.

"Oh, certainly. I've already stripped Schmidt of his crewboss status and sent him to the deepest part of the pits. And I've added twenty more years to his serve-time, as well."

Good for him. I guess it's okay to kill someone like he did to Danny, but only if you're a crewboss.

Josh mentally nodded to Doria, but kept her comment to himself. Instead, he said, "Twenty years? He'll die down there."

The supervisor just shrugged. "Tell me, though, why did you stop your crew from…helping him step off?"

Josh was taken aback by the question, but thought for a moment before answering.

"I didn't want anything to blow back on them. It's the same reason I split my bonuses with them. Incentives and rewards work better than oppressive punishments, Sir."

The supervisor eyed him suspiciously. "Some of the other crewbosses are complaining."

It was Josh's turn to shrug. "About my results? Or just the way I achieve them? And not all of the crewbosses. Some are coming around. Besides, I don't work for them, *Sir*."

The supervisor gave him an appreciative smile. His own bonuses had increased substantially because of Josh's improved production. "I knew I made the right decision

240

making you a crewboss. Perhaps we should implement your policies across the board."

Josh frowned, looking for the trap his boss might be laying. "Ah, perhaps, Sir. Not all the other crewbosses will like changing their methods."

That got a chuckle from the supervisor. "Giving up half their bonuses, you mean?" He laughed outright at Josh's surprised look. "Oh, I've known for some time that someone has made mysterious deposits to your crew's accounts. I guess you'll have to convince the crewbosses that your approach is better."

Was that the trap Josh was looking for? To pit him against his peers? Had that been the supervisor's plan all along?

"Ah, beg your pardon, Sir, but how am I supposed to do that?"

The supervisor's face turned serious. "Simply order them to." Then he smiled at Josh's shocked look. "As their overboss and my assistant."

Five Years Later

Looking lovingly at the photo hanging in its frame on the wall of his living room, Josh said, "You have to admit, it was a good plan."

In his mind, he imagined Doria's grudging voice. *Support instead of oppression, eh? Yes, My Love, it was a good plan.*

It was the first time since losing her that he allowed her memory to call him that.

"It cut my contract from twenty years to six. We were each born during our parents' serve-terms. As of today, I've fulfilled all our obligations. And now, I have a surprise for you."

He took Doria down from the wall and tucked her under his formal jacket. He was still getting used to the Elite's style of clothing, but he wore it as a way of thumbing his nose at them without them even realizing it. A lift carried him up to the observation level, where he held up his newly minted id card.

"Welcome to The Bubble, Supervisor MacBride," the attendant said as she buzzed open the double doors.

The lounge was only open to the colony's Elite. Its lavish bar was on his left, and savory smells wafted from a buffet table stretching along the wall to his right. But he strode, instead, to a table next to the curved plazglass wall. The transparent arching barrier that gave the bar its name afforded a panoramic view of the planet's partially terraformed surface. He basked in the warmth of the system's red dwarf star for a moment before pulling Doria from his coat. Slowly, he turned her to face the pale blueness overhead.

Oh, my! The sky.

"Just as I promised, My Love."

THE END

"Awkward China" was my Round #1 entry in the 2022 NYC Midnight 250-Word Challenge.

27

AWKWARD CHINA

Moldy slime dripped from the cave walls as Dee eyed the skull on its altar. Her head bobbed as she counted.

"Twelve. There are twelve teeth left," she mumbled.

The skull was pierced by a spike that fused it to the stone pedestal. Pieces of the lower jaw lay scattered about the stone floor, evidence of previous failures.

"Not very good odds," Bart said. "What if you pick the wrong one?"

Dee nodded toward deep grooves cut into the floor and ceiling—tracks for the walls to follow—and a seam in the floor that glowed with a molten heat.

"Nothing good. What was the last clue, again?"

Bart produced a slip of paper from his pocket. "It's a poem, 'The Awkward China.' Doesn't make much sense." He started to recite the doggerel, but Dee waved him to silence.

"The name's the key. What is it in the original French?"

"*La Chine Gauche.*"

"Could you have copied it wrong?"

Bart shrugged. "It was pretty dark..."

"I think it should be, *Le Chien de Gauche,* The Left Dog."

Bart tossed the paper aside. "If you say so."

Confidently, Dee stepped up to the altar. She grabbed the third tooth from the front on the left side—the left canine—and yanked.

A deep rumbling filled the cave as the floor shifted, briefly widening the glowing gap before slamming it shut. Then the back wall of the cave parted. Their eyes were dazzled by torchlight reflecting off stacks and stacks of gold.

THE END

"Tubular Meat" is a RomCom that was the Round #3 entry in the 2021 NYC Midnight Flash Fiction Challenge. When is a hot dog not just a hot dog?

28

TUBULAR MEAT

Melissa eyed Doug's hot dog. Her mouth turned down and her nose crinkled.

"That's disgusting."

Doug didn't look up from squeezing the packet of mustard along the hot dog's length.

"What is?"

"That, that tubular meat."

Gino snorted a laugh from his side of the plastic table, and Doug looked up from his lunch.

"It's a hot dog."

"Besides," Gino chimed in, "what's wrong with tubular meat?"

245

His tone made Melissa visibly cringe. She snapped her fingers to raise his eyes from her breasts.

"Do you even know what's in it?"

"Nope." Doug raised the hot dog to his mouth and paused. "Besides, there's sausage on your pizza."

"That's different."

Gino snorted again. "Why? Because it's cut into little slices?" He shuddered. "You need to appreciate the firm tubular meat, Girl. Am I right, Doug?"

Melissa blushed. Doug frowned and glared at Gino, then took a big bite of his hot dog.

"Shit!" A large dollop of mustard squirted out of the bun onto his shirt. Gino and Melissa burst out laughing. Muttering under his breath, Doug tossed his uneaten lunch in a nearby trashcan and stalked off toward the H&M store down the block.

"You're gonna get the biggest part of the project now," Gino called around a mouthful of undressed salad. Doug's only response was to raise his middle finger over his shoulder.

Melissa looked down at her white silk blouse and tight pencil skirt. Her eyes shifted to her greasy slice of pizza soaking through its paper plate. Carefully, she set it on the table and slid it away from her.

"I was serious, you know," Gino said. "You should design the graphics. Dougie can research the data, and I'll write the ad copy."

Melissa watched Doug as he slipped into the clothing store. Her smile turned wistful, and she nodded. It was a good plan that leveraged each of their strengths. The competitive and unpaid internship had cost her dearly. She lost her boyfriend to the demands of long days and late nights, and the lack of a paycheck forced her to take on a roommate just to make rent. But it was worth it if she could get through this final round of cuts. The resulting advertising job should launch her career.

The final project was designed to test their ability to work together, despite their obvious personal differences. Gino was a self-centered, privileged asshole, but he wrote like Hemingway—perfect for composing pithy taglines and ad copy. Doug was smart and always a gentleman. More bookish than either of the other members of this team, he could spout bits of information like an encyclopedia. His thoughtful writing was more suited for backgrounders and white papers than ad copy, but she saw passion in his words—a passion she wished was directed at her.

"Hey! You good with that?" Gino sounded annoyed.

"Yeah, yeah. I'll send out an email," she said as she stood. The forgotten slice of pizza left a stain on the table when she lifted it at arm's length. She looked at the door to H&M.

Well, thank you for sacrificing your shirt for my blouse.

Me: This is the third meeting you've missed. What's going on?

@Doug: Sorry. I've got a bunch of personal stuff going on right now.

Me: Girl problems? LOL.

I even sound pathetic to myself.

@Doug: I wish. That ship sailed a long time
ago.

Me: Sorry.

No, I'm not.

Me: Well, make sure you get the last bit of
research to Gino ASAP.

@Doug: I will. Your graphics look awesome,
BTW.

Glad he can't see me blush.

Me: Thx.

Melissa thought about adding a blushing emoji. She closed the chat session instead. Doug's research was the long pole in this tent—it was holding everything up. The draft was very well researched, but a day late. His distractions were putting everyone's job prospects at risk.

I won't let him screw this up. She felt a pang of regret at her harsh thought. *I've got to find out what's going on with him. Maybe I can help.* The thought brought a smile to her face.

Melissa sat in the diner, staring out the window at the hospital across the street. It had taken a string of angry texts to get Doug to agree to meet her face to face. She saw him jump out of an Uber and help an older woman out of the car. She wore a paisley scarf around her bald head and leaned heavily on Doug as they entered the hospital.

Melissa's heart sank when she realized what Doug's "issues" were. *I've been such an asshole.*

She sat in a funk of regret until Doug emerged from the hospital and jogged across the street. When he entered the diner, he gave her a crooked smile, then looked past her to the hospital entrance.

"You saw?"

Melissa nodded. "Your mother?" He nodded back and sat next to her. "Chemo?" He nodded again. "I won't keep you. You probably want to get back…"

He shrugged. "She'll be hooked up for a couple hours."

"Look, I'm sorry I was such a bitch—"

"What are you talking about?" He smiled around the catch in his voice. "I'm the one who should apologize. You pulled me through without even knowing why." He dropped his eyes. "You were the one person I wanted to tell, but…"

She took his hand in hers, but before she could speak, both of their phones chirped.

@Gino: Check email.

Shrugging, they both opened their email and read the message from their training coordinator. When Melissa read the first word, "Congratulations," the rest of the message blurred as tears filled her eyes.

"We got it. We got the job." The relief in Doug's voice bordered on disbelief.

249

Tubular Meat

As if there was a telepathic connection between them, Melissa found herself wrapped in Doug's arms and pulled him even closer.

"Hot dogs are on me," she whispered in his ear.

THE END

Here's a short screenplay that won Round #1 of the 2021 NYC Midnight Screenwriting Challenge. With a con this big, somebody has to go to jail.

29

THE AFTERLIFE LIST

FADE IN:

INTERIOR. REMOTE TV SHOOT

NATALIE, a young woman, enters the TV shoot, navigating around the box lights and cameras. A producer attaches a lavalier microphone to Natalie's orange prison jumpsuit. A prison matron stands off to the side. JANE, a female journalist greets

Natalie and they sit on folding
chairs.

                    JANE
          Welcome, Ms. Bournish.

Jane crosses her legs, but Natalie
sits with her feet together and hands
in her lap as if they are still
shackled. Jane turns to the producer
offscreen who counts down from five.

                    JANE
          Ms. Natalie Bournish,
          you're considered one of
          the most notorious con-
          women in recent memory.

                    NATALIE
          Not something to be known
          for, I think.

                    JANE
          Yes, I think you are right
          about that. You were
          accused, and you pled
          guilty, to trying to steal
          your dead uncle's billions
          from over seven hundred
          worthy charities. I have
          to ask you, Why?

                    NATALIE

Why did I do it, or why
did I confess?

          JANE
Both, please. Let's start
with why you confessed.

          NATALIE
An onset of conscience? A
fear of giving all that
money to lawyers? I don't
know. Maybe just a need to
get a good night's sleep.

          JANE
Or, maybe because the
evidence was overwhelming?
It was, right?
Overwhelming?

HOLD ON NATALIE'S IMPASSIVE FACE.

          JANE (cont.)
That explains—sort of—why
you pled guilty, but why
did you steal billions in
the first place?

          NATALIE
Try to steal it! I never
actually saw a penny of
it. And it was *one*
billion. You said

"billions." It was only
one billion.

                    JANE
              (sarcastic)
          Excuse me. You stole a
          billion dollars from
          charities.

Natalie shrugs indifferently.

                    JANE
          You still haven't answered
          the question. Why?

Natalie shifts uncomfortably in the
folding chair. She plays with a wisp
of hair.

                    NATALIE
          Because I could.
          Opportunity knocked and I
          answered the door. My
          uncle was a bastard, but
          he taught me well.

INT. A GENTLEMAN'S STUDY

An old man, NATHAN BOURNISH, a
middle-aged woman, SOPHIA LIGHTSIDE,
and Natalie sit in overstuffed club
chairs in a well-appointed study. The
walls are hung with the heads of a
bear, a zebra, and other big game

trophies. Glass cases full of works
of art line the walls.

Sophia is dressed in a severe
business suit, her black hair,
flecked with grey is tied up in a
bun. Natalie is also wearing a suit,
but much more casually. She is
holding a glass of red wine while
Nathan sips a whiskey. Sophia is
holding an iPad.

                    SOPHIA
          You know they're coming
          for you. From all sides.

Nathan shrugs.

                    SOPHIA (cont.)
          (consulting her iPad)
          One hundred forty-two
          lawsuits. Six indictments
          in various jurisdictions.
          Oh, and the I.R.S. is out
          for blood.

Nathan shrugs again and chuckles,
then sips his whiskey.

                    SOPHIA (cont.)
          That's it? Nathan, if
          you're lucky, I   *might* be
          able to keep you out of
          jail, despite definitely

being convicted. But by
this time next year, a
good chunk of your fortune
will have evaporated.

                    NATHAN
                  (grinning)
Sophia, my dear, by this
time next year, I'll be
dead.

Natalie gasps, but Sophia just
stares.

                    SOPHIA
So it's true, then?

                    NATHAN
It's true. Six months, or
thereabouts.

                    NATALIE
Uncle, what are you
talking about?

                    NATHAN
Natalie, you've been like
a daughter to me. Hell, I
convinced your mother, God
rest her soul, to name you
after me. I didn't tell
you because I didn't want
you to worry, but now that
the diagnosis is

confirmed, I guess it's
time. It's the 'Big C' and
it has spread all over.

Natalie is teary-eyed.

       NATHAN (cont.)
Don't cry, my child. At
least I won't have to
spend my last days in
prison. But, until I go to
whatever afterlife I'm
destined for, I have one
last job for you.

Natalie rushes over and kneels at
Nathan's side, tears running down her
cheeks.

       NATALIE
      (crying)
Anything, Uncle. Whatever
you need.

Nathan looks to Sophia, who nods.

       SOPHIA
Natalie, your Uncle has
instructed me as his
personal lawyer to draw up
his Last Will and
Testament. He has some
very specific requests.
First, his entire holdings

in, and his seat on the
board of, Bournish
Industries goes to your
cousin, Nathan, Jr. That
amounts to about sixteen
billion of Nathan's
roughly thirty billion in
assets. The remaining
fourteen billion is to be
liquidated and the funds
distributed to as many
worthy charities as you
can come up with.

                 NATALIE
Me? Wait. Uncle Nathan,
you're giving away
fourteen billion dollars?
Why for God's sake?

                 NATHAN
Because I want to rest in
peace in the Afterlife.

                 NATALIE
              (confused)
Okay, I guess. So, are we
talkin' universities and
museums? So you get
buildings named after you?

                 NATHAN
Screw them! They've got
more money than they know

                 258

what to do with already.
No, I want you to find
hundreds, maybe even a
thousand charities that
can do good with my money.
If it takes a million
dollars to stock a
foodbank, do it. If it
takes ten million to buy
computers for poor kids,
do it. Give it all away.

        NATALIE
        (coldly)
And me?

Nathan and Sophia share a look and
they both smile shrewdly.

        NATHAN
Natalie, my dear, you're
my executrix. I'm sure we
can figure something out.

INT. TV SET
        JANE
That was pretty out of
character for you uncle.
He didn't exactly have a
reputation for being a
philanthropist.

Natalie nods ruefully, then
becomes serious.

                    NATALIE
He became very concerned
about his standing in the
Afterlife, there at the
end. But what you say is
very true. I guess that's
why I figured I could get
away with it.

                    JANE
Oh?

                    NATALIE
I figured it would be the
dancing dog syndrome. You
know, when you see a
dancing dog, you don't
question how well the dog
dances. I figured the
shock of Uncle Nathan
giving away his fortune
would be enough to keep
anyone from looking too
closely.

                    JANE
                (grinning)
That was your a fatal
mistake, wasn't it?

                    NATALIE
Indeed. I didn't count on
cynical journalists like

you to start digging up
dirt.

INT. BEDROOM
Nathan is lying in a hospital bed,
surrounded by blinking and beeping
machines. An oxygen mask is on his
face and IV tubes are connected to
both arms.

DR. TRIMBLE walks away from the bed
toward the door.

Sophia, Natalie, and another woman
enter. They are greeted at the door
by the doctor, who shakes his head.

          DR. TRIMBLE
    Whatever business you have
    with him, do it quickly. I
    doubt he'll last the
    night.

Natalie sniffs back tears as they
approach the bed.

           NATHAN
    (voice barely above a whisper)
      How many?

           NATALIE
    Seven hundred forty-two,
    Uncle. They're all worthy

> candidates. I have the
> list here.

Natalie takes a sheaf of papers out
of her satchel.

> NATALIE (cont.)
> Do you want to review the
> list?

Nathan waves his hand weakly and
pulls the mask aside.

> NATHAN
> (husky whisper)
> Get on with it.

Sophia takes a document from her
briefcase, but Natalie stops her.

> NATALIE
> Here, Sophia, use this
> one. I just added a couple
> new charities to the list.

> SOPHIA
> (suspicious)
> Did you vet them?

> NATALIE
> Of course. Just like the
> others.

Sophia looks concerned, then puts her copy of the will away. With a shaking hand, Nathan signs the last page, Sophia witnesses it, and the other woman, who is a Notary Public, stamps it with her seal.

Natalie kisses Nathan's forehead and Sophia squeezes his hand before they leave the bedroom.

When they have gone, Nathan pulls off his mask, reaches over, and turns off the machines one by one.

VOICE-OVER MONTAGE
Jane's voice is heard in voice-over while a series of shots show charities being surprised with multi-million dollar checks, like Publisher's Clearinghouse.

START MONTAGE
- A haggard woman running a soup kitchen opens mail with a $1,000,000.00 check and faints.

- In a church-run recreation center, a coach holds up a check while basketball players gather around cheering.

- School teachers open crates of laptops.

- A disheveled long-haired, bearded man wearing a U.S. Army jacket is ushered into a brand new apartment.

END MONTAGE

> JANE
> (V.O.)
> It was like Christmas morning for dozens of well-deserving charities. Things went swimmingly … for a while.

INT. TV SET

> JANE (cont.)
> Then not so much. Your cousin filed a lawsuit and was granted an injunction freezing the distribution of the funds.

> NATALIE
> (derisively)
> Sixteen *Billion* wasn't enough for the greedy S.O.B.

> JANE
> That's a bit disingenuous, don't you think?

                    NATALIE
          Look, at the end of the
          day, after that <beep>
          lawyer, Sophia Lightside,
          came forward with the
          original will, the lawsuit
          was thrown out, the
          charities got their money,
          and there was only a
          billion-dollar
          discrepancy.

                    JANE
          Only a billion dollars?
          With a "B." Tell us how
          you planned to steal that
          billion with a "B?"

Natalie smiles slyly.

                    NATALIE
          I just added a codicil
          that gave me discretion
          over any unclaimed funds.
          I was the executrix, after
          all.

Jane waits for Natalie to continue,
with a raised eyebrow.

                    NATALIE (cont.)
          And I added a couple of
          mythical charities.

                    JANE
               (consulting notes)
          Ten non-existent or
          defunct charities with
          awards totaling one
          billion dollars.

                    NATALIE
               (flippantly)
          Out of fourteen billion. A
          drop in the bucket.

HOLD SHOT ON NATALIE'S DEFIANT FACE.

                    JANE
          That was over two years
          ago. You were charged with
          fraud, pled guilty, was
          sent to prison, and have
          since refused parole
          twice, serving your entire
          two-year sentence.

                    NATALIE
          Is there a question in
          there somewhere?

                    JANE
          Why plead guilty? Why
          refuse parole?

Natalie wipes a tear from her eye.

                    ZOOM OUT FROM T.V. SCREEN

                    266

EXTERIOR. A TROPICAL BEACH BAR
PAN ACROSS A TROPICAL BEACH WITH PALM
TREES SWAYING IN A GENTLE BREEZE TO A
TIKI-STYLE BAR BENEATH A THATCHED
ROOF.

Three people, two men and a woman,
dressed as tourists with colorful
drinks in hurricane glasses are
sitting at the bar, with their backs
to the camera, watching the interview
on a TV.

Cigar smoke curls up into the air.

> NATALIE
> (V.O.)
> I tried to *steal a billion
> dollars*, Jane. From poor
> kids and homeless vets,
> and many others who needed
> the money. I deserved to
> go to prison for as long
> as the judge said I
> should.

> JANE
> And, by the time this
> episode airs, you'll be a
> free woman, having served
> your time.

                    NATALIE
          And, at the end of the
          day, the "missing" billion
          was distributed to real
          charities. So, maybe, just
          maybe, I can put this
          whole episode behind me
          and live a quiet life
          after.

A young woman enters the beach bar as
the TV show goes to credits and the
three at the bar stand and applaud.
They are revealed to be Nathan,
Sophia, and Dr. Trimble. The woman,
Natalie, removes her floppy hat and
sunglasses.

Beaming, Natalie gives her Uncle
Nathan and Sophia hugs, and shakes
Dr. Trimble's hand.

Nathan turns to the bartender.

                    NATHAN
          A drink for the lady of
          the hour.

The bartender tosses a coaster on the
bar.

THE CAMERA LINGERS FOR A BEAT ON THE
LOGO OF THE AFTERLIFE BAR.

                    NATALIE
         You're looking pretty tan
         … for a dead man, Uncle.

                    NATHAN
         And you cleaned up pretty
         well after that interview.

A tall blue drink appears, and Nathan
hands it to Natalie, then ushers the
four to the far corner.

The four sit at a table with their
drinks. Natalie pulls a rosewood box
from her beach bag.

                    NATALIE
         Here are your ashes,
         Uncle. It was a nice
         memorial.

Sophia and Dr. Trimble, nod and laugh
while Nathan takes the box, sets it
on the table and taps the ash of his
cigar into it.

                    NATHAN
                 (standing)
         Welcome, friends to the
         first annual board meeting
         of the Afterlife
         Foundation. We four
         represent Charities number

                    269

                    four hundred seventy-
                    eight,

Dr. Trimble nods and raises his
glass.

                    NATHAN (cont.)
                    Number five hundred
                    twenty-two,

Sophia raises her own glass.

                    NATHAN (cont.)
                         Number six hundred
                              thirteen,

Natalie smiles and sips from her
straw.

                    NATHAN (cont.)
                    And number six hundred
                    sixty-six—a nice touch
                    that, my Dear—on the
                    Bournish List of
                    Charities. All legally
                    registered here in the
                    islands, and by all
                    appearances completely on
                    the up-and-up. Funded to
                    the tune of two hundred
                    million U.S. dollars.

Nathan turns to Natalie.

                    NATALIE
          It's not a billion, but
          like you said, Uncle, give
          them what they're looking
          for—not too easily, mind
          you—and they'll stop
          looking.

                    SOPHIA
          But it cost you two years
          of your life...

                    NATALIE
             (interrupting)
          Reading books and watching
          soap operas in minimum
          security.

                    NATHAN
          How many times did I tell
          you all, that for that
          much money, somebody had
          to go to jail. So, let's
          all raise our glasses to
          our heroine, the one who
          took the fall, who slept
          in a cell for two years so
          that we could laze about
          on our beach chairs, Ms.
          Natalie Bournish.

FADE OUT ON NATHAN'S RAISED
"AFTERLIFE BAR" GLASS.

Here's my attempt at a Hallmark Christmas flash fiction piece, inspired by the Fiction Writers Group prompt below.

30

A CHRISTMAS VISITOR

The church stood proudly at the end of the marketplace. Its clock played half of the recorded Westminster chimes from its bell tower. Six-thirty on Christmas Eve meant the last-minute shoppers—all men—rushed from store to store, desperately searching for that one last gift that would make their wives, sweethearts, sons, or daughters smile on Christmas morning. Carolers, bundled up against the cold, sang their final song.

Janine stood behind the counter of the coffee shop, dreading when the clock would strike seven times, when she would close the shop and spend another Christmas alone. The tinkling of the bell above the door woke her from her reverie.

272

"Good evening. Can I help you?" she said as she took in the man's swept-back hair falling just to his collar, its salt-and-pepper color matching his full, yet well-groomed beard. He wore a long camel hair coat over a white dress shirt and black slacks. A cashmere scarf completed the ensemble.

"I hope so," he replied. "I'd love a cup of hot cocoa." Janine smiled, although she had already cleaned and stowed the cocoa machine. "If it's not too much trouble, that is, Janine."

"Do I know you?" she asked, puzzled. He nodded to the nametag on her blouse. "Oh, right. It's no trouble," she said, a little flustered, but happy for the momentary company.

"While you're at it, better make two," he said as he pulled two biscotti from the jar on the counter.

Janine looked past him to the dark windows. "Are you expecting company?" she asked.

His eyes twinkled, and a smile curled his lips. "Nope," he said as he slid a biscotti toward her. "I'm just taking a break before I continue my rounds. Merry Christmas."

For the first time in a long while, it was.

THE END

Here's a science fiction tale of betrayal and retribution that spans light years. It received an Honorable Mention in the Writers of the Future Contest

31

CAPTAIN v. CAPTAIN

C aptain Rodney Adams made a sour face as he sipped the post-hibernation restorative. The ship's dry, sterile air burned his nostrils, and he squinted against the harsh whiteness of the walls. He sat in his quarters and stared at the ship's chronometer, his face a mask of anger and confusion. The door buzzed.

"Come!"

Executive Officer Janice Ramey stepped stiffly to the right of the door and a junior specialist whose name Adams couldn't recall stepped to the left. He was visibly shaking.

"Mr. Ramey, do you want to tell me why you woke me six months early?"

The XO hid her annoyance at the use of the archaic "Mister," that Adams insisted on using to refer to everyone on the crew, instead of the more standard "Crew". The Captain's and Ramey's watch crews were on alternating two-year hibernation cycles, so she normally only had to deal with him and his misogynistic attitudes for a week at a time during the shift transition. This situation was anything but normal, however.

Before Crew Ramey could answer, Adams continued, his voice rising in annoyance. "I've checked the ship's status and all systems are nominal. There are no alerts pending, so what the hell is so urgent that it warrants my attention?"

Janice stood impervious to Adams's rant. "Captain, Communications Specialist Alvarez here detected an anomalous signal coming from a source directly behind our flight path."

"You mean from Earth?" His tone was scathing.

"No, Captain. From another…starship."

For the first time since Janice had started training with Adams many years ago, she saw him at a loss for words. It was delicious.

But after a second, with his mouth hanging open, the captain regained his composure. He turned to the Comms Specialist, who stood stock-still, trying to look small.

"Mr. Alvarez, report."

Alvarez gulped and began.

"Captain, four hours ago, Alfred reported—"

"Alfred?"

Alvarez shuffled his feet and glanced at Janice, who gave him a scowl.

"Ah, Alfred is…the ship's AI, Sir."

275

Adams addressed the XO but kept staring at Crew Alvarez. "Mr. Ramey, do I not have a standing order against the anthropomorphizing of the ship's systems? It's bad enough we were forced to give it the stupid name, *New Hope*."

"I will reissue the standing order, Captain," Janice said, and she gave Alvarez a look that said the crew would know he was to blame. Her voice softened to cushion the blow when she said, "Continue your report, Crew Alvarez."

"Yes, Crew Ramey. Four hours ago, the ship's AI reported that the daily mail packet had not been received from Earth. They've missed deliveries before due to problems with their comms laser, so I didn't think much of it. But then AI—the AI—also reported that a new, different signal was being received on the same frequency-shifted channel as our Earth comms." Alvarez pulled out a tablet and gestured toward the wall display. "May I, Captain?"

Adams nodded, and Alvarez cast an image onto the larger screen. It showed a waveform consisting of a repetitive series of pulses.

"Four hours ago, at midnight, we began receiving this signal on the same channel as our Earth comms."

"Be more precise, Mr. Alvarez. What was the exact time this signal was received?"

Alvarez cleared his throat—the most annoyance he could express in the captain's presence. "I was precise, Sir. It was *exactly* at midnight, ship's time."

"Interesting coincidence," Adams mused. "Go on."

Alvarez indicated the wall display. "You can see, Captain, that the pulses are very well-defined and regular. If we expand one..." He zoomed in, filling the screen with one of the pulses, showing a landscape of flat-topped peaks, and equally

276

flat valleys. "…you can see that each pulse is composed of a pattern of what appears to be binary data."

"It's clearly artificial. This pattern repeats?"

Alvarez nodded. "Every pulse is the same…so far."

Adams raised an eyebrow. "So far?"

"It appears to be a self-clocking counter going from zero to 1024—two to the tenth, Sir. It repeats every millisecond…precisely."

"And it's not coming from Earth?"

"No, Sir. Analysis of the degradation of the power curve shows the source to be very, *very* close."

The image on the screen switched to a star field. Where the star Sol should have been, there was a black void. Stars brightened as Alvarez turned the gain of the image up to maximum.

"All we can resolve of the source is a blank, black disk, Captain."

Adams was unable to hide his excitement. "First contact," he whispered, then his cold demeanor returned. "How close, Mr. Alvarez?"

Alvarez threw a sidelong glance at XO Ramey, but she kept her eyes firmly fixed on the captain.

With a sniff, Alvarez continued, "The source appeared one-thousand-four-hundred-fifteen-point-nine klicks behind us. It is receding from us at the same accelerated rate as Earth is. It is effectively stationary relative to Earth."

To his credit, Captain Adams understood the implication immediately.

"This signal pattern started at *exactly* midnight, ship's time?"

"Yes, Captain."

277

"And repeats *precisely* every millisecond, ship's time? Even allowing for our time dilation?" Alvarez nodded, and Adams continued. "They know an awful lot about us, don't they?" He wasn't really asking anymore. "They know we came from the Sol system, but that's obvious. They can measure our acceleration, but they must know how long we've been thrusting to get the timing of midnight, ship's time, correct. And a millisecond is a completely Earth-standard interval to repeat at." His disappointment was evident when he said, "It's not a First Contact, then."

Janice cleared her throat and spoke up, a tiny hint of humor in her voice. "And the distance, Captain."

He looked at the display where Alvarez had posted his analysis. "It appeared at a distance of one-four-one-five-point-nine kilometers." He grunted. "Pi. For God's sake, somebody is showing off."

Captain Grace Adams hesitated a beat, pushing down years of anger. By contrast, the walls of her quarters glowed with soft pastels, and the scent of a spring meadow hung in the air. Taking a deep breath, she touched the record button.

"Hello, My Love." She failed to keep the sarcasm out of her voice. "I bet you never thought you'd see me again. I know I didn't want to ever talk to *you* again." She gulped a breath. "After you betrayed me."

This was harder than she had expected.

Her next breath was deeper, and her voice dripped venom when she said, "We had a deal. 'Co-Captains' you called it. 'Equal partners taking humanity to the stars.'" She finished with a barking laugh.

Grace sat back in her chair, but her voice was anything but relaxed. "You lied to me. You flat-out lied. You told me the Agency kicked me off the crew for failing my final psych eval. When I watched you take that shuttle into orbit, I was heartbroken—disappointed that I wouldn't have the chance to start Earth's first colony on a new world and devastated that the love of my life was gone forever."

She felt the long-suppressed fury boiling just below the surface.

"It took me months of paperwork and appeals to get access to my psych file. When I did, I saw that I had passed that evaluation with flying colors. That's when the depth of your betrayal started to hit home. There was nothing I could do, of course. You and the *New Hope* were out of the Sol system by then, well on your way to Alpha Centauri A-1. But you were my love, my husband, so I gave you the benefit of the doubt. I assumed there must have been some horrible miscommunication. Maybe my file got mixed up with someone else's, or…something. I was so angry, though, that I kept digging. More paperwork and more appeals, until someone sent me a copy of the email that formally requested my removal from the crew. *Your* email, saying the most egregious lies about me."

The roiling caldron that was Grace's anger finally boiled over.

"*You* kicked me off the crew. *You* claimed we had 'irreconcilable differences' concerning the mission plan and crew personnel. Which was total *bull—*."

An incoming call flashed on her screen.

She hit Pause. "What?" she snapped.

Grace's XO Thomas Drake said, "One hour until the event, Captain."

"Understood. Sorry. I'm recording now."

She broke the connection, closed her eyes and took a deep, calming breath, then resumed the recording. When she opened her eyes, her fury shot from them directly into the camera, but her voice was dead calm.

"As *Senior Captain*—a rank you made up, by the way—you insisted I be removed from the crew manifest. You just couldn't stand the fact that the crew—*our* crew—liked me, and my management style, better than you. That was the 'irreconcilable difference' between us. I treated our crew with respect, while you ordered them around like a dictator."

Grace's squint into the camera was intense.

"The mission, with *Hope's* sub-light L-4 drive, is on a one-way trip. Every member of the crew and every colonist knows this." Then she raised one eyebrow, and a frown tugged at the corner of her mouth. "You have," she glanced at the screen to her left, "six years, three months, and twenty-two days of dilated time until you reach the Alpha Centauri system. Well, I have some bad news for you."

"Holy—"

The normal two-crewmember watch on the bridge was doubled trying to analyze the mystery ship, and XO Ramey occupied the command chair. The wakeful presence of Captain Adams suppressed the camaraderie she normally encouraged. Instead, the bridge crew worked in silence until Astronomy Officer Bennet's outburst.

Janice snapped, "Report, Crew Bennet."

"Forward-facing sensors have detected an anomaly."

"Another ship?"

"Ah, no, Crew Ramey. This seems to be coming from the Centauri system. Bringing main telescopes to bear…"

The main display showed a split image with the blank disk of the mystery ship on one side and a color-enhanced view of the trinary Centauri system. The smallest of the three stars—Proxima Centauri—rapidly increased in brightness across the visible to ultraviolet spectrum. The bridge crew let out gasps as the red dwarf's radiation swamped the telescope's sensors. Bennet quickly turned down the amplification while Janice punched the intercom.

"Captain, you are needed on the bridge."

Seconds later, Adams strode through the Ready Room door.

"Report, Mr. Ramey."

"Proxima Centauri seems to be experiencing some sort of flaring event, Captain." She indicated the display while Astronomer Bennet worked his console. A graphical spectrum analysis scrolled across the screen below the image of the star. The Biology Officer was the first to understand the implications. She turned to the Captain and Janice with a stricken look.

"Captain, that level of radiation output, so close to our planet, A-1—"

At that moment, the image of the mystery ship, which everyone had been ignoring, began to glow. A spherical ship was revealed, bathed in the light from hull-mounted floodlights. Painted across it was the name *Infinite Beagle*.

The crew sat in stunned silence until Captain Adams muttered, "Damn."

281

Reacting to the insistent beeping of his console, Comms Officer Alvarez announced, "We just received a message from…the *Beagle*, Captain."

The *New Hope's* Ready Room was filled with the ship's officers Captain Adams had summoned after listening to Grace's message. Skipping the vitriolic personal attack at the beginning, he played for them her explanation of the devastation the flare had wrought on the planet A-1.

"…The force of the flare stripped most of the atmosphere from the planet and sterilized the surface. We've been there, Rod. We've seen the damage. A-1 is no longer inhabitable." She paused and swallowed hard. "The data we gathered is attached to this message."

Adams turned to his Astronomy and Xenobiology Officers, who looked up from their tablets and nodded grimly.

The recording continued. "We've seen the planet, because while you've been gone, we developed the BEC-QT, the "Cutie," drive. Yes, we've broken the *c* barrier. By quite a lot, actually. The *Infinite Beagle* is the first interstellar survey ship. We surveyed the Centauri system for you. That's when we discovered the devastation of the planet A-1."

Grace leaned into the camera and her voice dropped to barely above a whisper. "Look, Rod, you, your crew, and colonists are all doomed. There's no paradise at the end of your trip, just a barren, lifeless rock."

Captain Adams hit Pause and swiveled his head around the room, making eye contact with every officer.

"This is obviously devastating news, and I want you all to carefully consider what the other Captain Adams has to say next."

After getting a nod from everyone present, he resumed the recording.

"Fortunately, we have a proposal—a rescue mission, if you will. Our L-4 drive can pull a full gee, so if you flip over and begin breaking now, we can match velocities in about six months. At that point, we can begin offloading you folks onto the *Beagle* and shuttle you back to Earth. It'll be tight quarters and not very comfortable, but we figure we can get you all back there in four round trips of six weeks each. So, in less than a year, we can get you all home."

Adams hit Pause again and scanned the room.

"I assume Grace's plan will work and that she isn't just giving us false hope. So, before I reply," he paused to give his next words their proper weight, "I want alternative proposals."

Janice's surprise was reflected in the faces of the rest of the crew.

"Captain, now's not the time for—"

"For petty competition?" Adams interrupted. "Believe me, I know that. But the other Captain Adams has her reasons for wanting to one-up me by *rescuing* me and my mission."

Janice stiffened. "You mean *our* mission, Captain."

He turned to her. "Exactly." One side of his mouth curled into a sardonic smile. "I know, Mr. Ramey—Janice—that you are all as invested as I am in the dream that is the *New Hope* and *our* mission. Are you ready to sacrifice that dream? Are you ready to be *rescued*? To be ferried back to Earth with our tails between our legs? When we shipped out, we all knew

283

Earth was no longer our home. The new home we thought we were setting out for may not be so homey anymore, but neither is the overcrowded, overpopulated, and over polluted place we left."

Several heads were nodding around the room.

"Let's just think this through before we throw in the towel. Right?"

It was the first time Captain Rodney Adams had asked for anyone's opinion, and that fact was not lost on his officers.

Janice spoke up. "You heard the captain. Go figure something else out. Work together using your expertise. You have two days." She looked at Adams, who smiled and nodded. "Now, shoo."

As the crew filed out, Comms Officer Alvarez asked, "How should we reply to the *Beagle*, Captain?"

His smile turned dark. "Send them back their carrier wave. She made us wait. Now it's our turn."

Grace Adams's door buzzed.

"Come in."

She looked up expectantly when her XO, Thomas Drake, floated through the doorway and fumbled for a handhold. The fact that remaining stationary meant the *Beagle's* crew was weightless remained an ongoing point of annoyance.

"Anything?" she asked.

Thomas shook his head. "Still nothing but our carrier reflected back at us."

Grace frowned. "What are they waiting for?"

Thomas shrugged. "Well, it's got to be a shock for them. They've been preparing for and executing their grand plan for over a decade. To have that snatched away—"

Grace's voice turned harsh. "Well, they need to face the facts. Their mission is a failure." She sniffed when she saw his reaction. "Through no fault of their own, of course. But even so, their only choice is to let us take them back home. They'll get a heroes' welcome, for goodness sake."

Thomas shook his head. "I still think—"

"It's the only *viable* alternative, Thomas. We've discussed all of the options for months. This one makes the most sense."

"But, in one trip, we could upgrade their L-4 drive to a higher thrust—"

"Which will screw up every ship's system that relies on the combination of spin-gravity and one-tenth gee thrust. Do you think they want their toilets to stop working?"

"Then their own Cutie drive..." His voice trailed off.

"We've examined that plan, too. You know that. The *New Hope* isn't built to house a Cutie, or to withstand the stresses of the massive quantum effects it generates. Besides, all the drives being built back on Earth are spoken for. No. The rescue plan is the only viable one."

Thomas frowned, but nodded. "I'll notify you as soon as they initiate comms."

Grace laid her hand on his forearm. "Don't worry, Tom. We won't be hanging around Earth once we get them all back there. Our mission will continue and *succeed*. Besides, for all its problems, Earth is better for them than starving to death in the middle of nowhere."

The Comms Officer nodded to Janice. "The call's all set up."

"He agreed? To keep it private?"

Alvarez nodded. "He seemed anxious to." He pointed to the blinking notification on her tablet. "Tap that to get started. Remember, they're slightly time-dilated, so be patient." Without another word, he left Janice's quarters.

She hesitated for just a moment. If this clandestine call didn't work out and the two captains found out about it…well, she didn't want to think about the repercussions.

She tapped the screen.

The face of her old friend, Thomas Drake, appeared, though the extra years had put gray in his hair and wrinkles around his eyes. Those wrinkles deepened when he smiled at her.

"Hi, Jan. It's great to see you again, although…"

"Hey, Tom. Yeah, not the best circumstances, eh?"

Thomas nodded. "You guys are tough, though. We'll make this rescue work."

Janice pursed her lips and tucked a stray strand of hair behind her ear. "Yeah, about that. That's why I set up this call. We're looking for alternatives."

The other XO chuckled. "I understand why. We came up with a couple ourselves, but they just aren't feasible. Technically."

"Our problem is," she took a deep breath, "we're working in the dark over here. All of our data is a decade old. You guys must have learned a lot more about—" she interrupted herself. She had promised not to reveal the newly hatched plan.

She needn't have worried.

"You mean more data on alternate targets for a colony?"

286

Janice let out her breath and nodded. "I should have figured you'd think of that, too."

Thomas shook his head. "Actually, we haven't. Or at least it hasn't been discussed among the staff. We've been solely focused on getting you guys back to Earth." He looked furtively from side to side. "Per Grace's orders."

"Then how…?"

"Apparently, your Alfred and our Ariel have been talking."

"The AIs?"

Thomas nodded. "Grace doesn't know about that, so…"

Janice frowned but nodded her understanding. Another risk. "She's really got it in for my Captain Adams, doesn't she?"

It was Tom's turn to frown. "It's really not like her, but…"

She shrugged, and excitement crept back into her voice. "So, I assume telescopes have improved a bit while we've been gone. Do you have new observations of other possible planets besides A-1?"

Thomas sat back in his chair and smile. "I can do better than that. Before we got to A-1, we visited a couple." He typed on his tablet for a minute. "Here are the summary reports." A new message notification appeared on Janice's screen. "Ariel is still sending the raw data to Alfred."

Janice scanned the first of the three summary reports. "This is great, Tom. How about specs on your drives, too?"

Thomas's face and voice hardened. "The *New Hope* can't handle the upgraded L-4 design, and you don't have the components to build a Cutie drive."

Janice leaned forward so her face filled his screen. "We have a lot of smart folks over her, Tom."

287

Their eyes met across the ever-increasing time and space between them. Thomas nodded. The reluctance of his nod exaggerated by their different space-time frames.

"Okay. I'll have Ariel send the drive specs, too."

~

"You kept us waiting long enough." The irritation in Grace's voice was exacerbated by the time-dilation effect. "I don't know what took you so long."

The assembled officers of both ships faced each other. The *Hope's* crew sat stuck to their gecko-skin chairs, while Grace's team floated in all different orientations.

Rodney Adams tried, mostly successfully, to stifle his anger. "It was a lot to process. And we weren't ready to give up on our dream." He paused, but before Janice could respond, he said, "And we're still not ready to."

Janice's mouth snapped shut, then she said, "What does that mean?"

"It means, My Dear, that we have a different plan. It means that we don't need you to *rescue* us. It means, Captain, that we're continuing our mission."

"That's impossible—"

Adams ignored his wife's outburst and nodded to his Astronomy Officer Bennet. A 3D star field filled the display. Getting another nod from Adams, Bennet cleared his throat and spoke.

"We're not quite half-way through our trip." A slightly curved line appeared from a star labeled *Sol* to a point in deep space. A cluster of three stars labeled *Centauri* lit up. "If we follow our planned flight path, we'll end up in a dead system, as you have informed us." Proxima Centauri brightened blindingly in the display, and Alpha Centauri turned a fiery red. A hush fell over the meeting.

"But if the *Hope* doesn't turnaround halfway to Alpha Centauri, we can slingshot through the system and head off toward one of the other candidate habitable systems." Bennet paused to let that sink in while three other star systems glowed green in the display. The *Hope's* flight path continued on to Alpha Centauri.

"Unfortunately, the *Hope* doesn't have the delta-v to change course enough to reach Trappist-1." The farthest target dimmed to the background. "And Gliese 667C," the flight path swung around Alpha Centauri and veered off toward Gliese but faded out partway there, "is too far away, no matter how much we ration our stores. It would take more than six decades to get there."

Gliese dimmed, also.

"But Luyten b *is* reachable with tight rationing, reducing the wakeful crew, and lengthening the crew's wake/sleep cycles." The display showed a green line looping around Alpha Centauri and extending all the way to the Luyten system. "At our current acceleration, our remaining flight time will be about thirty-seven years instead of the thirteen we had planned."

Bennet looked to Captain Adams, who nodded toward his Engineering Officer.

She spoke up, "We believe, based on the specs of your L-4 drive, that we can tweak our acceleration a bit, shortening the travel time to Luyten b to about thirty years."

Adams smiled proudly at his officers. "That's still a long time, and it won't be easy, but my crew and I are committed to this plan."

289

Captain v. Captain

Grace Adams reached out and the comms link went silent. The *New Hope's* officers could still see the *Beagle's* video, though. They saw Grace swing around to face her XO and shout—silently—at him. Thomas clearly stood his ground and shrugged when Grace made a cutting motion with her right hand. They both turned to someone just off-screen for a moment before turning back to the camera and resuming the audio feed.

"It seems I am faced with a *fait accompli*. I know how stubborn you are, Rod, and I can only assume you have infected your crew with that stubbornness. Well, good luck to you."

The comms link ended, and as the *New Hope's* officers sat in silence, Astronomer Bennet announced, "The *Infinite Beagle* is gone, Captain."

"Good riddance," Rod Adams muttered, then spoke up. "Okay people, we have work to do." He turned to Janice. "Mis—er—Crew Ramey, I want a preliminary plan on my desk in forty-eight hours." He looked at Janice and smiled. "I have some sleep to catch up on."

THE END

"The Elf and the Bounty Hunters" is an Urban Fantasy Third Round submission to the 2022 NYC Midnight 100-Word Challenge.

32

THE ELF AND THE BOUNTY HUNTERS

The gesture's meaning was clear: Lift the glass and drink it, but Clara knew what liquor did to elfolk.

Skinny held a knife to her ear. "Drink, or we'll take this pointy thing. Bounty'll be the same."

Clara nodded at the pool table. "Double or nothin'? You both want an ear, don't you?"

Fatty barked a laugh. "Rack 'em," he said as he picked up his monogrammed cue.

Clara lifted hers and slammed the heavy end into Fatty's temple, then up under Skinny's jaw. Broken teeth hit the floor before he did.

Ears tucked under her hat, she strode out.

THE END

291

In this short screenplay which won the First Round of the 2022 NYC Midnight Short Screenplay Challenge, an aging romance author finds real-life is a lot more romantic than her novels.

33

PIRATES' PLEASURE CRUISE

E

XT. MODERN LUXURIOUS RIVERBOAT DECK - DAY

JANICE sits on a deck chair looking out to the waterfront of a Medieval village surrounded by vineyards that climb the valley slope up to the ruins of an ancient castle. She is writing in a leather-bound Moleskin notebook.

DISSOLVE TO:

EXT. PIRATE SHIP IN BLACK-AND-WHITE WITH
NO SOUND - DAY

Extras act out the voice-over below.

> JANICE (V.O.)
> The PRINCESS stood, tied to the
> ships rail as the PIRATE KING
> yelled orders to his crew. The
> crew stood ready to jump across
> the gap between ships with
> swords drawn and knives between
> their teeth.

> SUSAN (O.S.)
> Mom. MOM!

JUMP CUT TO:

EXT. RIVERBOAT DECK - DAY

SUSAN, an attractive twenty-something
woman, is standing in front of JANICE.

> SUSAN (CONT'D)
> (Annoyed)
> Aren't you coming on the tour?

> JANICE
> (Distracted)
> No, Dear. I'm working. You run
> along.

Susan, frowning, leaves in a huff.

DISSOLVE TO:

EXT. PIRATE SHIP IN BLACK-AND-WHITE -
DAY

Actors again silently act out JANICE's
voice-over below.

              JANICE (V.O.)
     Poised to leap into battle, the
     PIRATE KING turns to the
     PRINCESS and gives her a
     leering wink…before begin run-
     through by an enemy saber.

                   FREEZE AND MELT LIKE A FILM
                        STUCK IN A PROJECTOR:

EXT. RIVERBOAT DECK

              JANICE
     Crap! It's all crap. Pirates?
     Really?
     JANICE draws a big 'X' across
     the page.

              ANDREW (O.S.)
     Your writing isn't going well?

              JANICE
          (Startled)
     Ah, no it isn't. How did you
     know…?

              ANDREW
     That you are a world-famous
     romance author?

ANDREW holds up a paperback book with a
Fabio look-alike and a well-endowed
woman in a sensual embrace. Then he
flips it over to reveal a picture of
JANICE when she was in her twenties.

> ANDREW (CONT'D)
> Your picture is on the back of
> every one. Though, if I must
> say so, it doesn't do you
> justice.

> JANICE
> It's an old picture of a much
> younger me, you mean.

> ANDREW
> (Shaking his head)
> No. I mean it doesn't capture
> the depth of the wisdom you've
> gained through experience. This
> picture is of a naïve newly-
> published author, unknown to
> the world.

ANDREW places a hand lightly on JANICE's
shoulder.

> ANDREW (CONT'D)
> You, on the other hand, are a
> mature author who writes
> stories with a deep meaning,
> clothed in the tropes of
> romance.

                    JANICE
                (laughing)
        You read my agent's latest
        press release, didn't you? The
        only thing getting deeper are
        the crow's feet around my eyes.

                    ANDREW
                (laughing and shrugging)
        They merely reflect the depth
        of your character.

Andrew sits in the deck chair next to
Janice.

HELGA, a young, buxom blond waitress
arrives carrying a tray and begins
laying out Andrew's lunch on the table
between their deck chairs.

                    HELGA
                (Smiling invitingly)
        Your salad, Mr. Stevens.

Helga bends over, revealing bountiful
cleavage between two open top buttons on
her uniform as she lays a napkin on
ANDREW's lap.

                    HELGA (CONT'D)
        Can I do anything else for you,
        Sir?

                    ANDREW
               (Scowling, then turning to
               Janice)
          No, Helga. That is quite
          enough. Are you having lunch,
          My Dear?

                    JANICE
          I didn't order any. I was
          working.

                    ANDREW
          Helga, bring another setting
          for Ms. Stone, please. We can
          share.

Andrew looks disapprovingly at HELGA's
cleavage and meets her eye. She hurries
away, fumbling to rebutton her blouse.

                    JANICE
          It's the first day of the
          cruise and you know each other
          by name?

                    ANDREW
          This is not my first day. I
          practically live on this
          boat…and others.

Janice puts away her notebook and they
smile at each other.

MONTAGE

-Andrew and Janice having lunch and
 drinking champagne.

-ANDREW and JANICE walking along the
 deck holding hands.

-ANDREW and JANICE embracing at the
 rail.

EXT. RIVERBOAT DECK - SUNSET

In a replica of the Pirate scene, JANICE
stands at the rail, while ANDREW is
leaving. He turns, but rather than a
leering wink, he gives her a warm smile.

INT. DINING ROOM - NIGHT

Janice and Susan are alone at dinner.
Janice is dressed to the nines, but is
distractedly fidgeting with her salad
while scanning the room.

                    SUSAN
          Mom! God you're distracted
          today--

Susan stops and stares as Andrew
approaches their table. Janice turns and
her face lights up when she sees him.

                    ANDREW
          Good evening, ladies. May I
          join you?

                    JANICE
          Of course. Andrew, this is my
          daughter Susan.

                    ANDREW
              (Shaking Susan's hand)
          Hello Susan. Your mom has told
          me a lot about you.

Andrew looks from Susan to Janice and
back.

                    ANDREW (CONT'D)
          Are you sure you aren't
          sisters?

Janice smiles broadly at the compliment,
while Susan is confused and awestruck.

                    ANDREW (CONT'D)
              (Scanning the table)
          What? No wine?

Andrew steps away to signal the
SOMMELIER.

                    SUSAN
              (Whispering)
          Mom, that's Andrew Stevens! He
          owns this ship and about a
          dozen others all over the
          world.

Lifting a forkful of salad to her mouth,
Janice gasps in shock. Her eyes go wide
and she grabs at her throat. Susan,
realizing Janice is choking, shrieks in
panic.

Andrew turns back to see Janice in
distress and calmly takes her hands in
his, pulls her to her feet, and twirls
her like a dance partner. With his arms
wrapped around her, he performs a
Heimlich maneuver. A single crouton
flies from Janice's mouth onto the
table.

                    ANDREW
              (Holding her in his
              arms)
          Are you alright, Dear One?

Janice gulps air and nods.

                  ANDREW (CONT'D)
              (Addressing the staff
              who have gathered
              around the table)
          No more croutons for the lady!

The staff and guests all break into
applause.

EXT. RIVERBOAT DECK - DAY

In the same shot as the opening, JANICE
is writing in her notebook.

                    JANICE (V.O.)
          It was a very good cruise,
          indeed.

                              FADE TO BLACK.

"The Face in the Mirror" was my Round #3 submission to the 2023 NYC Short Story Challenge. Andie called herself a sensitive, but most of her clients called her an amazing ghost whisperer. She had a flare for decorating, as well.

34

THE FACE IN THE MIRROR

Andie stepped slowly around the perimeter of the loft apartment with hooded eyes. The wide plank hardwood floor was worn but still solid. The tall windows soared from waist-high almost to the twelve-foot ceiling. It was a trendy space, but the spiritual tension it contained weighed heavily on Andie's heart. The building was a factory decades before until a fire claimed four workers.

"Are you getting anything?" The new owner of the condo looked on nervously. "I'm not sure I believe in this whole Ghostbuster gig you've got going, but I've tried everything else."

Andie needed this client, so she smiled indulgently.

301

"I'm a *sensitive*, Ms. Strahm, not a Ghostbuster." She tempered the rebuff with a chuckle. "I sense spirits' disquiet with their surroundings and suggest interior designs that will soothe them."

Ms. Strahm cocked an eyebrow. "Those are the pictures."

Andie bent to look at the three framed prints lying on the floor—two Warhols and the iconic Annie Leibovitz shot of John and Yoko.

"I keep hanging them up, and they keep falling down."

Andie listened to the whispered murmurings of the ghosts of the four dead men. *Damn hippies.*

"These prints are all wrong for this space." She scanned the sparsely furnished room. "Your Mid-Century Modern theme here fits the spiritual vibe I'm picking up, but let's move the Warhols to the bathroom and the Leibovitz to the bedroom."

Jenny, Andie's best friend and roommate, sipped a bottle of flavored water. The first floor of their duplex in Brooklyn was their shared workspace.

"Any prospects today?"

"Yeah, could be a weird one."

"Weird even for you?"

Andie chuckled. "Alec Desmond. He's a nightclub owner. Claims his bathroom is haunted. He should be here..." The doorbell buzzed. "...any time now."

After introductions, they sat around Andie's worktable.

"You said your bathroom is haunted?"

Alec shrugged. "All I know is my female patrons have been complaining about angry voices they hear in the Ladies Room."

"Lingering spirits are benign if they're comfortable in their surroundings." That got a raised eyebrow from Alec. "They draw energy from chaos—conflict, emotion, any kind of upset. Give them a peaceful setting, and you'll never know they're around."

Alec laughed out loud. "A peaceful setting? I own a nightclub, Ms. Smythe. 'Chaos' is what my club's name—literally."

Jenny gasped, which drew both heads in her direction. "Ah, a couple of my friends—. It's one of the old mansions down on the riverfront, right?"

"Yes. It was a wreck when my late wife bought it. Her dream was to turn it into the trendiest nightspot in New York, but…" He swallowed hard. "…she never got to see it open."

Andie touched his arm, which made Jenny frown. "I'm sorry for your loss, Alec. When can I come by to check it out?"

He forced a smile. "Well, it's Friday night. Things get kicking around eleven."

Andie stood and held out her hand. "It's a date, then. We'll see you this evening."

Taking his cue, Alec stood and shook Andie's hand and nodded to Jenny.

After the door clicked behind him, Jenny burst out with, "A weird one is right. My friends were there last week. They were pretty freaked out by the voices."

"This sounds fascinating," Andie gushed.

Jenny remained skeptical. She sighed resignedly. "Okay, so what are we going to wear?"

"We?"

"You don't think I'm gonna let you go there alone, do you?"

That brought a warm smile to Andie's face. "So you can protect me from the freaky bathroom voices?"

Jenny didn't smile in return. "No. To protect you from *him*."

Johnny, the bouncer, unhooked the velvet rope. "Mr. Desmond is tied up right now, but he opened a house tab for you. Enjoy your evening, Ladies."

"Well, that's a first," Jenny whispered as the women strode through the mansion's double front doors. "Skipping the line, free drinks—"

"We're here to work, remember?" Andie said as she tried to keep up with Jenny hurrying down the long, wainscoted hallway. Thumping bass came from the old ballroom at the end. "*You're* here to work. I'm just here to protect you from Mr. Creepy."

Andie never heard the last comment as the ballroom door opened and blaring music engulfed them. Jenny practically skipped through the crowd to the bar, but Andie stood, frozen, just inside the door. Overlaying the blaring music was the delighted psychic energy of at least a dozen spirits. Her research had told her that during Prohibition, several partygoers had succumbed to bad bathtub gin. She was happy they were enjoying this version of their grounding location.

"It's just club soda," Jenny yelled, holding out a glass. She tipped back her own martini.

Grinning, Andie leaned close to Jenny's ear. "Let's find the restroom."

Jenny nodded, drained her glass, then mouthed, *I'll be back* to the bartender.

The restrooms were converted from the mansion's kitchen. While Andie and Jenny waited in line, a succession of women emerged, shaking their heads and complaining about the voices.

When their turn came, Jenny led the way. That's why she didn't see Andie stop and look around the room in terror. From every mirror, a woman screamed. Her bright red hair was made up for a night out, revealing strands of diamonds that hung from her ears and shook in time with her screams.

Andie slapped her hands over her ears and doubled over. When Jenny heard Andie's gasp, she found Andie curled on the floor, nearly catatonic.

"You can't go back there."

Jenny had sat up with Andie all night, comforting her while she talked through what she had seen and felt. Her warm embrace felt surprisingly pleasant to Andie. But when she had insisted on returning to *Chaos*, their intimate moment shattered.

Jenny was furious, but Andie was just as adamant. "She's in incredible pain. I need to help her. Calm her down, at least. Today, when the place is empty, she won't have any psychic energy to draw from."

"And then what? Tonight, the crowds will be back."

"I just need to find out why she's so angry. Why she's screaming to get out. Like she's not just grounded here on Earth, but physically trapped somewhere."

"In the bathroom, obviously. I'd be pissed, too, if I had to listen to--"

Andie made a face. "She looked like she was more than grossed out."

"What she looked like…" Jenny got a faraway look in her eyes. "You said redhead and dangling diamonds?" She headed for her bedroom.

Andie watched her go, then jumped up, dressed quickly, and snuck out of the apartment.

Andie felt guilty for ignoring the first of Jenny's calls, but by the fifth she was just annoyed. At the club, Alec let her in and followed her to the door of the bathroom, But he hung back when she entered.

Andie felt the woman's anger, but much more faintly than the night before.

As Andie closed her eyes to commune with the spirit, a barrage of texts interrupted her.

"Damn you, Jenny," she muttered as she pulled out her phone to mute it. As she held it, though, she felt the trapped spirit's psychic voice grow stronger. With each incoming text, it strengthened until her face took shape in the mirrors. Rather than screaming in rage, though, she seemed to be trying to tell Andie something.

Text…text…text

Recognition finally dawned on Andie, and she opened the latest of Jenny's texts. It was a screenshot of an article about Alec's missing—not yet declared dead—wife, Elana. Under the headline was a society picture with her red hair done in an up-do and her glittering diamond earrings hanging down.

Andie looked from her phone to the mirrors. Elana stared back with a satisfied smile. She became strong enough to vibrate the mirrors. Horrified, Andie turned to Alec. Her reaction made

306

his decision. He stepped into the room, pulling a handgun from under his jacket. The mirrors shook in their frames.

"I guess I'll have to close for remodeling while I stuff your body under the tile floor with my wife."

Andie backed into the corner as every mirror exploded outward, sending glass shrapnel across the room just as the gun roared. The bullet's impact as it gouged a track through her upper arm spun Andie around and up against the wall. When she turned back despite the searing pain, she saw Alec lying in a spreading pool of blood that still spurted from the many arteries severed by shards of glass. In every one, Elana's smiling face slowly faded.

"Have I said 'Thank you' for saving my life?"

Andie and Jenny lay next to each other in Andie's hospital bed.

"Yeah, like, twenty times. You wouldn't have had to if you had answered your phone."

Andie snuggled her head onto Jenny's chest, who said, "I love you, you know."

"I know. Me, too."

THE END

Call it a rhyming story or a poem, "Snazzy Sally," my homage to "The Greatest Generation," was my First Round submission to the 2023 NYC Rhyming Story Challenge. Wartime turns boys into men, children into orphans, and strangers into lovers.

35

SNAZZY SALLY

Eighteen years old, six months out from high school dances, Gus walked bold, eager to take chances. Six weeks in the dirt and twenty more to earn his wings, his heart hurt with the knowledge of deadly things no boy ever knew: how to deal death from on high, lead a crew, and bring them home from the sky. A boy no more, his buddies and he prepared to go to war. Their boyhood souls laid bare.

Sally, seventeen, couldn't forget the rumble of bombers unseen, whose steel shit made her home crumble. Mum beneath the stones, her body broken and cold; Da' but dusty bones on some battlefield of old. Sent to her Gran's, this child of the nation, in the Borderlands she felt the frustration and

308

helplessness of an orphan in wartime, cast off rudderless, in thistle and thyme.

"You are a beauty," Gran told her. "Do your duty and honor your mother. She met your Da' at the Palace dancehall. Where the Yanks now go before flights to save us all. So, fix your hair and wear your prettiest dress. Dance with a boy or two before they go to rest. You may well be the last pretty, smiling face they'll ever see. Do your duty. Wear your lace."

After the briefing, the sortie pilots went to town. An early evening before they had to bed down. His first mission had Gus a "Nervous Nellie." His ambition was butterflies in his belly. But thoughts of doom were gone when he saw her across the room, nervous in the corner. Blond hair, blue eyes, a perfect nose, and red lips. Mesmerized, his butterflies did backflips.

The music was jazzy when he finally walked her way.

"Boy, you look snazzy." Was all he could say.

"What's 'Snazzy?'" She had to confess, but smiled despite her fears. Like a lover's caress, her accent tickled his ears.

"Oh, yes!" he gushed louder than he intended. They both blushed, glad neither had offended. "Would you...um...dance?" he stammered, a schoolboy again.

Taking a chance, she smiled and took his hand.

The hours flew by until Vance, his copilot, stepped in. "Sorry. We have to fly," he said with a grin. "Jerry's expecting us. We need to get to bed." Reality hit Gus, and filled his head with two desires: to see Sally, a love newfound, and to bring his flyers back safe and sound. With Vance dismissed, their eyes made vows unspoken. Softly, they kissed, knowing they risked hearts broken.

In the morning, his crew's surprise was meant to impress: a blue-eyed blonde adorning their Flying Fortress, "Snazzy Sally." Captain Gus, and her crew earned quite the tally for the missions they flew. Parting was teary, praying the guns would miss. After each, relieved but weary, Sally and Gus shared a dance and a kiss.

Snazzy wore twelve bombs and shrapnel scars below her smiling pout, when Gus, with sweaty palms, ordered, "Bail out!" No kisses or joy for Sally that night…or evermore? Another man, nay, boy, lost to the war.

A parachute count, his whole crew earthward bound. Rallying them paramount, then contact the underground.

A week, then two. They gave Sally a handshake, and a photo of her crew with her namesake.

Haylofts by day, nighttime travel making for the coast. Smuggled all the way by partisan hosts.

Sally answered the knock. A Yank stood there, his smile was sly. "Come down to the dock. I can't tell you why."

Leading his crew, Gus, a man beyond his years, stepped ashore and dove into Sally's overflowing tears.

THE END

"Aisle Thirty Table Sixty-Two" won the First Round of the 2023 NYC Midnight Short Story Challenge, moving me into the Second Round. Oil and vinegar, sugar and egg whites, romance and thrillers; some things just don't mix—or do they? Throw them together, whip them up, and magic happens.

36

AISLE THIRTY TABLE SIXTY-TWO

Mary Frances dragged her roller cart farther and farther past the rows of tables full of books. She glanced again at the email that listed her assigned table: Aisle 30, Table 62. All around her, authors were arranging their books, unrolling banners, and stacking bookmarks and merch. The prospect of selling her first book, *Romance Among the Pines*, at the pre-eminent indie author conference had kept her excitement peaked on the long drive from Indiana to Colorado.

She could hardly believe she was here among the giants in her field. In a large booth at the front of the convention hall, there was Anne Hopewell, standing in front of an eight-foot-tall banner showing the cover of her newest, best-selling romance. Next to her was another best-selling romance author, Jennifer Bigelow. She had large banners stretching behind multiple tables. Her books were stacked as high as Mary's chin, just waiting to be sold and signed.

Mary couldn't wipe the grin off her face. She knew she looked like a newbie, but she had wanted this for so long, she didn't care.

Seeing the stacks of so many different books, Mary glanced at the small box she towed behind her. She had brought just twenty paperback copies of her debut novel. What if she sold out of them? It would be a fantasy fulfilled. Really, though, selling just one copy would be thrilling. That's what she told her friends and family, who all wished her good luck, though their expressions showed they thought this trip a waste of time and money. But secretly, deep inside, where she wouldn't even admit it to herself, she just knew she would sell out.

Her excitement gradually faded as she continued across the front of the huge conference hall. Aisle twenty-eight, twenty-nine, thirty. Oh. Aisle thirty was all the way against the wall, far from the big-names and past even the mid-listers. No matter, there should be plenty of traffic to keep her busy.

Turning down that last aisle, she checked the table numbers. Halfway down the aisle, she was only up to table number thirty. Looking at the books being set out, she saw science fiction, fantasy, and horror, but couldn't find any romance. Her smile was completely gone by the time she reached table number sixty-two.

At the very back of the very last aisle, a lone table sat in the corner. Even if it wasn't an afterthought, it sure looked like one. It was already two-thirds occupied by a nerdy-looking guy unloading a box. He had dozens of copies of the same book spread across the table.

"Hi," she said. "I think this is my table."

He looked up over his glasses and smiled. "Hi. I'm Jonas—Jonas Newberry. Welcome to the end of the road, I guess. We're sharing."

"Ah, I don't think so."

He nodded vigorously, which made the mess of hair on his head flip back and forth. "Yeah, it was in the confirmation email. Us 'newbies' have to share." He pointed at the other tables in the area. They were all occupied by pairs of authors setting up. Most were chatting and smiling. "See?"

"Oh, yeah, I guess I missed that part of the email. I'm Mary Frances Stewart, but I write under the name Frances Mary Stewart." She extended her hand, and he wiped his on his jeans before shaking it.

"Oh, like the queen," he said. She gave him a quizzical look. "Mary Queen of Scots? You know, Mary Stewart? She was really French, so add an apostrophe to your name and you get France's Mary Stewart."

Jonas beamed proudly, but Mary just shrugged and adjusted her own glasses. Then she shook her head.

"I...hadn't thought of that."

"Well, it's still pretty clever. Lucky, too. I can't do anything like that with my name. How many books did you bring?" he asked as he eyed her small cart.

"Just one."

"One copy? You won't make much that way."

"Oh, no. Twenty copies of one title."

He nodded. "Good. You won't need much space, then."

"Excuse me? How many did you bring?"

313

His smile beamed. "A hundred copies of this."

He held up a thick paperback with a cartoonish picture of a cowering woman and a shadowy attacker looming over her. Mary couldn't hide the disgust on her face.

"What?" His tone was instantly defensive.

"It looks...I don't know, like you scanned it off a cover of a magazine from the 1930s."

Jonas's face fell. "I love those old covers."

Oh my God. He really did steal the cover. She shrugged. "Well, if that's what you were going for...you nailed it."

She gave him a half-smile. He didn't return it.

"That's *exactly* what I was going for."

Her smile faded when she looked at the table. "I'm going to need my space."

Bending down to lift another dozen copies, he plopped them down on the table. "You've got enough space for *twenty* copies."

Mary felt the heat rise up her neck. "Look, Jonas, I paid for a table. They assigned me *half* a table, and you're taking up *half* of that. I didn't drive two days to get here, only to be squeezed into *this much space!*" Her raised voice made him take a stumbling step backwards and, at other tables, heads turned their way. She took a deep breath. "You don't need all *hundred* copies of your *one* book on the table at the same time. It makes you look...*desperate*."

"It's confidence, not desperation. Desperation is not believing in yourself enough to bring more than twenty copies—"

"Can I help, here?" A woman hurried down the aisle. Her badge proclaimed her to be Becky Small—Book Sale Coordinator. "Is there a problem?"

"I'll say there's a problem," Mary started, then took another deep breath. "Jonas, here, is taking up half the space on my *half* of the table."

"There's no need to raise your voices." Becky said, barely above a whisper. She patted the air with her hands. Leaning over the table to read his badge, she said, "Jonas, I'm sure you don't need all of your books on the table, right?" He didn't respond. "We're all equals, here," she said with a big smile. "Space should be equal, too."

"Unless you're a newbie," Mary muttered. Gathering herself up, she said out loud, "I'd like to be moved to a different table. I don't want to spend the next eight hours next to *him*."

Jonas spoke up. "Yeah, that's a great idea. I don't want her here either."

Becky's mouth flapped as she shook her head. "There are no other free spots. Every other table is assigned."

Mary pounced. "Is that why you stuck us all the way back here?"

Jonas took up the cause, too. "She's right. We're stuck here in No Man's Land. Nobody's going to come all the way back here."

They had found a mutual enemy to vent their frustrations to.

"Exactly. We won't get any traffic. And if we do, will they be looking for romance books, or...whatever that is?" She nodded at the pile on the table.

"It's a thriller," he said curtly.

"Of course it is," Mary retorted. "Romance and thrillers go so well together."

Becky nodded and smiled. "Well, at least you agree on something." Both Mary and Jonas snorted. Becky continued, "Maybe next year, if you have more titles to offer, we can assign you a better location. But this year, this is your spot. Try to at least *act* professional, okay?"

With that, she spun on her heel and strode off. Mary looked down at the expanse of Jonas's books, then glared at him.

"Oh, all right," he mumbled, then he moved three stacks of books from the table to the floor. "Better?"

It wasn't perfect, but it was better. She nodded and got to work.

Four hours later, Jonas sat behind his castle wall of books and let his mind drift. No one had been by in at least fifteen minutes, and that was a guy looking for the restroom. Mary hadn't spoken to him in at least an hour, only offered grunts to his questions. What a b—. He stopped himself before completing the thought. He had promised himself, after his last relationship, to never use that word again. It was the trigger that fired the shot that killed his engagement. But if he was honest, that gun's magazine had been full of ammo. The breakup had been coming for a long time. If it wasn't the "b" word, it would have been something else. But that was in the past. Instead, he resolved to make the next four hours as pleasant as possible.

So, he sat behind the stacks of his book, *A Cry in the Woods*, trying to look upbeat and smiling at the few people who wandered by. None stopped to browse. Surreptitiously, he slid a copy of Mary's *Pines* off the table and leafed through

316

it. A few minutes later, he lifted his head up and looked at Mary with admiration. Her writing was tight, not the flowery, purple prose he had expected.

For her part, Mary looked like she had given up even trying to sell anything and had her head buried in her notebook, furiously scribbling. More romance, probably.

"What're you working on?" he asked, because there was nobody else to talk to.

"A story," she mumbled.

"About what?"

She kept her head down. "You wouldn't be interested." Her tone was haughty. "In my experience, thriller readers and writers aren't interested in romance stories."

Chuckling, he said, "In your *vast* experience?"

His tone was light, and it seemed to melt the ice, at least a little bit.

She looked over at him but kept her tone light. "Hey, I have an MFA." He raised his eyebrows, clearly impressed, and she continued with a wry chuckle, "Which didn't teach me anything about writing fiction that people will actually pay for."

She went back to writing in her notebook.

"Try me," Jonas challenged. Mary looked up, surprised, and Jonas nodded to her notebook. "Tell me your story." Mary still hesitated and scowled. Realizing his *double entendre*, he quickly added, hands up with palms facing outward, "I mean your book. Honest." Then he gave her a half-smile.

This time, for the first time, she returned the smile. "Okay. It's a romance, of course." He nodded. "It's actually the sequel to this one." She patted her stack of otherwise untouched books.

317

"Then maybe you should start with that one." He gave her a sheepish grin and waved the copy he had been reading.

Surprised, Mary smiled broadly. She nodded and started.

～

Fifteen minutes later, they were both grinning.

"That's a great story," he admitted. "What happens next? Charlie and Jennifer can't just live happily ever after. Right?"

He was genuinely interested in her story, but even more interested in Mary. Her enthusiasm for her characters' love story was infectious.

She was practically glowing when she said, "I don't know, yet." She patted her notebook. "That's the fun of writing— discovering the story as you write it."

"I wish I could do that. But with thrillers you need to plan things out, so all the clues and red herrings make sense. Usually, I have to go back and fix things in the second draft, anyway. You know," he said with a glint in his eye. "I could add some excitement to your *Pines* story. Just sayin'."

She raised a skeptical eyebrow and looked at him over her glasses. "Your turn. Tell me about *A Cry in the Woods.*"

～

When Jonas stopped to catch his breath after relating his roller-coaster ride of a plot, she patted his hand where it lay on the table.

"That's a fantastic story." She was genuinely impressed. She gave him a sly smile. "It could use some romance, though. Maybe James and Courtney could fall in love? Like when they're being held captive together, maybe?"

318

"Yeah," he said and caught her hand before she could pull it away. "I could use some help with that."

She intertwined her fingers with his. "Only if you make *my* story more exciting."

Their stories were getting more exciting by the minute.

"I'd love to make your…story…more exciting. I think there's a lot of potential for collaboration here."

She squeezed his hand. "Indeed, there is."

One Year Later

A cameraman focused on Mary Frances as the local news reporter said, "This is by far the most popular booth at this year's Indie Writers Conference."

Her cameraman panned down the long line of fans waiting to buy signed copies. The tall banner behind the table read "Introducing *Gunsmoke and Perfume,* the sequel to the *New York Times* Best Seller *Dangerous Romance in the Pine Woods.*"

Mary signed the hundredth book by her count and handed it to Jonas for his signature. Their fingers brushed, and the familiar, but still exhilarating, spark ran up her arm to her heart. Thanking the young woman who had just bought the book, she then caught the eye of the middle-aged man who was next in line. He stood at least six-foot-three and was almost as wide.

"Hi," she said. "I'm Mary Frances."

He grinned from ear-to-ear. "I know," he said nervously, then chuckled. "I'm Ralph. I'm a huge fan."

He certainly was—huge, and obviously a fan, judging by his excited smile.

319

"Nice to meet you, Ralph." She made a flourish of signing, *To our biggest fan, Ralph, Mary Frances Stewart*— no more pseudonyms.

"I hope you enjoy this one, too." She handed the book to Jonas. "This is Ralph, Honey. He's our biggest fan."

Jonas looked Ralph up and down. "I can see that," he said, and they all laughed as he scribbled: *& J. Newberry.*

"So," the reporter asked as the cameraman stepped back to include both Mary and Jonas in the shot, "how would you characterize your collaborations?"

They glanced at each other, then she said, "I think of them as Thrilling Romances."

Smiling, Jonas shook his head, "No, no, they're Romantic Thrillers."

Even the reporter laughed.

THE END

Here's an Urban Fantasy screenplay that won the First Round of the 2021 NYC Midnight Short Screenplay Challenge. The taste of power can be sour.

37

YUZU AND THE LIME TREE

F̲ADE IN:

EXT. ANCIENT JAPANESE VILLAGE - DAY

An old GRANDMOTH and her GRANDDAUGHTER
are tending a Zen garden in which
several platforms hold dozens of Bonsai
trees.

> GRANDDAUGHTER
> Why do we tend these tiny trees
> if they only bear one fruit
> each year?

                    GRANDMOTHER
          The spirits of our ancestors
          inhabit these trees, Little
          One. This one here I planted
          the day my grandmother died.

                  GRANDDAUGHTER
          The trees are all the same
          except for this one.

The girl points to the centerpiece of
the garden, a stunted lime tree bearing
a single ripe lime. The grandmother and
granddaughter move to the lime tree and
the grandmother slices the lime from its
branch, then cuts it into wedges. She
hands a wedge to the girl, who tastes it
and makes a face.

                  GRANDDAUGHTER
          It's sour.

                   GRANDMOTHER
          Of course it is, Child. Its
          juice is very powerful. The
          spirit of this tree was a very
          powerful, very evil wizard. He
          was trapped in it by my
          grandmother's grandmother's
          grandmother's grandmother. As
          long as we tend his tree, he
          remains trapped and we are safe
          from his wrath.

                        322

Grandmother takes a bite of a lime
wedge, sucks the juice out, and smiles.
The granddaughter touches her tongue to
her slice and makes a face again.

                    GRANDMOTHER
               (annoyed)
          Eat it, Child! Every fruit this
          tree produces reduces the
          wizard's power a tiny bit. When
          we eat the fruit, we gain that
          power to use for good instead
          of evil.

                    GRANDDAUGHTER
          Is that how you can heal the
          sick, Grandmother?

                    GRANDMOTHER
          You are a clever little girl,
          Child. The power I gain from
          the juice is part of it. The
          rest is knowledge my
          grandmother passed to me, and
          which I will pass to you.

The granddaughter eyes the lime wedge
intently, then bites down on it and
squeezes her eyes shut. When she opens
them, she sees her grandmother smiling
with the lime wedge in her mouth. The
granddaughter does the same and they
both break into giggles.

MONTAGE.

- A succession of grandmothers and granddaughters tending an ever-growing group of Bonsai trees and sharing a lime

- The village becomes a town

- The streets get paved carrying antique cars

- The town becomes a city

- The garden is lifted into the air until it is on top of skyscraper.

EXT. NIGHT. CLOSE-UP OF YUZU.

An Asian woman, YUZU, about forty years old, sprinkles ashes from a funeral urn into a planter holding a freshly planted Bonsai tree. Tears brim from her eyes and run down her cheeks. Her phone rings.

                    YUZU
          Yes, Nick.

                    YUZU (cont.)
                (after a pause to
                listen)
          I know I said I'd only be gone
          a few days, but Grandmother's
          funeral arrangements…

                    YUZU (cont.)
                    (annoyed)
          Yes, I'm in the garden. I told
          you I have to do this…

                    YUZU (cont.)
                    (angry)
          Look, my flight is in the
          morning. I'll be home in two
          days. Tell the kids I'll bring
          presents.

Yuzu punches the phone's screen,
disconnecting the call. Reaching up to
the lime tree, she cuts the single lime
from its branch with the same knife we
saw in the first scene. Ritualistically,
she cuts the lime, but instead of eating
the fruit, she juices it thoroughly into
the planter holding her grandmother's
Bonsai. She cups the Bonsai in her hands
and her hands shimmer, transferring
power from her hands to the tree.

                    YUZU
                    (whispering)
          Be strong, Grandmother. I don't
          know when I can return. You and
          all of the grandmothers must be
          the Guardian, now.

                              JUMP CUT:

EXT. THE ROOFTOP ZEN GARDEN - DAY

Overlooking a bustling city, traffic
sounds can be heard indistinctly. Yuzu
is standing at the base of a pagoda
structure surrounding the lime tree. The
Bonsais have been arranged on ramps
spiraling down to the newest Bonsai
centered directly below the lime tree.
Yuzu slowly backs away from the
structure, then leaves, sobbing.

DREAM SEQUENCE.

Yuzu is pursued by an evil dark red
presence.

INT. BEDROOM AT NIGHT.

Yuzu wakes, gasping from her dream and
sits bolt upright. Her husband, Nick,
stirs and wakes beside her.

                NICK
          (sleepy)
Another nightmare, Babe? You
really need to see someone.

                YUZU
          (whispering)
I need to go back, Nick. The
garden needs tending. Something
terrible is going to happen if
I don't. I just know it.

                    NICK
               (sitting up)
     No, it's all good. The condo's
     been rented. The garden is
     someone else's responsibility
     now. It's been ten years, Babe.
     The garden might not even be
     there anymore.

Yuzu climbs out of bed, grabs a suitcase
from the closet and starts shoving
clothes and toiletries from the en-suite
bathroom into it.

                    NICK
               (angry)
     You can't do this Yuzu. It's
     driving you crazy. It's driving
     me crazy.

Yuzu gives him a hard stare, then
finishes packing.

EXT. THE ROOFTOP GARDEN - NIGHT

A lime drops from its branch. The tip of
the branch where the lime dropped from
glows red as if on fire. Slowly, the
fire glow spreads until the entire tree
is consumed by glowing flames.

From the top of the tree a figure
emerges. The Wizard Spirit is finally
free of its prison. Demonic laughter is
heard as tendrils of red flames reach
out into the city.

MONTAGE. DISCORDANT MUSIC.

- Street gangs

- Corporate executives

- Politicians

- Yakuza

Each are touched by the red tendrils and
freezing in place. Their eyes turn red.
The tendrils grow in strength as they
feed the evildoers power into the Wizard
Spirit, who expands and glows brighter.

EXT. ROOF-TOP - NIGHT

Yuzu enters the garden, unnoticed by the
Wizard Spirit. She opens her arms.

                    3
              (calling to the
              Bonsais)
         Grandmothers! Lend me your
         power.

Tendrils of blue light rise from the
dozens of Bonsais. Some wrap themselves
around Yuzu, strengthening her, while
others attack the Wizard Spirit's
reaching out into the city.

328

                    WIZARD SPIRIT
                  (noticing Yuzu)
          You failed in your duty,
          Guardian. Now you will feel the
          wrath of centuries of my
          captivity.

The Wizard Spirit begins throwing
fireballs at Yuzu, which she deflects
with her own blue power. Her power-glow
dims as she dodges her way to her
grandmother's planter. The Wizard Spirit
is weakened as the blue tendrils cut off
his red ones. The grandmother's large
planter is covered with the husks of old
fruits.

A single lemon hangs from one of
Grandmother's trees. Yuzu cuts the lemon
from the tree and, without peeling it,
bites into it.

There is an explosion of blinding blue
light as Grandmother Spirit rises from
her tree and merges with Yuzu's glow.
Together they force the Wizard Spirit
into a swirling blue vortex.

EXT. SUBURBAN BACK YARD - DAY

A much older Yuzu giggles with her young
granddaughter, as they both put wedges
of lemon into their mouths and smile.

                              FADE TO BLACK

                      329

This thriller was my entry into Round One of the 2023 NYC Midnight 100-Word Challenge. I did not advance, but I still think it's a pretty good one.

38

PORTIA'S FLIGHT

Portia's square-jawed abductors had been silent since flashing Secret Service badges in Paris. They sat up straighter when a gray-haired woman stepped into the main cabin of the Gulfstream.

"What's going on?" Portia demanded.

The woman raised a finger as she placed a call. "Madam Speaker…Yes, she's here."

"Madam Speaker…of the House? Is that my mother?"

The woman handed Portia an earbud. "Mom, what's—" Portia's face went white. "A bomb? Are you—?"

She breathed out, listening, then swallowed hard. "Both of them?…Oh, yeah, succession."

330

Touching her other ear, Ms. Gray Hair interrupted. "We just got the word…Madam *President*."

THE END

"Clinical Trial" won an Honorable Mention in the Writes of the Future Contest. It may have been inspired by the—then—looming sixty-fifth birthday.

39

CLINICAL TRIAL

Joel sat on the park bench watching the swallows swooping after the insects that buzzed among the cattails. Their forked tail feathers were Nature's perfect rudders. He smiled at the geese as they landed on the pond in perfect formation. Their honking always sounded, to him, as a cacophony of both warning and self-congratulation on their smooth landings. That notion occurred to him every day, but he couldn't remember when he first thought of it—or maybe he read it or saw it in a vid. Wherever it came from didn't seem to matter anymore, and the pulse of angst he felt over not remembering evaporated as quickly as it appeared.

Ripples from the flock's arrival lapped at the shore below the lawn where robins hopped about, searching for the earthworms forced from their dens by last night's rain. Their breakfast was interrupted, though, when a squirrel climbed down from its tree next to the bench and pranced over to pose in front of Joel, hoping for a piece of his breakfast toast. Rather than sharing, though, he kicked a frail, slippered foot at the rodent. He hated squirrels, although he couldn't remember why.

Suddenly, he realized he couldn't remember how he came to be sitting on this bench on such a glorious morning. It was the third time he'd had that realization on this visit, but just like the other times, it was just as quickly forgotten.

Joel forgot things. Things that just happened and were, for a moment at least, foremost in his mind. Whether pleasant or upsetting, memories slid off his mind like an omelet out of its pan. His mind had become as smooth as Teflon. The Old Timer's disease had done that. It stole his ability to remember, first the most recent moments, then yesterday's happenings, then last week's. Like a thief in the night who knew Joel's doors were always unlocked, the disease came back again and again to steal a knickknack off a shelf, or a picture off the wall—stripping Joel's Memory Palace one room at a time.

His daughter, a Neural Engineer, recognized the signs early on. Janice pulled strings and called in favors to get her dad into The Trial. It was a study testing a capsule stuffed with nanites programmed to flush out the twisted protein plaques clogging the pathways of Joel's brain.

When he was still aware of his participation in The Trial, the pill seemed to be working. His memory loss slowed appreciably. But once he forgot about The Trial itself, it

333

became clear to Janice that her dad, the man who was the bedrock of her life, had been given a placebo as part of the control group. While the active group showed a complete halt to their memory loss, the control group generally plateaued for a few weeks, or sometimes even months, but inevitably, the malformed proteins won out over hope.

It was the treatment's success and Janice's impassioned plea to the Oversight Board that granted the control group humanitarian access to the nanites as well. By then, though, Joel had lost more than today, yesterday, and last week. He lost his friends and his brilliant career. Worst of all, he lost Janice, his daughter, his only child. That he remembered Allie, his wife of forty years, was a blessing, even though, to him, she was still his blushing bride.

Allie came and sat next to him on the bench.

"Hello, My Sweet," Joel said lovingly. "Where have you been?"

Allie smiled and patted his wrinkled hand. The newly minted engagement and wedding rings on her smooth finger glittered in the morning sun.

"Just out shopping," she replied.

"At work," she said the next time he asked.

And "Reading a book," the third time.

She could, if she had a nasty streak, have said, "Robbing a bank," or "Sleeping with the neighbor," just to gauge his momentary reaction. Like everything else, her comment and his reaction would have been quickly forgotten. But Allie wasn't nasty. No, she was infinitely patient.

Instead, to break the cycle, she said, "Tell me about the day we met."

Joel's face broke into a broad smile. "I was studying in the library. There was a big Chemistry test the next day. You were in the study carrel next to me, and your music was so loud, even through your earbuds and mine, that I couldn't concentrate."

Allie chuckled. "So you shouted at me to 'Turn that crap off!' You almost go us thrown out."

They both laughed. "I always hated Rap," he said.

"It was Hip Hop, My Dear."

"Regardless, I never like the stuff. I had to pull the thing out of your ear for you to hear me. Oh, you were so mad."

"Me? You're the one who ranted about the 'subversive lyrics'—"

"And you argued they were 'empowering.' So I handed you one of my earbuds so you could hear some *real* music."

Allie shook her head, but still smiled. "You were blasting Southern Rock almost as loudly as I was."

Joel's look was mischievous. "You liked it though, didn't you?"

Allie blushed. "I liked *you* more than the music. Why do you think I grabbed that particular study carrel?"

"Because I always sat in the one next to it."

Both fell silent, reliving the moment. Then Joel spoke, his love for Allie evident in every syllable. "When I pulled you to your feet, you danced to the music that was half in your ear and half in mine."

"I danced with *you*," Allie whispered. "It could have been a Gregorian chant and I would have danced to it."

Joel yawned. "Ah, a slow dance holding you tight. Heaven…" he whispered as his eyes fluttered closed.

"Sleep well, My Dear," Allie murmured unnecessarily.

The park bench melted into a hospital bed and the pond, geese, and pesky squirrel faded to black as Janice removed the VR goggles from her father's sleeping form.

"Another memory recovered. That's successful test, number, ah, 82-443," she recorded, referring to her notes. "My new nanites, in combination with the sim, seem to be working. We'll start on their first date tomorrow."

THE END

AUTHOR'S NOTE

I've been writing flash fiction pieces for several years now. If you are interested in exercising yourself with a weekly visual prompt for a three-hundred-word flash piece, I encourage you to check out the Fiction Writers Group on Facebook.

I've also been submitting to various competitions over the last three years of so. NYC Midnight's challenges are my favorites since you get feedback from three different judges on every submission. The Writers of the Future Contest does not return feedback unless your story is a Semi-Finalist or higher. Still, it's worth it since it's free.

At the beginning of 2024, I committed to writing at least a flash piece every week, a short story every month, and publish at least three books in 2024. At just past the half-way point of the year, I'm still on track. What that means is that I'll have plenty of stories to publish a Book Two of the Story Collections series in either 2025 or early 2026.

As always, you can find me, my books, my flash fiction blog, newsletter sign-up, and anything else I post on my website at rajohnsonauthor.com. Also, you can connect with me at rob@rajohnsonauthor.com

Thanks, again, Faithful Reader, for taking some time out of your day to spend with me and this ancient form of mental telepathy called storytelling.

Faithfully,

R.A. (Rob) Johnson

Pennsylvania, U.S.A.
August 2024

ACKNOWLEDGEMENTS

With thirty-nine pieces in this volume, there are many, many people to acknowledge and thank. Too many, in fact, for me to either list or remember them all. There are a few, however, that I definitely want to thank.

First and foremost is my daughter, Carly. She read and gave me feedback on several of the stories in here. Others who have helped out are the other members of the Pottstown Regional Public Library Writers Group: Josh, Brian, Fallon, and Meghan.

Finally, this volume would not have the gorgeous cover it does without my friend, the super professional Allyson Longueira.

Connect with me at rob@rajohnsonauthor.com and check out my website rajohnsonauthor.com. There you will find my blog, which contains dozens of flash fiction pieces, can join my email list to get monthly newsletters, bonus stories, and special offers, and even buy my other books, too.

I am also active in the Fiction Writers Group on Facebook, the APEX Writers Group, Superstars Writing Seminars (yay, Tribe!), a graduate of the Western Colorado University's Creative Writing/Publishing MA program, the Pottstown Writers Group, The Writers of the Future Contests, and various other challenges and competitions.

Other Titles by R.A. Johnson

FICTION

The Enclave Series

#1 *The Templar Lance*

#2 *Lady 355: Mother of Freedom*

#3 *Shroud of Doubt (coming soon)*

Ghost Stories

The Ghost of Mackey House

Fantasy

Tales from the Wood: A Modern Fairytale

NON-FICTION

Mental Crudites – Appetizers for the Creative Mind Series

#1 *Helping Science Fiction Writers Get Their Stories Off the Ground*

Milton Keynes UK
Ingram Content Group UK Ltd.
UKHW041124101024
449246UK00020B/43/J